Vine Around My Hart

Greenleigh Adams

Cover by Wicked by Design

Published by Greenleigh Adams

www.GreenleighAdams.com

To the other pancreatic cancer warriors-

Cancer is a word, not a sentence.
—John Diamond

Cancer cannot cripple love, it cannot shatter hope, it cannot conquer the spirit.
—Author Unknown

Chapter 1

Ivy, age 7

Almost everyone I knew hated the first day of school, but I loved it even though it meant summer had ended. The first day of school was the start of so many brand-new things.

This year, I'd actually get letter grades on my report card. I mean, the Os for outstanding on my report card were fine, but I wanted to see As and Bs. Okay, I really only wanted to see As. I bet I'd get way more As than my best friend, Carrie.

First grade was a big deal. A lot of things would change, and I couldn't wait. My mom took me shopping for new clothes and school supplies. I wasn't a baby anymore. I needed a real backpack this year to carry all my stuff. It wasn't heavy now, but I hoped by the end of the day, there would be a million things in it for me to bring home and show off to my parents.

I wore my new book bag over both of my shoulders and had my new matching lunch bag in hand as I waited for the bus. I picked both things out of a catalog, and my mom ordered them with my name stitched onto both bags. The pretty blue-and-white checkered pattern had tiny daisies scattered all over the front.

My mom held my hand as we stood on the corner of our street, waiting for the school bus to pick me up. Waiting for the large yellow vehicle to turn onto my road had my belly feeling funny, like butterflies flapping their wings against my insides.

I was practically dancing with joy when the bus showed up. I looked up at my mom, grinning happily, and she smiled back at me. She told me it made her heart happy whenever I was happy, and this morning, I was bursting with happiness.

I released her hand, and after a brief goodbye, I climbed the stairs onto the bus.

"See you after school, Mom," I called to her over my shoulder as I hurried to find a seat.

There were several kids already on the bus, including my best friend, Carrie.

She flagged me over and pointed to the seat on the bench next to her.

Her family lived one block away. It was close enough that I was allowed to ride my bike there. I had to wear my helmet, and my mom or dad had to watch me on my ride. We could see Carrie's house from the edge of our front yard, so one of them would watch as I rode my bike there, and much like today, I would give a quick wave and then slip inside.

Carrie smiled at me as I walked down the aisle toward her seat. She'd lost several teeth this summer, so her smile had some empty spaces, and other parts had big teeth that didn't look like they fit right.

I hurried toward her and sat on the bench. She slid over closer to the window to give me more space.

A few older boys who lived on my street got on the bus next. They were third graders, and I didn't like them at all. They talked loudly and laughed even louder. I tried to ignore them and looked over at Carrie sitting next to me, hoping they didn't sit near us.

Luckily, they moved to the back of the bus and took seats far away from where we were sitting. We stayed at my bus stop for what felt like forever. Usually, the bus would be moving, and we would be on our way to school by now. I had no idea why we were sitting here.

But then I heard the crying. I leaned over Carrie to peer out the window toward the door of the bus, where a little boy held on to his mom's pants while he cried. She tried to pull him off her and get him onto the bus.

I didn't understand why he was crying. The bus took us to school. And I loved school.

He eventually gave up the fight and climbed the stairs onto the bus. I quickly sat back down so he didn't know I saw him crying all over his mom.

His pink face still had big tears running down his cheeks. His blue eyes had red in them, and his straight blond hair was sticking up all over the place from the wriggling he had done with his mom.

"Who's that?" Carrie asked. "Do you think he's in kindergarten?"

"I don't know," I whispered. I didn't want the boy to know we were talking about him. He was sad, and I didn't want to make him feel worse.

He passed our bench and sat on the empty one directly behind us.

His sniffles continued even after the bus began moving a few moments later.

"Blondie's a crybaby," I heard one of the older boys from the back of the bus say.

Of course, that jerk's comment made the boy shake and cry again. My heart hurt for him.

"Carrie, I need to sit next to the new kid for a minute."

She nodded, knowing that I'd be back, and mouthed *okay*.

I left my book bag and my new lunch box on the bench next to my best friend, and I slid around to the bench behind me, hoping the bus driver wouldn't see me. He didn't like for us to move out of our seats once the bus was moving.

The boy had his face practically smushed against the window, watching the road outside, which gave me plenty of room on the seat to park my butt while trying not to be seen.

He twisted his head away from looking out the window, and his light blue eyes met my dark brown ones.

"Hi, I'm Ivy," I said while I gave my best friendly smile.

Snot leaked out his nose, and he swiped it away with the back of his hand. "I'm Fl...Fl...Fletcher."

I wasn't about to shake his snotty hand, but I did reach for his clean hand and covered it with mine. "Are you scared of going to a new school?"

He nodded, and large teardrops fell down his face.

"Are you worried you won't have any friends?" I asked.

He nodded harder in response to my second question.

"I'll be your friend," I said, hoping to make him feel better and less scared. "And so will Carrie."

Carrie popped her head over the back of the bench and waved at him, showing her big, toothy smile. "Hi," she said quickly and then slid back down into her seat.

"Ivy has a boyfriend. Ivy has a boyfriend," one of the

older boys yelled from the back of the bus like he was singing a song.

They annoyed me, and I was tired of their mean behavior. So I sat up on my knees and twirled around to face them. "He's not my boyfriend, but he is my friend."

"Well, you're friends with a baby," Kevin, the boy with bright red hair and a million freckles over his chubby cheeks, said with hate in his voice.

"Really, Kevin?" I squinted my eyes because he made me so mad. "What do you call someone who pees his pants in second grade?"

His eyes became bigger when he realized I could tell his embarrassing secret to all the older boys in the back of the bus.

"It was one time," he whispered, and the boy sitting next to him scooted far away from him and almost fell off the seat.

"Leave my *friend* alone," I said, grinding my teeth, warning Kevin not to tease Fletcher anymore or he'd be sorry.

Fletcher stopped crying, and when I slid back down into the seat, his mouth had fallen open as if he were surprised. Then his lips curled into a half smile.

I wrapped my arms around him. I wasn't sure if I was trying to make him feel better or me. But making him smile made me super happy, and I just wanted to hug the heck out of him.

I also wanted him to know that he didn't need to be alone or nervous. I didn't believe in being afraid of much, and I wasn't going to let anyone tease or make fun of him.

I let go of him after a few seconds and pointed my finger at his chest. "You don't have to be scared of anything when you're with me. I won't let anything bad ever happen to you."

He nodded, and his smile got bigger.

~

We stayed together for the rest of the bus ride. With Carrie on one side and Fletcher on my other, we walked into the elementary school unafraid on the first day of first grade. Carrie and I were in different classrooms, but Fletcher and I had the same teacher, so he and I waved bye to Carrie and walked across the hall to our room.

The three of us found each other again on the playground at recess and took turns on the swings, then climbed the monkey bars. Fletcher didn't seem to mind spending time with two girls instead of finding other friends.

I thought eventually, he would go to the side of the playground where the boys played once he felt more comfortable at a new school. The older boys had teased him, but the boys in our grade were okay. I didn't hate them. They were sometimes gross, but at least they weren't mean.

Hopefully, Fletcher wouldn't end up being gross like some of the others that liked to have burping and farting contests where they got points for how loud they were or how long they lasted. Of course, there were boys who ate boogers and didn't always wash their hands.

Basically, I just wanted to see him happy—even if that meant he became a gross first-grade boy. I never wanted to see him cry again. I promised to stand up to the mean kids and chase them away. I could be brave for myself and him also.

Chapter 2

Ivy, 15 years later

I missed my college gym already. I scheduled my workouts like a class. I went during certain times of the day, and I always knew who would be there and what the atmosphere would be like.

I was unfamiliar with the workings of this place. I needed a place to exercise now that I wasn't in college anymore, and after returning to my hometown of Villpointe, I had a few ideas about which gyms to try out.

I was already annoyed that at seven o'clock in the evening, there wasn't a place to park in the lot near the exit, so I would have to walk in the dark out to my car when I left. I wasn't going to completely write this off as a possibility based solely on parking availability, however.

I was just considering trying again at a different time of day. The facility was clean and modern. The equipment appeared to be new, and there were enough treadmills and stair climbers that I didn't need to wait for a turn.

I had to time my workouts at the gym in college around those busy times. It was super annoying to be on a limited period of time in between classes and not have the ability to use the equipment I needed to fit in my workout.

So, other than the parking situation, this place had already checked off an item on my pro list as far as I was concerned. And honestly, walking in the dark wasn't horrible. I walked on campus in the dark all the time. I walked from the gym to my apartment off campus numerous times, so I shouldn't be making such a big deal of walking a little distance away from the main building out to my car at night.

My hometown was safe. After going to college in North Carolina for four years, I was still uncertain where I wanted to put roots down, so I returned to the eastern shore of Maryland, where I grew up.

I hadn't been home since the summer after my freshman year. I worked every summer at a resort in North Carolina after that, so I didn't make the trip back. My parents came to me, loving the warmer weather during the holidays, and stayed at the resort I worked for every summer for a week of vacation.

The people seemed different between the two states. Perhaps I hadn't noticed before, or maybe things had changed since I was away. But no one greeted me or even attempted to speak to me when I searched for an available piece of equipment and finally settled for an elliptical machine.

I kind of enjoyed the silence, even if it meant the regulars weren't receptive to a newcomer. I wasn't really new per se, but I wasn't a member of the establishment.

Maybe being able to go in and readily get out without needing to even bother with a hello wouldn't be bad.

"Hey, you're new."

Well, there goes my appreciated silence.

"Hi," I said with a small wave. I broke my hand away

from the handle to send a quick greeting to the sweaty guy in a T-shirt that was most likely too tight on purpose and mesh gym shorts.

His brown hair was damp with perspiration, and even though he had a nice smile, I was basking in the ability to blend into the background. Although I was an extroverted person, there was something to be said for grateful moments of quiet.

"I'm Colton, but you can call me Colt."

I was no longer looking at him but rather focused on the man sprinting on the treadmill in front of me.

"Nice to meet you," I said but didn't return my gaze to him.

"I haven't seen you here before."

Dear Jesus. I wasn't interested in having a conversation. I nodded and picked up my speed on the machine, hoping to send him the message that I was more interested in working out than holding a conversation.

"I can give you a tour...perhaps spot you in the weight room."

What the hell? Is this guy for real? "Thanks, but I'm good." I cut a glare at him then. He obviously wasn't going to accept polite avoidance. I needed him to see the displeasure in my eyes.

I returned my focus forward again. The man in front of me slowed his pace to a walk. I wondered if he was in the cooldown phase or whether he was doing interval training, where he would walk and sprint for certain times or distances.

"I can tell by the shape of your body that you are serious about working out. How about we meet outside of the gym then?"

"I don't shit where I eat. It would be really awkward to

date someone from the gym. You know that whole mixing business with pleasure thing." I slowed down my revolutions, and I was pissed at myself that I allowed this guy to be the reason I had to alter my workout.

This wouldn't be the gym for me. I would happily go to a place with older equipment and no parking than be harassed by a patron on my first day.

"The pleasure would be all mine." His creepy smile would have been attractive if his mannerisms didn't make my skin crawl.

I shuddered when he gripped my leg before anger seeped out of my pores. I stopped the cycling motion on the machine and kicked his hand away. "Don't touch me."

This was too much. Not only was he persistent, but he also thought he could put his hand on me.

The man on the treadmill in front of me jumped off without bothering to stop the belt. *Great. Some guy thinks he needs to be chivalrous.*

I could defend myself. I hopped off the elliptical and wagged a finger in his direction before the other man could follow through on his need to halt Colt's advances. "Listen, Ponyboy. I'm. Not. Interested."

Rather than wide eyes full of shock or surprise, his dark eyes narrowed with utter disgust. "You're going to be sorry."

"I know I didn't just hear you threaten a woman." A throaty, growly voice triggered a warmth to disperse throughout my core. I had only seen his backside, but I knew that voice must be from him. His ass was delectable, so of course, his voice would be sexy also.

"Back off," Colt hissed. "I saw her first."

Lord, how I wanted to get away from this situation. But being the person I was, I couldn't ever back down from a bully. He wouldn't see me cower. I didn't glance over my shoulder at the man attempting to save me from this nightmare.

"It's not going to happen, Little Horse." I squared my shoulders with him and raked my gaze up and down his torso. "And for the record, you need to spend more time on your legs. Your upper body doesn't match your lower half. Considering everything below your waist is smaller compared to the rest of you, I'm definitely *not* interested." I shrugged and snorted with a condescending laugh.

Colt's face paled before inflaming with a deep shade of crimson. And after a huff and frustrated stomp of his foot, he spun on his heel and treaded away heavily.

"Absolutely won't be coming back to this gym," I muttered under my breath as I watched Colt retreat to another area of the gym.

"Don't let one man turn you away," sexy voice said.

I had all but forgotten he was near me.

I swung my gaze around to meet the owner of the husky tone. I had intended to let him know I could fend off unwanted advances without help, but I was met with a set of pale blue eyes I hadn't seen in nearly four years.

Upon his discovery of my identification, his jaw slacked, and he shook his head full of blond hair with disbelief. "Why are you here?"

I hadn't expected any kind of reception from him, but certainly not a warm one, so his questioning of my existence in his vicinity wasn't completely unwarranted.

"Moved back home with my parents while I decide what I want to do next." I knew there was a potential I would run into him when I returned to town, but I hadn't exactly planned what I would say at our chance meeting. I decided to go with the truth. "You look good, Fletcher."

No wonder I was drawn to his ass on the treadmill. I

had been attracted to him most of my life. Which was essentially since the onset of puberty.

My compliment didn't seem to make him happy, though. A scowl scarred his chiseled face. "I guess you'll be moving onto your next adventure soon enough then, won't you, Ivy?"

The use of my actual name falling from his lips was meant to hurt me. He hadn't called me Ivy since I was fourteen. He was reiterating my insignificance in his life by the lack of utilization of my moniker.

"Well, I plan to at least stay for the summer, so we may run into each other again sometime."

A sarcastic laugh rippled through the air. "I retract my earlier statement. You should find another gym." A twitch fluttered along his jaw. *I guess he still grinds his teeth when he's upset.* "I would really rather not run into you again."

I expected that. I hurt him, and obviously, time hadn't healed that old wound yet.

"No problem." I nodded. "I'll find somewhere else."

I hurried to gather my water bottle, keys, and phone off the machine and made the split-second decision to hightail it out of there without even bothering to disinfect the equipment before leaving.

"At least I'm reassured you don't need anyone to scare away the bullies." His hoarse voice had me meeting his gaze again before I could propel myself away. "But then again, you never did."

I offered a weak smile and tilted my chin upward, keeping up the strong front I was feigning.

His blue zircon eyes shook with longing but quickly transitioned to anger. "I'm engaged."

I swallowed hard. That was the final arrow straight through my heart. He blurted out those words to slice into me. It wasn't bad enough he called me Ivy, but he practically announced that his heart belonged to someone else in an effort to pour salt into old wounds.

"Congratulations." I cracked a disingenuous smile and drew in a deep breath unknowingly. "I'm glad you found your happiness."

I released the air from my burning lungs, and a sheen of water clouded my vision as I proceeded out of the gym without looking back.

Somehow, I managed to be in my car halfway home before the sobs broke free from my chest. I made a trip through the drive-through at the local fast-food restaurant chain to pick up a fountain soda before I completed my commute to my parents' house.

Although some people chose alcohol or ice cream when depressed, I'd always found my guilty pleasure to be cola. But not from a bottle or can. It needed to be from a fountain machine. There was nothing like that flavor and the bubbles mixing perfectly as it hit my tongue and tickled my nose.

I didn't feel much better emotionally, but at least I wasn't crying any longer when I reached my childhood home.

"Mom?" I called after entering the house and shutting the door behind me. I was still clutching the paper cup of soda in my hand. It was slippery from condensation and still had a straw sticking out of the lid.

I passed through the living room, surveying as I walked, searching for my mother. I slurped one more time from the cup within my grasp and emptied the ice from the now-empty cup into the kitchen sink.

"Mom?" My assessing gaze still hadn't located her.

Her car was in the driveway, so I figured she was home. My dad might not be home from work yet. It was after seven o'clock in the evening when I left the gym. I had glanced at the clock in my car when I started the ignition, realizing I had spent less than thirty minutes at the gym in total. The time I had checked in, worked out on the elliptical machine, spoken with that asshat Colt, and had my heart stomped on by Fletcher all equated to less than half an hour of my life.

I felt like the whole experience moved forward at a snail's pace, but twenty-seven minutes dragged out like twenty-seven thousand minutes, and twenty-seven million fragments of my shattered heart broke into splintered pieces during that short span of time.

"Mom?" I called again as I headed to the hallway where my dad's office-slash-den was located.

"Honey, I'm upstairs." My mother's voice finally responded to my repeated requests.

My best friends used to live in this town, but although I kept up somewhat with social media, I hadn't seen or talked to them in years and, therefore, had fallen out of touch.

So, without another person's shoulder to cry on, I sought out the refuge of my mother's, hopefully, welcoming arms.

However, climbing the stairs and pushing open the door to the master bedroom, I found my mom amid piles of clothes strewn haphazardly over her bed.

"What are you doing?" I asked, no longer swept away in my deep cesspool of pain and regret.

"Your father received a call from a hospital in Houston. They're revamping their emergency department and need someone with experience establishing a different throughput system."

My dad had been a hospital administrator for over two decades. Although I didn't understand exactly what he did, I knew he took calls in the middle of the night sometimes and had to make visits beyond his normal working hours to the hospital to deal with issues that arose.

I was always interested in taking care of patients, while it seemed he enjoyed being one of the people behind the scenes that kept the hospital running smoothly.

"So, you're leaving?" My voice cracked.

"For just a little while. Maybe a month or two." Her brow drew downward, and her lips frowned, causing faint lines to form around her mouth and across her forehead. "You'll be here for at least that long, right, sweetheart?"

"What? I mean, yes. But..." I shook my head. I couldn't deal with running into Fletcher and my parents' abandonment on the same day. "I just got home, and I thought we would be able to spend some time together."

My mother released the hold she had on the blue cardigan she had in her hand and tossed it onto the bed in a pile containing her other items of clothing. "Ivy, are you okay?"

"Of course." I huffed out a humorless laugh.

"I can stay behind and have your dad go by himself." She sat on her bed and tapped the mattress next to her, encouraging me to also sit.

I reluctantly plopped myself alongside her and sighed. "You don't need to do that."

"Do you need me to be with you?" She nudged me in the shoulder by leaning into me, then withdrew and eyed me suspiciously with a quirked eyebrow as if speculation had just struck her. "What has you so shook up anyway? There's more than my going away that has you rattled."

"I ran into Fletcher." There was no reason to withhold

the truth from her. She obviously realized being alone or away from my parents had never bothered me before.

Her dark eyes softened with understanding.

I'd told her years ago that I didn't want her to speak of Fletcher in my presence, and she had respected my wishes all this time. So she sat quietly, awaiting words to leave my mouth.

"He was my best friend, Mom." Tears burned the back of my throat.

She embraced me, wrapped her arm around my shoulder, and pulled me close to her side. Then she dropped a kiss on my temple. "Maybe you will be again."

"He told me he's engaged." I sniffled but refused to let tears break free.

"Are you upset about that?" she questioned with a whispered tone.

I rolled my eyes forcefully enough that my head turned away also.

She released a small, empathetic laugh. "Are you upset because you think that means he can't be your friend anymore or that he can't be more than a friend?"

Chapter 3

Ivy, age 11

"I don't want her to move!" I wailed and slammed my bedroom door when my mom asked me to come downstairs and say goodbye to Carrie.

She had been my best friend since pre-k, and now, the summer before beginning middle school, the parents of my best friend decided to snatch her away from living in a house I could literally see from my front porch to somewhere in Florida.

I'd been to Disney World and that was a long car ride to an airport and what felt like a long flight in a plane to get there. She was moving to a town named Jacksonville. I had no idea where that was in relation to Orlando, where Disney World was, but I knew it was far, far away compared to the place where she had lived as long as I could remember.

I knew crying in my room and throwing a good old-fashioned temper tantrum would not prevent the evitable, but I was a ball of emotions, and I couldn't seem to be okay with this.

I lifted my head from the pillow on my bed when the door opened. My mom twisted the knob and pushed against the wood, causing a squeak to be emitted from the hinge. My sad tears had transitioned to angry ones by that point, and my mother was throwing herself into my line of fire.

"Go away, Mom," I shouted through my sniffles and sobs.

She, of course, didn't retreat. She sat on my bed next to me, and I flipped from my stomach to an upright position and glared at her.

"I know you're upset right now, but Carrie really wants to say goodbye to you, and right now, you're being selfish."

"Selfish?" I guffawed. "Her parents are being selfish, taking her a thousand miles away from her home!"

"It's okay, Mrs. Hatfield." Carrie's form came into view, emerging from the hallway outside my room. "I've got this."

My mother's soft, chocolate gaze bounced from Carrie to me and back to my friend. "Okay." Then, with a soft pat against my upper arm, my mom's weight lifted from my mattress as she stood and left my friend and me alone in my bedroom.

Carrie's mouth twitched with a weak smile, and she tilted her head empathetically.

Why isn't she upset about this?

"I always thought you were the strong one," she said and shook her head a few short times, causing her long blond curls to bounce with the brisk movements.

I slid closer to the end of my bed, where she stood, and grabbed at her wrist, pulling her down.

She willingly sat on top of my comforter and shifted her hand so my fingers were no longer wrapped around her wrist but intertwined with hers. "You will always be my very best friend, no matter where I live."

Her blue eyes shone from their coating of unshed tears, and she blinked repeatedly, most likely fending off the water about to be shed.

"I don't want you to go." My shoulders slumped with shame. I had voiced my opinion on the matter repeatedly, and after letting the words tumble from my mouth this time, I finally realized not only was my statement not going to change the outcome, but they also weren't words of comfort and my beautiful friend sitting next to me needed that.

She had said I was the strong one and I hadn't been so far. I found out about her upcoming move at the end of sixth grade. We swore to have a summer to remember forever, but I pouted so many times I probably hadn't made our last few months together happy memories.

I should have filled our days with laughter and fun, but I withdrew, sulked, and moped. And now I couldn't take any of those moments back. I couldn't relive those missed opportunities and change them.

But I could change my attitude now. She needed me to be brave, and I could do that for her.

So, I freed the grip she had on our hands, and I draped my arms around her, embracing her with a lifetime of friendship. "My mom said I'll be getting a cell phone soon, and then we can text or talk all the time."

Warm water stuck to the side of my face, but the streaming moisture wasn't from me. Her cheek was pressed against mine, and the evidence of her crying was now adhering us together.

I pulled away, and she swiped her eyes with her fingers.

"I'm going to miss you." I forced my lips upward into a somewhat wayward smile. "But you are going to have a great time at a new school and make new friends." I reached for her hands and squeezed them tightly. "And you'll have warm weather all of the time."

She released the smallest hint of a laugh and gave a tight nod. "I wish I didn't have to go."

My broken heart needed to be strong. I had already made things difficult enough for her, and even though all I wanted to do was tell her how much I didn't want her to go also, I needed to bolster enough courage to provide her with words of encouragement.

"You know where I'll be. You can visit anytime and sleep right in this bed with me." I turned my neck slightly in the direction of the pillows lining my headboard.

"We've had a lot of good times in this room and sleep-overs in this bed." She laughed again, and more tears sprang from her eyes and slid down her face.

"That fingernail polish is still a pink stain on my carpet. And I won't ever be able to watch scary movies again without you next to me, hiding under the covers during the scary parts."

"But at least your room will be free of snack food from now on." She twisted and folded her leg onto the bed to face me better. "Your mom would get so upset with us for the crumbs."

"And the loud belches from the soda we would sneak up here." Both of us let happy memory giggles lift into the air.

"Maybe every once in a while, drink a soda in your room and burp really loud for me," Carrie said with a constant flow of tears sliding down her cheeks at this point.

"I promise."

And with one final hug, she left. I stared at the door she shut behind her for only a moment before sprawling back out onto my stomach with my head down on the pillow and allowing my tears to escape again.

I must have fallen asleep. My emotions had exhausted me. I had never understood the saying about "crying myself to sleep," but I did now. I had experienced it firsthand.

I probably would have still been asleep if a hand against my upper arm hadn't startled me.

My eyelids were somewhat adhered due to the salty tears I had shed, so it took a moment for my eyes to open and finally establish focus.

Fletcher.

"Your mom said it was cool if I came up to your room to check on you."

Fletcher had never been in my room before. Although we had been friends for years, my parents didn't think it was appropriate for a boy to be in my bedroom. So, typically, Carrie, Fletcher, and I would hang out in the family room together downstairs if we weren't outside.

But here he was—not just in my room but sitting on my bed next to me. A sympathetic smile tugged at the corners of his mouth, letting his teeth covered in braces peek through. His blond hair had darkened, and his once-stick-straight hair now had some wave to it, curling on the ends. His bright blue eyes were still the color of blue zircon gemstones.

"She's gone, Fletcher." I couldn't cry anymore. All the water had run out, but my throat was still clogged with choking sobs regardless.

And that's when I received my first hug from Fletcher, right there on my bed the summer before the start of middle school.

He enveloped his arms around my torso, and I leaned into him. He stroked the back of my head like my mom did when I didn't feel well. "I'll always be here for you. I'll never let my parents take me away. We will forever be together. I promise."

He never broke his promise.

I did.

Chapter 4

Fletcher, age 22, present day

I had thought if I ever saw Ivy again, I would immediately resort to the lovestruck teenager I'd once been and melt into a puddle the moment our gazes connected. But anger flowed through my veins the moment my brain and heart recognized her.

At first, I merely wanted to save the damsel in distress because what gentleman doesn't want to help a woman fend off the bad guy?

But that second, when she was identified as the girl that shredded my young heart, I couldn't deal with the fury bubbling through my core. I was infuriated she was in the same place, enclosed by four walls as me. The area seemed too small to contain all my emotions, as well as the two of us.

The fact that she looked beautiful only irritated me further. Her dark hair was pulled up into a messy bun on top of her head, just like she had worn it when we were younger, and the irises of her dark brown eyes were still outlined with the faintest hint of green. They were by far the most exotic-colored eyes I'd ever seen in my life.

If the tongue-tied, Jello-legged pubescent boy from years ago didn't appear with love in his heart, I would have thought indifference would have made me nonchalant. I mean, it had been *years* since she left me.

I'm engaged to another woman for chrissake! I'm over Ivy Hatfield. I'd moved on and shouldn't care whether she came around within my presence or not. *Yeah, I'm totally over her.*

So why am I so resentful? Why am I so aggravated by our chance meeting? Why does her proximity provoke my exasperation?

I didn't know the answers to any of the questions in my mind. I was still trying to figure out how I even noticed the new curves she seemed to have with slightly larger breasts and the appearance of curvier hips but still a tiny waist.

I shouldn't have detected the subtle changes in her body even though, once upon a time, I was well acquainted with every inch of her as she was with me. We were inseparable, and now we were utter strangers. Feelings I had kept locked up for years bubbled to the surface in unrecognizable forms. I'd loved that girl with every bit of my heart, body, and soul, and she demolished everything inside me.

I was grieving so badly when she first left; all I could think about was how much I missed her and how much I wanted her back. I never wanted to hurt her. I loved her.

But the instant I saw her after all this time, hurting her was my intention. I blurted out that I was engaged, which, although true, shouldn't have been something I could have gutted her with.

She would have to care about me for the mention of my moving on to affect her. And if she hadn't loved me all those years ago, why would she feel anything different now?

She probably went home grateful that I'd moved on so she could continue to live her life guilt-free.

But as well as being accustomed to her voice, her touch, the feel of her skin, and the smell of sunshine and flowers that was uniquely her, I was familiar with how easily she wore her emotions.

And the light that sparkled within her brown eyes dulled when I made my confession. I wanted to stab her heart with my words, and the dim flicker within those chocolate orbs confirmed I had succeeded.

Even though I was confident I had accomplished what I had set out to do, I didn't feel good about fulfilling my intention. I had been the recipient of pain from another person's actions, and I was feeling guilty and remorseful now.

Apologizing didn't feel right in this situation. Technically, I hadn't done anything wrong. I made a factual statement, even if verbalizing the truth was delivered with malicious intent.

I didn't want to believe that the guilt stemmed from the misguided, idealistic perspective I had as a teenager. I thought I was going to marry Ivy, and some of my guilty twinges probably stemmed from the ridiculous feeling that I was cheating on her.

My dreams of a happily ever after with her died a long time ago, so my heart and my brain needed to get over the delusion of us getting married and having a family together.

My future was going to be with Amilyn. We'd been together for nearly two years. Although we hadn't set a wedding date yet, she was wearing a ring I purchased, and we'd discussed what we wanted from life.

Maybe I needed to go see my fiancée. Maybe if I spent some time buried deep inside her, I'd forget about Ivy. Was that what I had done for all these years?

Damn. I really hoped that wasn't true. Admittedly, moving past Ivy had been the hardest thing I'd ever done, but I think I've finally been able to love someone else. My heart belonged to another woman now.

And with that realization, I drove to her apartment.

Amilyn lived in a tiny apartment. It was considered a one-bedroom, but the bedroom was barely large enough for a twin bed and a nightstand. She had a pull-out couch in the living room because her square footage was virtually nonexistent. She had a kitchenette and a bathroom with a small stand-up shower and a single sink and commode.

I knew that was all she could afford, but I'd offered to have her move in with me into my house; however, she didn't want to take that step until we determined a wedding date.

My house wasn't huge, but it was a lot bigger than what she was currently living in. I reminded myself she'd be moving in soon enough, so I'd keep my mouth shut because the more I suggested she leave her apartment, the more she pushed to stay there.

"Hey, beautiful," I said as soon as Amilyn answered the door after my three consecutive knocks. She hadn't given me a key to her place even though she'd had a key to my house and my parents' house for years.

I was graced with a wide smile, showing me she was happy to see me. I definitely needed that. I needed to feel like someone was delighted with my presence, and thankfully, she obliged me.

I wrapped my arms around her, but she pushed out of

my hold. Her blue eyes narrowed, and her brow furrowed. "What's wrong?"

"I just needed a hug, Aim." I could feel creases settle into my forehead as a result of her suspicion regarding my display of affection.

"Okay, we've done that. Now tell me why you need a hug." Her arms crossed over her body protectively as we continued to stand at the threshold of the entrance to her apartment. I stood on one side of the doorjamb, and she stayed rooted on the other side while maintaining an arm's length distance.

"May I come in?" I probably shouldn't have to request entry into my fiancée's home, but I tried to be respectful and not just barge in.

She swept her hand out, gesturing me to enter, so I walked past her into the living room. She clicked the door shut behind us, and I turned to face her.

I studied the soft lines of her face and jaw and her shoulder-length blond hair with curls skimming against the skin near her throat. Her eyes begged for my honesty, and I decided to be forthcoming.

"I saw my ex today at the gym."

Her sapphire eyes widened with astonishment before she whispered, "Ivy?"

We'd been together long enough that I'd shared everything about my past relationships with her, even though she hadn't revealed much information about her exes.

Guilt riddled me, causing me to slump my shoulders and drop my head down. "Yeah."

"And what happened?" Her voice remained soft and curious.

I pulled my head back up and met her gaze. "I yelled at her, and she practically ran out of the gym."

Her lips fell to a flat line, and she stared blankly at me, suddenly mute. Her soft voice was so much better than silence. When she asked questions, I could follow her train of thought. But when she didn't choose to speak, I had no way of knowing where her mind was going.

We stood on opposite sides of her tiny living room for several beats before she found her voice again. "Did you kiss her?"

"What? No." I shook my head. Although I could hear her words, I still didn't have any idea where her imagination was taking her.

"You're looking pretty guilty to me, Fletch." Her tone was still low and controlled. She hadn't raised her voice; curiosity still laced her softly spoken words.

I took a moment to quietly digest her accusation. I was feeling guilty, but because I was sorry I had yelled at Ivy, not because I wanted to kiss her. I hadn't even thought about kissing her.

Of course, now that Amilyn had planted that seed, I was bombarded with memories of kissing Ivy, and suddenly, I couldn't stop thinking about kissing Ivy. *What the hell?*

"I don't believe in having any secrets from you, so I wanted to let you know that Ivy was back in town." Perhaps my reassuring words could convince her, even though I didn't sound convincing to my own ears.

"Am I going to have to worry about you going back to her?" Hurt flashed in her eyes.

Somehow, I had managed to cause pain to two women today. One that I loved a long time ago and one that I was engaged to presently.

I shook my head. "Aim, I love *you*. I want to be with *you*." I gobbled up the two paces with short strides before reaching her. I cupped her face with my palms and pressed a kiss to her full lips with a gentle peck. "I'm going to spend the rest of my life with you."

Chapter 5

Ivy, present day

It only took five days after my parents left for me to be itching for something to do. I attempted patronizing another gym, but after I had been on a treadmill no more than twenty minutes, some asshole pulled the emergency stop string that I didn't have clipped to my body, thankfully, and said I was using *his* machine.

Once I recovered from nearly flying off the treadmill due to the abrupt stop, I exchanged some words with him about his name not being on the machine. I also said something about the reason he was acting like such a big dick was probably because the one in his pants was so small...but whatever.

Apparently, I wasn't meant to utilize my time at a gym right now. So, I decided to pursue something different from my original plan. I elected to obtain a job rather than take a couple months and figure out what my next step in my life would be.

I went to college to be a nurse and even sat for the Maryland board exam since I was technically a resident of Maryland, even though I attended college in another state.

Although I passed the board exam, I hadn't fully committed to beginning my career this summer. Originally, I wanted to take some time to decide where I wanted to live and work. I figured I could visit some places and determine where would be a good fit for me.

But my restlessness had me contemplating something more structured to do with my idle time. I considered taking a job as a waitress in the ocean resort town, where I worked every summer during high school. But after working the past four summers in a restaurant as a waitress in my college town, that option was not so appealing. Because after eight years as a waitress, I truly desired something different.

I wanted something that was more than just a paycheck. I wanted to do something that was meaningful. So I bit the bullet and called up my dad to inquire about a nursing position at the hospital in town.

I could have made phone calls myself, but I figured with my dad's position at the medical center, he had the ability to move things more quickly than I could on my own. His job revolved around quality improvement and efficient processes, after all.

So, a mere two weeks later, I was sitting in an auditorium filled with other hospital new hires. The first day I sat through organization topics applicable to all employees. I listened to spiels on corporate compliance and sexual harassment, as well as a whole slew of additional lectures that had nothing to do with being a nurse.

They fed us lunch that first day, and we were visited by hospital executives. But on the second day, laborious tests were administered, and classes on equipment and computer access processes were put into place, and chart documentation highlights were taught.

I thought I had returned to nursing school. We were on

our own for lunch every day, and although we went to the cafeteria as a group each day for the following four days, I hadn't exactly opened myself up to making friends with any of the women in my classes, so I ate by myself Tuesday through Friday.

I had no problem making friends in college, but my hometown hadn't been very welcoming, so I most likely retreated into my own space, unwilling to put myself out there. It was no wonder I kept to myself. My parents essentially left a hot second after I arrived home from college. With my less-than-receptive run-in with Fletcher and butting heads with the two jackasses at the gyms, my hesitation to interact with other people seemed warranted.

But after the grueling and truly boring week of hospital and nursing orientation, I was finally walking into the emergency department for my first shift.

I walked in through the sliding glass doors at the rear entrance near the ambulance bay. No one greeted me or asked if I needed anything. I guess since I was so excited about this new adventure, I expected someone else to be excited with me.

Instead, other nurses pushed past me, and when I couldn't remember how to get to the time clock, I attempted to ask someone, only to be ignored.

I can't believe my dad works for this hospital. No one was friendly, and I wasn't enjoying anything about this place so far. The orientation week was a mixture of boring and stressful. I hadn't made any friends, and now, within my own department, I felt out of place.

Coming home had been one disaster after another. I'd always stood up for myself before, so I needed to do that now. No one else was going to look out for me, so it was time

I took charge of my life. Instead of things happening to me, I'd make them happen *for* me.

Since all the nurses in the department wore mint-green scrubs, the others were easy to identify. If no one would speak to me, then I would just follow the next nurse to walk into the department. Surely, he or she would need to clock in for the night shift also.

So I fell in line behind the next person who entered the department wearing the same color scrubs. She was a woman maybe a decade older than me who walked at a fast pace. Her legs weren't as long as mine, but clearly, she planned to get to wherever she was going in a hurry.

Her strawberry-blond hair was tied in a ponytail, and her curly hair bounced as her pace picked up to a brisk jog.

I fell into step behind her and continued to trail behind her to the time clock. I mimicked her by swiping my badge and pressing the *in* button. Then, I maintained my position as her shadow and slid into the huddle room after her.

Fake it until you make it. I'd figured things out so far.

"You Ivy?" a woman in her forties with jet-black hair and dark-rimmed glasses asked me.

"Yes, ma'am." I nodded.

She dragged her scrutinizing gaze up and down me in some kind of weird assessment.

"You'll be with Dawn tonight," she said and led into a speech about the assignments for the night shift.

I didn't receive an introduction to Dawn, but then again, she hadn't introduced herself either. I examined everyone in the room as the nurse I presumed was in charge spoke to the pack of us wearing mint green.

Once she finished sharing the itinerary for the next twelve hours, she scrunched her nose, hopefully just to move her glasses further up her nose and not as a sign of disgust.

Jeez, can I at least run into one nice person in this whole town? I used to like it here. But things had certainly changed.

"So, I guess you're with me tonight?" the strawberry-blond nurse I followed into the department said as she cracked gum loudly several times.

"You're Dawn?" I quirked my eyebrow, slightly astounded that she hadn't introduced herself when the charge nurse made the declaration that she was to precept me tonight.

"Yep." She shrugged and then trotted out the door with her ponytail once again bouncing with each of her paces.

Little did I know when I followed her into the department that I would be following her for the entire night.

~

The night passed fairly quickly, but by the end of my first shift, I was completely exhausted and craved my bed with its fluffy duvet and plush pillows. I had just changed the sheets yesterday, so I knew the fresh-from-the-laundry smell still lingered on the fabric.

I sniffed the air and wrapped my arms around myself while squinting my eyes shut, standing right in the nurse's station, imagining my clean sheets, comfy cover, and soft pillows.

"Ivy, stop the daydreaming and get into room one." Dawn's voice had me snap my eyes open and startle from my fantasy, which embarrassingly was of my bedroom... sleeping alone.

I nodded once in recognition of her demand and stepped in the direction of the minor care area. Mostly, we had helped with splints, bandages, crutches, and the like. Dawn and I had been assigned the lesser acuity patients since I was new, I guess.

The most exciting thing I had done all night was to clean some bad road rash with some saline and brush out the small bits of gravel from a teenage girl's knee after she took a tumble on the asphalt, chasing after some high school boys on her bike. Luckily, she had been wearing a helmet, so other than a wound that would heal on her knee and being a whole lot embarrassed, she would be fine.

I must have been half asleep on my feet while dreaming of this shift being over because I didn't even notice the triage nurse had brought a patient back to our area.

Dawn had paid attention, and she scowled at me when my gaze connected with hers. She had been an ER nurse for fifteen years, and although I had no doubt she was skilled and knowledgeable, she wasn't exactly warm and fuzzy.

But that was okay. Since being back in Villpointe, I hadn't met many friendly people. I supposed work was going to be no different.

So, after I broke my gaze free from Dawn's threatening grimace, I inhaled a deep breath and headed into room one to take care of what felt like my hundredth patient of the night. And it wasn't even night anymore; it was six a.m. I knew the emergency room was always open, but this was ridiculous.

"Hi, my name is Ivy, and I'm going to be your nurse. What brings you here tonight..." When I observed the man holding a white T-shirt stained with blood over his lower leg, I wasn't speechless because of the continued bleeding.

I lost my words because of who the patient was. Sitting on the stretcher was Fletcher Hart.

My tongue was dry and refused to move and formulate anything that resembled speech.

I thought Dawn's scowl was angry, but Fletcher's glare shot daggers in my direction. Those light blue eyes were icy and cold, not warm and inviting as I once viewed them.

I cleared my throat, hoping to free the words that were lodged somewhere deep within my vocal cords when another voice echoed in the room. "Hi, Ivy. My name is John. And this is Fletcher."

I twisted my neck hastily toward the deep baritone of the man speaking. I hadn't even realized there was anyone else in the room. But it wasn't completely unheard of for me to have blinders on when it came to Fletcher.

I used to only see him, even in a crowded room.

When I glanced at John, he jutted his hand in my direction.

I swept my gaze down to his hand and then over to Fletcher again.

However, once my brown eyes focused on his blue ones, I instantly shook myself free from his unwavering glare and quickly moved toward John, grasping his hand awkwardly and pumping twice.

Without averting my eyes back toward Fletcher, I asked John, "What happened?"

"That idiot cut me with a saw."

John's eyes widened, but his lips hadn't moved from their downward tug at the corners.

The comment was made by the man who had once owned my heart.

I once again swung my gaze back toward Fletcher, who was still pressing a shirt to his lower leg.

"May I take a look?" I asked softly, trying to calm the angry man sitting on the stretcher before me in a room that suddenly felt extremely too small for me and the two men in it.

Fletcher clenched his jaw and hissed through his teeth.

He didn't deny my request, so I took that as nonverbal consent and squatted on the floor next to him and touched the white fabric splattered with large drops of crimson.

He flinched away from my touch and kept his fingers firmly in place, holding the shirt against his skin.

I placed my hand over his and peered up at him, and this time, he didn't pull away from me.

His eyes softened, and he released a short breath accompanied by a low grunt. It wasn't an angry grunt, though; it sounded more like one of the noises he would make when he was satisfied with an accomplishment, like after he scored a goal in soccer or a home run in baseball.

I licked my lips and drew in a breath at the memory of his satisfied grumbles.

When I pulled his hand away, I dropped my gaze down as I removed the fabric, which revealed a four-centimeter laceration that was slowly dripping blood. I replaced the fabric and instructed him to keep it in place while I grabbed several four-by-four gauzes.

Once I had a good stack of gauze piled, I replaced the shirt with the clean medical compress and once again directed him to hold pressure on the area. Our fingers grazed each other's several times during the exchange, and he didn't withdraw from my touch at any point.

"You're going to need stitches," I said as I stood. "I'm going to go get the doctor."

"Thanks, Ivy," John said from the side of the room, but my eyes remained zoned in on Fletcher.

Fletcher only gave a tight nod, and I turned on my heel to leave the room.

I was barely across the threshold, still recalling how his hands weren't soft like they used to be but calloused and rough when I heard *his* voice.

"Don't even think about it, jackass."

"Why not? You know how I have a thing for nurses," John replied.

"You have a thing for any woman that acknowledges your presence."

"You're just jealous because I can still play the field, and you're tied to one woman."

John's comment stung, and I should have continued walking away from the room, but as the glutton for punishment that I am, I slowed my steps to an eventual halt just so I could hear how the rest of the conversation was going to go.

"I'm definitely not jealous. You can go stick your dick in whoever you want, as far as I'm concerned. Just leave Ivy alone."

John released a rumble of laughter. "Then give me a reason why."

After a few beats of silence, I walked away and alerted the physician of the suture potential.

Doctor Gibson and I returned to Fletcher's room, and after assessing the patient, I was instructed to prepare the patient for suturing.

I grabbed the necessary supplies and assisted the doctor without Dawn even making an appearance. I had no idea where she had gone, but I guess she figured I could handle cleaning a wound, helping the physician during the suturing procedure, and covering the repaired laceration with a clean dressing on my own.

And typically, I would have felt confident to handle that kind of patient. But I was *not* confident in handling Fletcher Hart anymore.

Chapter 6

Fletcher, present day

I was too stunned at the discovery that Ivy was my nurse for my unfortunate injury that I was unable to be angry at the sight of her. I tried to deliver my most intimidating glare, but once she touched me, a sense of calm settled over me. She was so familiar and comforting.

I could hate myself for letting the mere brush of her fingertips resolve all the years of pent-up frustration regarding Ivy Hatfield. But I utterly crumbled beneath the gentle contact of her hand on top of mine.

If I had a different nurse, I knew the feel of a soft hand on my wound wouldn't have felt so intimate, but because it was *her*, I was washed with a flood of memories.

Ivy's hands roaming and exploring every inch of my body.

Ivy's lips trailing kisses over any and all exposed skin.

Ivy's naked body...

Shit, I need to get ahold of myself.

I was engaged. I shouldn't be having any of these thoughts regarding another woman. A long time ago, she was my best friend, and then she was so much more than that. She was my first kiss, my first girlfriend, my first everything.

Even now, I'd only had sex with two women ever. Ivy was my first, and if I had my way, she would have been my only. When she broke up with me and left for college without me, my heart had been so damaged I didn't think I'd ever recover.

John insisted the way to get over one woman was to bend over another. He and I became friends shortly after Ivy and I split. He only knew as much as I told him, and I was so hurt I didn't want to share much. The pain was too great. Anytime I mentioned her or anything about her, another tiny fissure cracked through the wall of my heart.

John was good at providing a distraction. He took me out to have drinks, and although I never hooked up with women like he did, I probably wouldn't have left my house if he hadn't insisted on taking me to dinner or a bar for a couple of beers.

For that, I would always be grateful that he came into that incredibly painful time in my life. But I definitely didn't believe in his wandering ways. He tested too many waters for my liking. He had no desire to settle down, where I'd always known I would get married and have a family one day.

Of course, I'd thought that would happen with Ivy. But regardless, I never would have been interested in a casual relationship. I wanted to be committed, which is probably why I've pushed this engagement on Amilyn.

She said she wasn't ready to set a wedding date, but as long as she was wearing my ring, I'd told her I was okay with that.

Why is it that the only two women I've ever been serious about brush me off when it comes to the long-term kind of love?

These thoughts continued to invade my brain as I lay in bed the following night. I wondered what happened to change Ivy's mind about us.

I was convinced she felt the same way about me that I felt about her. We had been friends since first grade, had seen each other at our best and worst, gone through milestones together, and wanted careers where we helped people and a family to come home to every night.

At some point, she must have been lying to me because I still didn't understand how she could have meant what she said about having a forever with me, only to be tossed aside the summer after our senior year of high school.

She'd told me she loved me. She'd shown me she loved me. But then I'd let her words cut through me. I hadn't examined what her actions actually said to me.

They say actions speak louder than words, but I'd let her words determine our fate.

Maybe I shouldn't have walked away after what she said. Perhaps if I had insisted, we could have worked through anything and genuinely tried to make that happen. Things could have possibly been different.

Maybe it wasn't even about me. Maybe she had some scary shit she was dealing with, and I walked away. If I hadn't cooperated and agreed to go our separate ways, would we still be apart?

What if I had hugged her and kissed her like I did for every other tough situation she went through her whole life? Would she have confided in me or continued to push me away?

Then, as if I'd willed her to speak to me, my phone

vibrated against the wooden tabletop of my nightstand, and when I lifted the device, Ivy's name illuminated the screen with a text message.

> Ivy: I'm not sure if you'll get this text or not, but I just wanted to check in with you. I hope your laceration is doing okay.

I had no idea if I should respond or not. Of course, she was uncertain if I'd get the message. She called and texted me several times over the past four years, which always went unanswered. She probably thought I blocked her number. I considered it—I really did. But I couldn't seem to do it. Because even though she destroyed me, if she ever needed anything, I couldn't deny her help.

> Me: I'm good. Thanks for your help today.

Three dots danced across my screen like she was formulating a response, but then they stopped. After thirty-two minutes, the dots didn't reappear, and no text came through from her.

Great. Now I was worried about her. I hadn't worried about her in years, but after a retracted text, I wondered if she was okay. She hadn't reached out to me in a long time. Was checking on me just a cover? Did she really need a friend?

I wiped my hand across my face and then was in my truck before I could talk myself out of it.

~

"Fletch, what are you doing here?" Her hair was piled on top of her head like I remembered how she used to wear it, and she was wearing short flannel pajama shorts with a tight-fitted tank top.

Her surprise transitioned to concern swiftly. "Are you alright? Is your leg okay?" She reached for my upper arm and grasped tightly, pulling me toward the open door to her house, and I willingly allowed her to propel my body into her living room.

I kicked the door shut with the bottom of my foot like I had so many times over the course of my life. Being around her became associated with so many memories— good memories, not just the one that broke my teenage heart.

I made a quick perusal of the living room and noted everything seemed to be in the same place as the last time I saw the interior of her home.

"Fletch."

Ivy's voice snapped my wandering eyes back to focus on her face. Her mouth tugged downward in the corners, and worry creased lines across her forehead. Those chocolate eyes danced with concern, and I wanted to just hug the crap out of her and assure her everything was okay.

"I'm okay, Ivy." Saying her given name suddenly felt foreign on my tongue. I spewed it out before attempting to strike a nerve with her.

I told her about Amilyn in an effort to hurt her. But I didn't want to upset her. No matter how much she broke me, I didn't want to cause her any emotional harm.

"Then what are you doing here?" Her nose wrinkled, and one of her brows shot upward as concern switched to confusion across her face.

"I wanted to make sure *you* were okay."

Her fingers still gripped my upper arm, but when I broke my gaze from hers and glanced down to where her palm rested against my bicep, she dropped her hand promptly to her side.

"Why would you think I wasn't okay?" She nervously propped the same hand to her hip as if she didn't know what to do with it after breaking contact with my arm.

"You texted me," I retorted plainly.

She released a small sigh that was so familiar I felt my heart squeeze at the simple sound. "I didn't expect you to respond."

"So you sent me a text because you didn't think I would text you back?" That didn't even make sense to my some-times-twisted brain.

She dropped her gaze down to her bare feet.

I couldn't help but follow her line of sight and took notice of the pink polish on her toes. And once again, my heart tugged, but this time, my throat constricted with emotion.

She always wore shades of pink on her toenails. Never blue, green, purple, or even red. She only wore pink. Her toes were always adorable and now was no different.

"You're not okay, are you?" My voice came out softer and raspier than I intended, but somehow, words were lodged in my throat and squeaked once sound was emitted from my vocal cords.

Her shoulders shook, which was always a predictor of falling tears shortly after. So I did what I always did when she cried.

I wrapped my arms around her and pulled her close to my chest for an embrace, pressing the side of her head against my heart. Her sobs were quiet, as were the sniffles she attempted to stifle.

But I was powerless to her tears. And soon, I was stroking my hand over her hair and whispering in her ear that everything would be okay. She would put on a brave front around everyone else, but she always let me see her vulnerable side, and rather than purposely wound her when her walls were down, I chose to comfort her. That's just how our relationship had always been, and it was so easy to fall back into the Fletcher-Ivy relationship of the past.

Chapter 7

Fletcher, age 15

"You don't have to be tough around me," I said to Ivy as she lay on the stretcher in the emergency room of our local hospital.

I didn't dare look down at her wrist, but I was told by her mom that it was deformed and obviously broken.

Her dark eyes held a sheen of water over the chocolate orbs from unshed tears. She squeezed my hand awkwardly since she needed to use her left hand because her wrist injury was on her right.

One salty drop fell from the corner of her eye and slid down her cheek. I wanted to take away her pain, but all I could literally do was wipe away her tears. So I brushed my thumb across her cheek with my free hand and chased the evidence of her pain away.

Her parents were outside the room, speaking with the doctor. They asked if I could stay with her while they did.

They didn't need to ask me. I would always be with her when she needed me, and right now, she needed me.

I witnessed her fall on the soccer field. The boys' soccer team always watched the girls' home games after our practice if we didn't have a game ourselves. Most of my team would chatter among ourselves and not pay a whole lot of attention to the girls' games. Our presence was enough support as far as most of them were concerned. But not for me.

I was there to support my best friend, just as she had always supported me. I cheered louder than anyone for her, causing more than a few of my teammates to roll their eyes over my enthusiasm, but I didn't care what they thought.

And when that girl tripped Ivy, watching her outstretch her right arm and land on her hand played like slow motion until I heard the crack that resonated in the air.

Ivy jumped back up like the tough girl she'd always been, and after regaining possession of the ball, she drew her leg back and had a beautiful shot on goal that struck the upper right corner of the net, putting our school ahead by two goals.

There were only two minutes left in the game, but my girl gripped her wrist after she scored and headed to the bench. That's when I knew she was injured. She wouldn't have been looking to be replaced by a sub on the field if she wasn't really hurt.

I leaped from my place on the bleachers surrounded by my teammates and jogged down several stairs till I was level with the playing field. A chain-linked fence separated me from where she sat on the team bench as she was given ice and the trainer taped and splinted her wrist.

I totally wanted to hop the short fence and be with her, but I restrained myself from doing so. That was until the ambulance arrived. Then, I cleared that fence like a hurdle jumper on the track team.

Her parents weren't at the game because her dad's sister, Ivy's aunt Charlotte, was in labor, so she needed to ride in the ambulance with the assistant principal. At least her mom and dad were already at the hospital, so they would meet her, rather us, at the hospital. Because I was getting in the back of that ambulance with her.

"Mr. Hart, what do you think you're doing?" Mr. Briggs, the vice principal for our grade, asked.

"Mr. Briggs, Ivy is my best friend. I know about her medications and allergies. Without her parents, I'm the next best person to provide her medical history," I said while climbing into the ambulance.

The paramedic shrugged and exchanged a look with Mr. Briggs but didn't refuse my entry, so I took that as implied approval and slid onto the bench next to Ivy.

"I'm scared, Fletch." Her eyes shook with apprehension, and my heart fell into my gut at the look of sheer terror within her gaze.

I scooted closer to her and grabbed her hand. "I'm right here like always. I told you we would be forever together. No one will ever split us apart."

"Your boyfriend is a romantic," the female paramedic said, reaching over me as she placed a blood pressure cuff around Ivy's upper arm on the side where I was currently seated.

I released her hand and nonchalantly told the paramedic, "I'm not her boyfriend. I'm her best friend. She might have lots of boyfriends someday, but they'll come and go. I'm always going to be right here...forever at her side."

The woman laughed and shook her head at humor I didn't contemplate. "It's going to be challenging for her to have a boyfriend if you're forever at her side."

After a chuckle, she inflated the cuff and completed her assessment of Ivy while we were en route to the hospital.

Our high school was only two miles away from the local

hospital, so we arrived at the back door of the emergency department in a matter of a few minutes.

~

Ivy and I were still alone in her room in the emergency department while additional tears fell from her soft brown eyes. She lay on a gurney, and I was seated next to her in a plastic chair dotted with stains that were hopefully from just regular dirt and not bodily fluids. Her broken arm sat across her waist, still immobilized in a splint with a fresh ice pack over the wrist.

The water fell down her cheeks with more frequency, and I could no longer brush them away. "You're going to be okay," I reassured her as I gave her hand an additional squeeze.

"Are you okay?" A weak smile tugged at her pale lips as her silent crying continued.

I couldn't help but release a slight chuckle. She was injured, and she was worried about me. Although typical of her character, her selflessness was one of the reasons why she was my best friend.

Emotion clogged my throat at her concern for me, and I leaned in toward her, bringing my face only inches from hers.

The smile she had started to wear only a moment ago flattened, and I swear she leaned forward, closing the last bit of distance between us.

When our lips met, soft and gentle, she sighed, but I drew in a breath. My nerves had me holding my breath while she seemed to feel a sense of relief.

Our mouths pressed harder, and I didn't know if she

pushed into me or if I pulled her toward me, but I knew that moment would be tattooed in my brain forever.

She reached for the back of my neck with one hand, and soon I was hovering over her with my ass now seated alongside her hip on the stretcher.

When she parted her lips, I delved my tongue against the slightly open seam and tasted her. She welcomed me and opened further for me to deepen our kiss.

We weren't each other's first kiss, but this was *our* first kiss. Her first kiss was with a boy named Billy during summer camp after sixth grade, and mine was with a girl named Lucy, who was my girlfriend in eighth grade.

I didn't know why I was thinking about who our first kisses were while I was kissing Ivy.

I'm kissing Ivy.

She was my best friend, and I was kissing her.

And I was enjoying it tremendously. Our tongues slid over each other's, and our mouths fit together so perfectly that I didn't understand why we hadn't kissed before now.

"Thanks for keeping Ivy company while we spoke with the doctor." Ivy's father's voice broke our lip-lock, causing me to jump off the bed and land my ass back in the plastic chair next to the stretcher.

I was certain we appeared like two kids caught making out, which I guess was true to some extent. I was mortified. I had no words. *Should I apologize? Should I pretend nothing happened?*

Thankfully, Ivy spoke first. "He's good at distracting me." A sly smile pinched at her cheeks, and I wanted to die of humiliation.

"Is this new?" Ivy's mom bounced her index finger from Ivy to me several times. "Or has this been going on for a while?"

"Mom, that was our first kiss," Ivy said with an exaggerated eye roll.

Ivy's dad glared in my direction, most likely awaiting my corroboration of her statement.

"She's telling the truth, Mr. and Mrs. Hatfield." *Hopefully, I don't piss myself before I can finish.* "I'm sorry I kissed her before asking your permission."

Mr. Hatfield huffed out a short laugh. "You were going to ask permission before you kissed my daughter?"

"No, sir." I gulped down the golf ball-size lump lodged in my throat, uncertain whether he was going to kick my ass or approve of my request. "I was going to ask permission if your daughter could be my girlfriend."

The laugh lines at the corners of his eyes disappeared, and his dark eyes blinked several times rapidly as he attempted to absorb what I had just asked.

"That is adorable, Fletcher." Mrs. Hatfield clapped her hands several times in excitement. At least I had the support of one of her parents. "You and Ivy have been friends forever, and now you want to be boyfriend and girlfriend. That's precious. Right, Jim?"

Ivy's dad shook the shocked look off his face, and a stern gaze bore into me. "I guess Ivy could do a whole lot worse."

Thanks for the compliment, Mr. Hatfield.

The sound of a ping rang in the room, and Mrs. Hatfield grabbed her phone from the purse she had on her wrist and a bright, wide smile lit up her face. "Charlotte is pushing, Jim. We're about to be an aunt and uncle."

His forlorn expression clearly marked how torn he was at the situation at hand. He wanted to be in two places at once. I was familiar with how protective he was over his much younger sister. She had married a few years ago. I went to the wedding with Ivy so she would have someone to hang out with at the reception.

Charlotte was only ten years older than Ivy and me. And Mr. Hatfield was fifteen years older than his only sibling. Considering how protective he was of his sister, I would expect him to be even more so with his daughter.

"Jim, I'll stay down here with Ivy, and I'll call you the moment anything happens." She delivered a brief peck to his cheek.

And then, with a tight nod, he was gone without even an "I'll be back" or "See you soon" to his daughter. I guess he figured she was in good hands.

It was kind of crazy that Charlotte was born when her brother was our age, and now he was running to the labor and delivery area of the hospital department again to see her give birth.

"I'm going to run to the ladies' room and I'll be back," Mrs. Hatfield said before shuffling out the room as well.

"Seriously, Fletch?" Ivy sat up further and reached across to slap my arm with her good hand. "You asked my dad to be my boyfriend?"

"Yeah, so?" I said, rubbing my arm from where her unexpected slap stung my skin.

"So now we're going to have to pretend to be boyfriend and girlfriend." Her dark eyes were stormy and irritated.

"Who says we have to pretend?"

"How else are we going to cover your lie?" She blew out an exasperated breath.

"Who says I was lying?"

Her jaw slacked, and her eyes softened into a wistful glimpse of understanding. "What are you trying to say?"

"You know me better than anyone. You know exactly what I'm trying to say. But I'll give you the benefit of the doubt since you might be under the influence of pain meds and therefore not able to understand as quickly." I grabbed her hand and brushed my thumb along her sensitive palm while connecting my gaze with hers. "I want to be your boyfriend. Will you be my girlfriend?"

Maybe I shouldn't have asked during a vulnerable time or a time when she wasn't able to make decisions clearly because she was on some pain medications, but she said yes, and I transitioned from just her best friend to her boyfriend. I retained the best friend title too.

Unfortunately, I lost both labels simultaneously at the worst time of my life. Not only did I lose my girlfriend and best friend, but I lost them both when I needed them the most.

Chapter 8

Ivy, present day

Fletcher had hugged me probably thousands of times, but this time felt like a first. Maybe because it had been so damn long since I felt the warmth and comfort from one of his hugs.

I would have said that I had forgotten what one of his embraces felt like, but as I stood here in his arms, I could remember with vivid clarity. He felt like the best memories, a cozy blanket and hot chocolate on a cold night.

Not only did I melt into him, listening to the soothing sound of his heart's beating rhythm, but I let the tears openly fall like I only could in front of him.

I chose to have everyone just see the badass part of myself. I could fight my own battles, and I would never give anyone the satisfaction of seeing me as weak. But with Fletcher, I could show my vulnerability.

When we broke up, although at the time I thought it was for the best, I cried in the shower or alone in my bed for months after I left for college. I missed him so much I didn't think I'd survive. But somehow, I did.

And now, in his arms, I couldn't fathom how I made it the past four years of my life without him. Because I didn't even know I needed him tonight, and yet he did. And here he was, giving me the hug I so desperately craved but didn't even know I wanted.

My sobs grew louder, not because of the original reason I began crying, but due to the realization of the thoughts that slammed into my brain. I had this beautiful man as my best friend, my boyfriend, my other half...and I left him.

I really thought I was being selfless and doing the right thing. He needed to be home and not follow me to college, but no one ever said that being selfless would feel good.

Whoever said, "If you love someone, then set them free," should have said how miserable you'd feel when you did it. Supposedly, if you loved someone, you cared more about their happiness than your own. Unfortunately, Fletcher and I were in a no-win situation, and I made my decision based on what my young heart and mind thought was best.

"What's going on, Vine?" Fletcher asked with a softness to his tone as he gently cradled my jaw with his hands, and his light denim-blue gaze connected to my tear-filled brown one.

My old nickname falling from his lips had sobs shaking my shoulders even harder. This was more than showing my vulnerability. This was pent-up sadness that had been buried deep inside me, rushing out like a busted pipe. I couldn't seem to stop it.

"Has someone hurt you?" His concern ripped my heart open further. He had been the only one to hurt me, and I had no one to blame but myself.

"Are we going to be able to be friends?" I questioned with a hiccup.

A hint of a smile appeared, and his white teeth peeked through his pink lips. "I don't know how I thought it would ever be possible to stop being friends with you."

"Everything has been awful since I've come home."

Fletcher dropped his hands from my face and grabbed my hand, pulling me toward the couch, eventually urging me downward to sit next to him.

We both plopped down onto the cushions, and I recounted the past few weeks. The gym disasters, my parents' departure shortly after I arrived, and the unfriendly people at work.

"The worst part is my best friend hates me." I swiped at both of my cheeks, feeling how wet and sore the skin had become from the salty waterworks.

"Who's your best friend? Someone you met at college or someone I know?" His teasing was obvious, and the relief caused me to smack his arm, falling into our old patterns.

"Thanks for coming over, Fletch. And thanks especially for knowing I needed you. I've never had another friend like you, and I probably won't ever again."

I felt a million times better since Fletcher had shown up at my parents' house last night. He listened to me and then gave me one last brief hug. It felt like old times, yet something new and different at the same time.

I was okay with that. Just having him back in my life as a friend had me feeling like being back home wasn't so bad after all. I wondered if he told his fiancée about his late-night visit to my parents' house, but I didn't want to let my mind go there.

Because if she didn't want him to be friends with me, I

figured he would choose her wants over mine. And I didn't want to think about him choosing another woman over me.

Although I knew we could never go back to how our relationship was before, rebuilding our friendship was something I felt like we could do. Fifteen years of friendship couldn't be just forgotten that easily. I was relieved to discover our friendship could withstand the bad stuff in life.

I was still reminiscing in the memory of last night and the rekindling of our friendship when Fletcher appeared through the back door of the emergency department. Only he wasn't a patient this time.

He was dressed in a navy-blue fire department-issued button-down shirt with navy slacks that hugged his ass. Damn, he had grown into a fine-looking man.

His smile lit up his face when his gaze connected with mine, and I could feel my lips curling up into a grin as well.

I was thinking about him, and he appeared.

He pushed the stretcher with a middle-aged patient toward an empty room after being instructed by the charge nurse. The man dressed in similar attire that stood alongside the gurney, I recognized as John—the friend that brought Fletcher in when he required stitches.

"Fifty-five-year-old man with shortness of breath," Fletcher reported to the ER staff that followed him into the large trauma room. "History of chronic bronchitis and COPD."

"Page respiratory," the physician standing at the head of the bed directed to a girl dressed in tan-colored scrubs.

She nodded and left the room.

Fletcher finished his verbal report, and once the ER team took over care of the patient, he and John left the room.

"So, I guess you became a firefighter after high school?"

I said as I stood in the threshold of the EMS room several minutes later.

Firefighters, EMTs, and paramedics had a room within the ER for them to complete their electronic reports. The room wasn't that large, but it did have a few computers, a little kitchen with a fridge, and an equipment closet.

Fletcher looked up from the computer screen, and that wide smile stretched across his face once again. "Yeah, and I went to paramedic school also."

"Nice to see you again, Ivy," John said with a quick wave.

"Hi, John. Glad to see you as well." I only gave him a second of my attention, and then I shifted my focus back to Fletcher. "How's the leg?"

Fletcher pulled up the leg of his pants and revealed a Band-Aid covering the laceration on his lower leg. "It's fine."

"Do you check up on all of your patients? If that's the case, I may need to step on a rusty nail or something." John's comment earned him a glare of disapproval from Fletcher but a small laugh from me.

"Fletch and I were friends a long time ago. I was a little shocked to see him the other day because it had been a while, but his persistent stalking has worn me down. I've agreed to be friends with him again."

John's gaze bounced back and forth from me to Fletcher and back to me.

"I didn't stalk you," Fletcher said with a loud chuckle.

"Please. You've shown up at my work twice and came over to my house last night," I guffawed.

"Whaaaat?" John's eyes widened, and he once again shifted his gaze back and forth between Fletcher and me.

"You showed up at my gym first," Fletcher teased back.

"Ivy Hatfield, you bitch."

And just like that, the friendly teasing and rebuilding of our relationship was silenced by the shrill female's brash comment.

I swung my torso around to identify the owner of the voice, and I immediately launched myself at the woman, who openly welcomed my hug, wearing a smile too big to be considered cute and demure.

But my friend Julie was never a girly girl. She was a tomboy through and through.

"Watch it, calling me a bitch where I work," I said while shoving out of the physical assault I had instigated.

"Hey, I work here too," she said, spinning slowly to showcase her teal-colored scrubs. "I'm a respiratory therapist."

"Nice." I spun on my heel, too, as if I needed to explain my occupation also.

"Let me guess." Julie tapped her chin contemplatively and then snapped. "ER nurse?"

"Is it that obvious?" I shrugged.

"Well, you're hanging out in the EMS room, so I'm hoping it's just to talk to Fletcher and not because you're planning to let John get in your pants." She always spoke without a filter, but I couldn't help the flash of heat in my cheeks following her comment. "I didn't realize you two got back together."

Now Fletcher's cheeks had a red hue as well.

John's rumbling laughter broke through the suddenly tense moment with an inappropriate amount of loudness and misplaced humor. "Ivy's the girl that broke your heart, isn't she?" he coughed out in between his fit of chuckles.

"Damn, I guess there's a story there," Julie said with a

hand propped on her hip. She scrunched her nose and waved indifference with her other hand through the air, killing John's insensitive laughter. "So you're single?"

Her comment was directed at me. She had gestured that the men were not to be part of our conversation any longer.

I nodded, and her face glowed with happiness, just like when we were in high school, and something wonderful occurred.

She clapped once, again breaking our stunned silence. "Perfect. We'll go out this weekend. I'll bring a couple of my male coworkers." She winked in my direction, indicating this would be a set up.

Julie had a way of creating awkward situations without even trying. "Give me your phone," she commanded like she always had when we were younger.

I dug my cell out of the back pocket of my scrub pants and handed it over, unlocking the screen before I did.

She tapped against the screen several times and shoved it back in my direction. "I put my new number in there. I mean, it's not really new...but you didn't have it, so text me. I gotta run."

She waved once and jogged off, leaving me alone with Fletcher and John again.

"Are you really going out with Julie and some guys?" Fletcher's nostrils flared just like they did when we were kids. When we were little, it was how I knew he was angry. But as we got older, it was his tell regarding jealousy.

This time, I thought the gesture revealed a little of both.

"Let me know where, and I'll meet you," John offered, I'm sure just to poke the bear.

A low sound emitted from Fletcher's throat that resonated like a growl.

"You could come, too, Fletch. You could bring your fiancée." I suppose I wanted to poke the bear as well. If he was jealous, what did that say exactly?

"I'm not available for your every whim anymore, Ivy." His gravelly voice wasn't sexy; it was spat with venom.

"I thought after all this time had passed, we were working our way back to a friendship," I whined at a higher pitch than I intended when I spoke.

"I guess I realized it's better if we go back to not speaking or seeing each other."

My heart cracked with his icy words. "Okay. I won't text or call you anymore."

"You should have taken the hint five years ago when you incessantly texted and called. If I had wanted to speak to you, I would have." He stood to his full height and pushed the plastic chair he had been sitting on beneath the counter more aggressively than necessary, causing the metal legs to scrape loudly against the linoleum floor.

"It's only been four," I cried without tears. *Seriously, what's up with the high-pitched voice?*

"It feels like it's been a lot longer," he retorted with sheer malice.

Gone was the man who held me as I wept last night.

I nodded in agreement. It felt as if a lifetime had passed since we were the Ivy-Fletcher team. "At least you were able to move on with someone else." My voice quivered even though I managed to reduce its octave. "I'm glad you've found happiness because I certainly haven't...maybe that will give you some satisfaction."

I glanced at John, who was still sitting in a chair, taking in the scene.

"Good to see you, John. Maybe we'll run into each other

again." I offered a weak smile and walked away from my previous happiness just like I did over four years ago.

But when you loved someone, their happiness was supposed to be more important than yours, so once again, even though it hurt like hell, I did the right thing. I walked away even though it broke my heart to do so.

Chapter 9

Fletcher, 14 years old

I vy sat next to me at lunch every day for all of middle school, and today, she sat next to a girl named Julie.

We had other friends besides each other, but I liked that we were always each other's first pick, whether it was the kickball team in gym class, a seat at lunch, a field trip partner, or someone to go to the movies or grab something to eat with.

Ever since Carrie moved three years ago, it'd just been the two of us. Our friendship had been unconventional, but even our parents had realized that we were each other's best friends, which meant we spent most of our time together.

I'd even spent the night at her house. Not in her room like she and Carrie used to, but in a sleeping bag on her living room floor, eating popcorn and watching movies until we fell asleep. And then the next day, Mrs. Hatfield made us a huge breakfast, and I went back home.

Although my parents had offered to let Ivy to spend the night at my house, her parents weren't comfortable with that. I guess they thought my parents wouldn't keep as close an eye on us as they did.

A lot of kids at school had questioned our friendship, but we didn't care. The ones who had known us since elementary school were aware we'd been best friends since first grade, and even though the newer ones had tried teasing us, we'd let their comments roll off our backs.

However confident I'd been in our friendship, today I felt alone, which was not something I'd ever had happen before. Not since before first grade, anyway.

But I guess she had a new friend now. Today was the first day of high school, and she met stupid Julie in first-period biology class.

She spent all of second-period gym class with me, telling me about the friend she made in the class prior.

Then they apparently had computer science class third period and decided to eat together during fourth period lunch. When I approached the table, Julie literally shooed me away, stating she and Ivy needed to get to know each other better.

I couldn't believe it, but Ivy went along with it, and I sulked away with my tail between my legs to sit with guys from the soccer team. I was friends with them, too, but I wanted to eat with my best friend, just like I had done every year since first grade.

After soccer practice that day, my mom picked up Ivy and me and drove us home.

"Ivy, since your parents have that fundraiser this evening, why don't you stay for dinner at our house?" my mother asked her by peering in the rearview mirror.

I was seated in the passenger seat up front with Mom, and Ivy was seated in the back seat.

"That sounds great, Mrs. Hart. But maybe I could shower and change at home first?" she tentatively asked.

"Of course, dear. I'll drop you off at your house and you come by once you've had a chance to clean up." My mom smiled into the mirror as if Ivy would really be paying attention to her expression within the rectangular reflection.

I was thrilled my mom had suggested Ivy stay for dinner because I wanted to have some time with her to myself. I mean, sure, my parents would be there, but we would mostly talk to ourselves anyway, like we always did.

But during our meal, Ivy was extremely talkative with my parents. She talked nonstop about Julie, the new girl-friend she made at school. I wanted to vomit my mom's meatloaf, and I loved my mom's meatloaf. But I just couldn't stomach all the Julie talk. *Julie this and Julie that. Julie likes pizza like me, and Julie is afraid of heights, and Julie has a golden retriever.*

I was so sick of hearing about Julie. By the time dinner was over, and the dishes were finished, my mom insisted I walk Ivy home since it was getting dark.

I knew if one of my guy friends walked home, it wouldn't be expected for me to walk any of them home. But my parents recognized that Ivy was a girl, and I needed to act like a gentleman, so I always complied without any hesitation.

However, this evening was different. I couldn't listen to one more word about Julie, so unless she promised to stay silent, I wasn't interested in being a gentleman tonight. "I'll walk to the end of my street and watch you go the rest of the way home to make sure you get there safely."

Both my mom and Ivy twisted their necks so rapidly they could have gotten whiplash, and then stared at me with wide eyes.

"You will do no such thing, Fletcher Hart." My mother's authoritative voice surfaced, and her lips, which had quickly formed an *O* from shock, transformed into a scowl. "You walk Ivy to her door like the young man I've raised you to be."

"Fine," I huffed and strode out the front door, forcefully pulling it closed behind me.

I stood waiting on my porch for Ivy to emerge from the house for a couple of minutes, all the while stewing about her new friend Julie.

"What's wrong with you?" Ivy asked once she set foot outside, and we were alone on my porch.

I rolled my eyes and descended the three steps from my porch onto the walkway that led to the sidewalk.

I walked swiftly, and I heard her footsteps quicken to catch up.

"Hey!" she called, but I didn't decrease my pace. "Fletcher!"

I was being a dick, and I didn't care. I kept my set pace and walked furiously, clomping against the pavement toward her house.

But a shuffled noise resonated behind me, followed by a "crap" from Ivy.

I halted my speed walking and peered over my shoulder to see Ivy sidestep some trash and blow out a frustrated breath. She hadn't fallen, so I resumed my forward momentum, only I didn't hear her footsteps behind me. When I swiveled my head back toward the direction where I last saw her, she was still in the same spot with her phone in hand, scrolling the screen like she didn't have somewhere else to be.

I stomped angrily back toward her. "What are you doing? I'm supposed to walk you home."

"Is that what you're doing, Fletch?" She shoved her phone into the back pocket of her jeans and glared her dark eyes at me. "It feels more like you're running away from me, and I'm trying to catch you. So either tell me what's going on, or I'm going to call your mom and tell her you left me alone near this trash pile."

"You wouldn't." I returned a glare at her. Telling on me to my mom was low.

"Try me." Her eyes narrowed, and in the setting sun, her hair reflected red and gold highlights over her brown hair, giving the appearance of fire.

"I'm a little angry with you," I finally confessed.

"Duh." She plucked her finger against my forehead. "But why?"

"You're going to be upset with me." I tucked my hands into the front pocket of my hooded sweatshirt.

"I'm already upset with you, Fletch." Her arms crossed over her chest at that point, and she grumbled her annoyance.

I dropped my head down and drooped my shoulders at the same time. "I'm a little jealous."

"Jealous of what?" she wailed as if she might start to cry.

I brought my gaze back up to hers, and the anger that I saw across her features just a moment ago was replaced with sadness.

"I'm jealous you have a new friend," I admitted and shrugged.

"Do you mean Julie?" Her confusion baffled me. *Of course I meant Julie.*

"You know you'll always be my best friend," she said and reached for my hand.

"No, I don't know that. We're in high school now. You'll

have new friends, and they'll take you away from me," I shamefully self-proclaimed.

"No one is ever going to take me away from you. Remember, we will forever be together." The corners of her mouth tipped upward in the hint of a smile. "I'm more worried you'll be the one who finds new friends and doesn't want me anymore."

"Why would you even think that?" I felt my brow furrow with her ridiculous statement.

"You'll have girlfriends, and they won't want me hanging around you." She sucked in a breath before continuing. "And one day, you'll find *the one,* and she'll tell you it's either her or me, and you'll pick her."

"That's impossible," I said as I grabbed her other hand so we were facing each other, and I squeezed both of her hands gently. "You aren't just Ivy. You're my vine. You're wrapped around everything in my life. You're wrapped around my heart."

And that was the first time I witnessed my best friend shed a tear. She sniffled a few times, and a couple of large, wet water droplets slid down the sides of her face.

I pulled her in for a hug, along with a promise that no one would ever split us up.

Julie and I basically tolerated each other during the rest of high school, but when my relationship with Vine changed from best friend to boyfriend, there were definitely a few hard times and a few hurt feelings, but eventually, we made it work.

Chapter 10

Ivy, present day

The two guys that Julie and I met at *Thursday's Bar* that Friday night were cute and fun. But I was still thinking about Fletcher. In fact, whenever I was around a cute and fun man, I thought of him. This was a situation that repeated itself too many times to count over the past four-plus years.

The tall blond one named Dean acted interested in me. He was smart and worked as a respiratory therapist at the same hospital as Julie and the other guy named Allen, so we had some things in common.

Maybe if I hadn't run into Fletcher so many times over the past couple of weeks, I would be willing to give Dean a chance. But he really had no shot in hell because my mind, body, and heart were still locked up with another man.

I still smiled and contributed to the conversation. Allen cut in a few times, which was fine with me but seemed to annoy Dean somewhat. I didn't know what Julie had in mind when she said she would bring a couple of her male coworkers along. Was she trying to set me up? Was she trying to hook up with one of these guys herself?

I probably should have inquired a little bit before blindly agreeing to meet. I would have told her I wasn't in the right headspace to hook up with anyone and I definitely wasn't ready to start a relationship with anyone.

If I hadn't been ready for the entire four years of college, it wasn't going to happen on a random Friday night. But only when I was away at college, there wasn't a chance that Fletcher would show up at the place where I was.

But tonight, while I was trying to concentrate on what Dean was telling me, I saw his masculine form walk through the glass door with John at his side.

I instantly sat up straighter and leaned closer into where Dean was sitting at the table across from me, as if what he said piqued my interest.

"His wife came back and thanked me the next day," Dean said with a wide grin, revealing his straight, perfect, white teeth that his parents probably spent thousands of dollars on.

"That's awesome," I said, but I truly hadn't been paying attention to the story he just finished.

I lifted the tumbler containing my whiskey and Coke and pressed the glass to my lip before taking a healthy swallow.

Fletcher's feet approached me. Of course, I was watching him without appearing like I was truly observing every aspect of him. Like how his flip-flops clopped across the faux wood floor of the bar. *I guess he still wears flip-flops with jeans.*

And his jeans were delectably worn in all the right places. His chest stretched the gray T-shirt he was wearing, revealing the broad expanse of his torso along with chiseled pecs. He had filled out since high school, and holy crap, he was hot.

"Hey, Julie," a male voice said.

I turned to my right and recognized John standing near my friend. I guess since I was attempting to focus on Dean and surveying Fletcher in my peripheral vision, there was little of my eyesight left to notice John had approached our table as well.

Julie huffed and rotated her neck away from where John stood.

"I don't think she's interested in speaking to you," Allen said with a tick in his jaw.

"Ignore him, Al. He'll move on to another woman to bother." She waved him off and returned her attention to Allen.

"Jules, we used to be friends. But I get it. I was good enough to study with at community college, but I'm not good enough to speak to in public." My gaze darted from John to Julie and then to Allen, who seemed to have become uncomfortable and began fidgeting in his seat.

Julie slapped the wooden tabletop and stood abruptly from her seat, causing the chair to scoot across the floor. "You *were* my friend until you started fucking every nurse at the hospital where I work." She had a finger pressed into his chest by that point.

But John wasn't ready to surrender.

Allen's and Dean's eyes widened at her reaction.

Fletcher and I exchanged a knowing smile. This was typical Julie. She was fiery and hotheaded. Her stubborn streak ran a mile long, and she would fight anything she held conviction for with all possible effort.

"Are you jealous?" John freaking winked at her, and I cringed, awaiting the fury that he certainly would unleash from my high school friend.

"Jealous of what? A ride that isn't worth the time?" She

retracted her finger but drew closer to him. "I heard you're like the disappointment after waiting in line for a long time when the ride doesn't live up to the hype. That's why no one ever rides more than once."

John's nostrils flared, and I waited for steam to blow out of his nares and probably his ears too.

"You know, you can be a real bitch sometimes, but I would have never said anything like that to your face or behind your back because I thought we were friends." John's eyes narrowed, and his gaze swept up and down Julie with scrutiny that showed a hint of disgust. "I'm a loyal friend, and I would have always had your back. Clearly, our friendship was one-sided."

John withdrew his body from her proximity by taking two steps backward, but then he shot his gaze toward me. "Watch your back, Ivy. The second you do something she doesn't approve of, you'll no longer be good enough to breathe the same air as her." Then he strutted toward the bar, and Julie retreated to her chair, dropping herself onto the wooden seat with an ungraceful plop.

"Sorry for that outburst, guys," she said and blew out an exasperated breath, causing her bangs to lift off her head with the force.

Allen and Dean muttered their "no worries" and "that's okay." I downed the rest of my drink with one swallow and set the rocks glass on the table.

"I'm going up to the bar to grab another. Anyone want anything?" I asked as I stood.

"The waitress will be back shortly. We can just order another round when she does." Julie scrunched her nose and eyed me suspiciously.

"I need something now, so I'll be right back."

Before anyone could refute my insistence, I was already

headed to the bar and approached the seat to the right of where John was seated. Of course, I noticed Fletcher was seated to his left.

"Well, that was awkward," I said as my butt hit the vinyl-covered stool.

"For you?" John said as he tossed back a shot of brown liquid.

I waved the bartender over, and once I had his attention, I flashed my best flirty smile. "I'll take whatever he had." I hitched my thumb in John's direction.

The extremely attractive bartender in his mid-thirties with full sleeves of tattoos only nodded in response to my request.

"Julie has no filter," I said to John, but I kept my eyes locked on the bartender pouring my drink. His hair was pulled up into a man bun, and although I didn't usually go for that, he rocked it well.

I wondered how many girls went home with him at the end of a night of drinking. I could understand if he had a different woman every night.

I suddenly liked my seat at the bar a whole lot better than the table with Julie and her friends.

Handsome bartender man placed my shot in front of me on the shiny bar. "Put it on his tab," I said with a smile, motioned to John, and then lifted the glass in salute and threw back the shot. "I'll take another." I winked at the bartender, and I heard a grumble from Fletcher before John spoke.

"If you're going to shoot whiskey like that, I hope you have a ride home."

"Would you take me home if I needed a ride, John?" I swiveled in my seat and placed my hand on his knee.

"What the hell are you doing, Ivy?" Fletcher's gravelly voice cut through the air with a low treble.

I cut my gaze to him and glared. "What business is it of yours?" I took notice he had returned to calling me Ivy.

"I really don't want to get in between whatever is going on between you." John swiveled his neck from side to side. "I'm hitting the head," he said as he slid off the bar stool and quickly stepped away from us as if he expected a detonation of emotions to fly out at any moment.

"What are you doing here, Fletch? Checking up on me? Or maybe you're stalking me." The bartender sat my next shot in front of me, and I again smiled seductively at him and saluted before swallowing the brown liquor. "My name is Ivy."

"I'm Calvin." He had a hint of stubble on his jaw that moved as his smile widened, and I wondered what those bristly short hairs would feel like against my skin.

"Back off, Calvin." Fletcher's irate voice grew with more indignation.

Calvin narrowed his gaze, and I rolled my eyes. "Protective older brother," I offered, and Calvin nodded in acknowledgment.

Fortunately, Calvin was called over by another customer on the opposite side of the bar.

"I'd only say one of those three is right," Fletcher stated plainly.

I craned my neck away from him as if I was ignoring his comment.

"Protective absolutely. But you're older than me by two months. And brother?" He released a condescending bark of laughter. "Pretty sure the things we did as teenagers should *never* be done between siblings."

I had no idea why I didn't immediately jump up from the stool and return to Julie and the others, but for some reason, when Fletcher and I were insulting each other, it was more like old times and not truly being nasty to one another.

So I turned back toward him and reached across to his drink, swiped the tall glass from the bar in front of him, and sipped at the beer. "You didn't answer my question."

"I'm here to grab a beer with my friend—a friend you chased off, by the way." He shrugged nonchalantly. "In case you didn't realize, I'm old enough to drink in public now...not just in the woods behind the school with our friends."

Damn him and his teasing. The exchange felt so normal. It was natural for us to rib each other.

"Well, now your beer's gone, and so is your friend," I said, giggling into his glass as I sipped more of the lager.

Fletcher peered over his shoulder at the table I had fled from, and then his gaze settled back on me. "It appears your friend is gone as well."

I jerked my head back in that direction, and just as he reported, Allen and Dean were conversing between themselves, and Julie was nowhere in sight. "She probably just went to the ladies' room or something."

"Or she's hooking up with John in his truck in the parking lot."

His comment had both of us lifting our shoulders as we attempted to hold back laughter.

It felt so good to share a laugh with him. We shared so many inside jokes, and I missed those times when we snickered and no one understood what we were giggling about except the two of us.

"Julie's not like that," I said in between my short laughs.

"John totally is, though."

Suddenly, the laughter died on my lips. "Were you ever like that?"

He pulled the beer I had been clutching out of my grasp and took a long pull. "No. I've never been that kind of guy."

"Serious relationships for you only?" I asked, although I already knew the answer.

He shrugged, and I nodded.

Tension weighed heavily between us, and I wished cute bartender would come back over, John would return from wherever he snuck off to, or the floor would open up and swallow me whole.

"How about you?" he asked but flinched slightly as if he expected me to hurt him with my response.

"No relationships...serious or otherwise. I was really in love with this boy in high school, and I was never able to get over him. I was stupid, though, because for some reason, I assumed we'd get back together and end up with a forever."

I guess the alcohol gave me the nerve I needed to get my thoughts out in the open.

I watched Fletch's Adam's apple bob up and down at my comment.

"I know you didn't answer my texts or calls, but I assumed you would have heard something from your dad that would make you want to talk with me. I guess he never said anything to you about our breakup?"

I already knew his father hadn't offered him any insight, but I was still hurt that he never gave me the opportunity to explain things to him.

And, of course, hurt and alcohol lead to anger and sometimes spiteful comments, so I couldn't help myself. "I haven't been with anyone else since you, but maybe tonight will be my fresh start."

Then I slid down from the stool and returned to the

people I had abandoned earlier in the evening and pulled out the seat next to Dean. I placed my hand on his shoulder, and he smiled warmly at me.

Julie made an appearance back at the table a moment later, and coincidently, John reappeared at the same time and sat next to Fletcher at the bar. However, his friend had already tossed several bills on the slick surface where his now-empty beer glass sat, and he stormed out of the bar clad in his flip-flops with John in tow.

John's friendly wave of departure didn't make up for the angry scowl Fletcher glared at me on his way out.

Chapter 11

Ivy, present day

I ended up calling an Uber shortly after John and Fletcher left the bar last night. I knew that Fletch could wield a hurtful dagger straight through my heart, but I couldn't believe I had the same amount of hate within me.

He had every reason to hate me. He didn't know the truth, but I did, and I made the decision based on what I thought was best for everyone involved. *I* made the choice. He didn't do anything but love me like no one else in my life ever had, and I just spewed out hurtful words that he didn't deserve.

He deserved to know the truth. And now that we were living in the same town, it seemed we were destined to continue running into each other. So maybe the universe was giving me chances to come clean.

It was completely obvious he still cared about me. I just needed to draw some energy from that and get him to come over. I was sure if I called and told him I needed him, he'd be unable to stay away.

I would need alcohol, though. Just like last night, I would need some liquid courage to get things off my chest.

And I didn't think a case of beer was going to cut it. I was going to need the hard stuff.

So, I made the drive to the liquor store on the outskirts of town. The places within the city limits only sold beer and wine, and this situation called for whiskey, rum, vodka, gin, or perhaps all four. A combination of dark and clear liquors might do the trick.

Thankful I had grabbed a handheld basket, I dropped one of each bottle into the plastic container that rested on my forearm.

"Damn, that's heavy," I mumbled as I shifted the contents while turning to head toward the register and practically plummeted into a patron's shopping cart when I did.

"I'm so sorry," an older man's voice said.

I was all set to let him know I was okay when I met the gaze of the person who had altered my dreams forever.

A set of pale blue eyes stared back at me as my hardened gaze locked with his.

His hair was grayer than it was when I left for college and was thinning on the top. His face had several days of stubble, and his body had thinned, but I could still see the man who shared DNA with the boy who owned my heart.

"Mr. Hart," I said vehemently.

"Fletcher said he ran into you." His steely expression angered me.

"Yep, he has, and you know what? He has no idea why I broke up with him. Why haven't you told him?" Resentment filled my gut, and rage settled in my core.

"I thought you loved him." He hissed between his teeth.

"That's why I broke up with him. You preyed on that young love and destroyed the happiness we could have had together."

"Yeah, well, that time has passed. He's happy now, Ivy.

Let him go. If you really loved him, you'd let him get married and be happy. I know you're probably jealous, but you'll have that for yourself one day."

Is he serious? "I'm not jealous," I guffawed. "You are, you old vindictive man."

"I just want my son to be happy, and he is, so leave him alone." I understood where Fletcher got his low growl from, but I wasn't deterred by the older Hart's snarl.

"Does Fletcher know you drink this much?" I asked, waving my hand at his cart after my thorough perusal of its contents, which included two gallons of vodka. "Unless you're trying to burn down someone's house, I'd say that's more than an average person would drink in an entire year." I dropped my gaze toward the inside of his basket and then lasered my focus back to his eyes, which happened to be the same light denim color as his son's.

"I've had a hard time losing the love of my life." His stern expression softened, and there was a slight tremble to his hands against the handle of the shopping cart.

"And you stood by and forced your son to lose the love of his life?" I shook my head in disgust. If he was trying for empathy, he wasn't going to get it.

"Ivy, I was going to tell him, but I was having such a hard time. I needed to lean on him. I couldn't tell him. He would have been furious with me and left." Now his voice quivered with emotion. Although there was no doubt in my mind he truly needed Fletcher during that time, it didn't explain why he hadn't said anything to him four years later.

"We were miserable men for a long time." He sighed and stared into the distance as if revisiting a painful memory, but I repelled any empathy that could have been retrieved at this point.

I rolled my eyes and huffed an exasperated breath.

"Yeah, I bet you loved that. Misery loves company and all." I shook my head, appalled at his excuse.

"Unlike me, he was able to break free from the grief and despair, and now he's happy again. So I'm begging you...just leave him alone." If I wasn't so upset about Fletcher's feelings being completely dismissed by his father, I might have felt sorry for the old man.

"Are you drinking because you miss your wife, or is it because of the guilt you've carried for all of these years?" I just couldn't find it in myself to sweep this situation under the rug. "Fletcher has a right to know what really happened."

A tear fell from Mr. Hart's eye, but I kept my resolve.

"You have a week to tell him, or I will." I gripped the heavy basket tighter and began taking steps toward the front of the store when I heard the desperate voice.

"You're not the Ivy and Fletcher team like you once were. He'll be upset with both of us, but I'm his family. He'll forgive me. You'll be discarded like clothes that no longer fit, and he'll get married to Amilyn."

He may marry another woman, but he wasn't going to go to that altar without knowing the truth, even if I had to stand up during the ceremony and be all dramatic when the pastor asked if there was anyone who objected to the marriage.

Chapter 12

Ivy, junior year of high school

The juniors and seniors played this stupid game every year with water guns. The premise was to eliminate players in the game by shooting them with water. All students who wanted to participate paid twenty dollars, and the winner received half of the money collected as a prize while the other half went toward covering the cost of prom. There was no prize for second place, so unless you were the last man standing, you lost.

Each week, every student was assigned a mark. You could eliminate said mark with any form of water you liked. It could be with a bucket of water, water hose, water gun, dunking in a pool, or any other means of soaking your opponent.

There were rules, obviously. None of the eliminations could take place on school grounds, church, a student's workplace, or going in or out of doctor appointments.

Any other place was considered fair game.

At the beginning of the game, most students formed allies to establish the location of marks and join forces to eliminate opponents with help from each other.

Clearly, Fletcher and I were a team. We were always a team, no matter what. We had been since the first grade.

So I helped him eliminate Jimmy Wright because I knew he always picked up his sister from dance class on Tuesday evenings, and he helped me eliminate Carla Winters because she always had a crush on him, and he flirted with her when she was at a fast-food restaurant after track practice, so I could attack her while she was distracted.

Just like every year, there were feuds that developed, and some friendships suffered over this stupid game because feelings got hurt and allies changed due to deceit and the ultimate desire to win.

But I didn't care if I won. I just didn't want to be eliminated in some humiliating way because, of course, in order for the elimination to count, it had to be captured on video. And once it was posted to social media, everyone could see how your classmate abolished you.

Thankfully, Fletcher and I have been able to keep our alliance, never having each other as a target. Things had been progressing well. He shielded my body twice from incoming fire by water, and I pushed him out of the way once, which, of course, drenched me instead.

But with the elimination of both of our targets last week, Fletcher and I were the last two standing.

"You should just shoot me and get it over with Fletch," I said to him at lunch the following Monday.

"I can't believe you would say that after you dodged me and avoided me that entire week I had you as my mark," Julie said while chewing the sandwich her mother most likely packed for her. She had the kind of mom who still cut the crusts off her sandwiches and sliced her apples into eight equal pieces. "Then Fletcher took a hit for you when I went for the garden hose at your place."

I shrugged and giggled at Fletcher, who was wearing a smile so big he squinted and creases appeared at the corners of his eyes.

"You two are disgusting." She made a gagging sound, and I was glad she swallowed the food bolus she had been chewing, so I didn't have to see any regurgitated sandwich make an appearance. "Best friends, boyfriend slash girl-friend, classmates, homecoming king and queen, partners in crime, et cetera...I could hurl."

Fletcher leaned over and delivered a peck to my cheek, and I squeezed his knee when he did.

"I'm seriously going to have to sit somewhere else for lunch. You two make me want to puke," she said while scooping up her paper bag and its contents and stood before climbing over the bench seat and walking away after a brief shake of her head.

"One day, she's going to find her other half, and she'll understand." I sighed whimsically.

"If that's only half of Julie, I'm not sure I want to meet her other half," Fletcher commented after she walked further away from us.

I slapped his upper arm, and he flinched but laughed at my light smack.

"Why don't you shoot me, and then you can win the prize money, Vine?" he asked, intertwining the fingers on one of our hands together.

"Because I want *you* to win."

"Vine, I can't win if you lose. It doesn't work that way."

"Fletch, that is literally how it works." I exaggerated an eye roll, which made me slightly dizzy. "We could both forfeit, but then neither of us would win."

"Then neither of us will win the money." He tapped his finger against his chin a few times before a devious smile curled his lips. "How about you shoot me, and we split the money? Then we could both win."

"You could shoot me, and then we could split the money."

"Fine, stubborn girl."

~

That afternoon after school, Julie prepared her phone to capture our water gun elimination on video. I told her Fletcher would be shooting me, but she thought it would be more dramatic if we both had water guns in hand and staged a shoot-out.

"As long as you see him pull the trigger first, you can fire because he'll get you first. I'll be focused on your face, so all anyone will see is how your face is wet," she explained.

She handed me a red water pistol that was so full it dripped liquid, but I tested its range anyway, even though it didn't matter.

"He's behind the bush in your backyard to your left," she said as she pulled open the sliding glass door that led to the deck outside my house.

With her phone already recording, she gave me a nod, urging me out the door, so I stepped onto the wood planks, awaiting Fletcher to make an appearance.

The bushes weren't that tall in my yard, so I could see his white T-shirt moving as he crouched down and shifted his weight.

I pretended I wasn't aware of his exact position and proceeded toward the middle of my yard, certainly making me an easy target.

Fletcher stood then from behind the hedge with his blue water gun pointed in my direction, and the moment his finger pulled the trigger, I lifted my gun and pulled against my gun's trigger and released several streams of water.

His face and shirt became wet, and he turned his face from side to side as the shooting streams of water continued to strike and saturate him.

As he pulled his gun's trigger over and over relentlessly, I expected to be soaked thoroughly, but my face wasn't wet, and my clothes remained dry.

I dropped my hand at that realization and released my finger from the firing position on my gun, then ultimately tossed it onto the ground.

His big, goofy grin dripped with water, and his blond hair had large droplets clinging to their ends. "Did you get that on camera, Jules?"

His blue gaze never left my face, but he asked my filming friend.

"Yep," Julie said, popping the *P*.

"I saw you pulling the trigger. Your gun couldn't have misfired that many times." I grabbed the gun from his hand and tossed it to the ground. "Fletcher Hart! Your gun doesn't have any water in it."

He shrugged, and that silly smile that still clung to his face remained in place.

"You two set me up!" I squealed as I let out a loud peal of laughter.

"I thought you'd be happy Julie and I finally got along well enough to create a plan like this."

I charged toward him, and when I jumped, he caught me.

I wrapped my legs around his waist and kissed him as I snaked my arms around his neck.

"Alright, I'm out," Julie called. "Things have progressed beyond PG. See you both tomorrow."

Fletcher's wet shirt soaked through to my cotton top and denim shorts as he deepened the kiss.

I closed my eyes as our tongues slid against each other.

We stood there kissing. Me with my legs wrapped around my boyfriend's waist and his strong arms draped across my back.

When we finally broke away from the contact of our lips, Fletcher kept one hand behind me, still holding me in place against his torso, but placed a thumb and forefinger on my chin, angling my gaze upward to his gray-blue eyes.

"I love you, Vine."

My heart damn near exploded at his declaration. And I only waited maybe half a second before I blurted out, "I love you too."

He pulled my arms away from his neck, and I slid down his body until I was standing on my own two feet with my legs supporting my weight.

Then he reached down onto the ground and grabbed the red water gun, aimed, and fired repeatedly at me, causing me to squeal and run away.

But he caught me and tackled me to the ground, and before I knew it, we were back to kissing on the lawn of my backyard, rolling around on the grass while laughing and breathless through fits of giggles.

Chapter 13

Fletcher, present day

August in Maryland was always a scorcher, and as I made my weekly shopping trip, I took notice of only one case of water left at the grocery store when I glanced down the aisle I was currently in.

But rather than reaching down, I decided to reach up first and grab the electrolyte drinks that were located a few shelves above it and tossed them into my cart. However, when I reached down to grab the case of water, a body squatted below me and reached for the same case of bottles.

I retracted my arms and stood back to my full height. The young woman startled when she felt my presence over her, and she stumbled and nearly twisted her ankle trying to right herself back to a standing position.

Then she pushed her dark hair out of her face, revealing those chocolate-brown eyes I used to dream about. She released a small sigh, and my throat constricted from just that little sound. There were so many faint noises that were uniquely Ivy, and each of them squeezed at my heart.

She stared blankly at me, blinking her thick, inky

eyelashes. "Sorry, I didn't realize you were reaching for the same thing as me."

We used to reach for each other at the same time too many times to count. But that was the past, and this was the present.

"You can have it." I guess I'd never be able to take anything from her. "I can put it in your shopping cart for you."

"Nah. You take it." Her despondence was evident as she pivoted from the spot across from me and took a couple of strides toward a shopping cart a few paces away.

I lifted the case of water, used my long legs to my advantage, and ate up the distance toward the cart she had just reached. I placed the water bottles into the basket of the cart and caused the wheels to halt their forward progression as she pressed against the added weight she was now pushing.

"Fletch. I told you to take it." Her soft brown eyes appeared apologetic, and I didn't like that one bit. I preferred it when her eyes were playful or content or lust filled.

Shit. I had no idea where that thought came from.

"I can't take something from you." I couldn't believe I had even been able to intentionally hurt her with my words or actions. "Besides, I owe you one."

She quirked an eyebrow at my comment.

"I didn't get to hit you with water junior year of high school. So I owe you some."

Once the hint of a smile cracked her melancholy disposition, I felt my chest grow lighter. Her heartbreak had always been my heartbreak, and her happiness was my happiness.

"Fletch, you don't owe me anything." Even with her lips

slightly tugging up at the corners, she still wore a somewhat poignant expression. "I'm so damn sorry."

And then my chest was constricted again. "Vine." And I couldn't have stopped myself from taking those two steps toward her if there was a wall of fire between us.

"Holy crap. Ivy Hatfield." A female voice rang in a loud cadence from behind me.

Ivy's eyes widened with shock, but the surprise appeared to be a favorable one by how her lips changed from an O shape to a bright smile that reached her eyes. "Carrie?" she said way too loudly to be a question and without even a hint of hesitation.

I peered over my shoulder and instantly recognized the blonde beauty standing behind me. Her hair was curled and hung around her shoulders. She had filled out with feminine curves and was wearing denim cut-off shorts with a sleeveless, button-down shirt tied at the bottom, revealing a small area of bare skin across her abdomen. The girl whom I spent so much time with in elementary school had become a beautiful woman.

"Damn girl, you grew up and got hot," I said, teasing her. I noticed the eye roll Ivy gave me, as well as the little nostril flare.

"Come over here, Fletcher Hart, and give me a hug." Carrie waved toward herself, and I stepped in that direction to receive the quick embrace she offered. "You still let this guy hang around you, Ivy?" she said, hitching a thumb at me once she had released me from the tight yet brief squeeze.

"Well..." Before Ivy could provide any kind of explanation, Carrie had lunged at her, wrapped her arms around her shoulders, and pulled her in close to her own torso.

Ivy wrapped her arms around Carrie also, and they held

each other for several seconds. This was quite a different reunion compared to the one she had with Julie.

"If you girls go to second base, I'm getting my phone out to record it." I chuckled, and they both cut me a glare that softened immediately because they were well acquainted with my teasing ways.

"What are you doing in town?" Ivy asked after they separated.

"My great aunt Maureen died, so the whole family came up for the funeral. There's an outdoor reception following the service, so Dad wanted me to grab some Gatorades and water so the older folks don't get dehydrated."

Ivy and I exchanged a knowing look. We were once again operating on the same wavelength. We knew what the other one was thinking without needing to say anything.

So I reached into Ivy's cart, lifted the last case of water, and placed it into the cart Carrie had next to her, but unlike Ivy and me, her cart sat empty, while the two of us had several items in ours.

"There was only one case of water left, but you can have it," Ivy said to Carrie.

"So are you two still friends...or is there more here?" Carrie asked, bouncing her finger back and forth between us.

"Uh..."

"We're friends," I said, cutting off Ivy's attempt at an explanation.

Relief washed over her face at my clarification regarding our relationship description.

"Aww, that's amazing. We should get together tomorrow night and catch up." She dug around in her purse and pulled out her phone, then after a swipe of her screen and a few presses of her finger, she handed the device to Ivy. "Put your name and number in my contacts so I can text you."

After a beat, Ivy accepted her cell and typed in her information before handing it back to Carrie.

"We have tons to catch up on." Then, after she grabbed a few twelve-packs of Gatorade and dropped them into her cart with a thud, she waved goodbye and promised to reach out later that evening.

"I didn't expect that at the grocery store today," Ivy said with a sigh of confusion.

"Yeah, I got a couple of surprises myself." I *hmphed* at the absurdity of the whole exchange that had transpired.

Her chocolate gaze left its distance stare from its dream-like state to focus back on me.

I took a step closer to her so I could see the green flecks within those brown irises. I always loved how her eyes appeared one way to the world but, upon closer inspection, held some hidden treasure. And only those people that sought out that closeness with her got to experience the wonderment of the gems.

She sank her teeth into her bottom lip just like she always did when she was holding back words. *What does she want to say but is holding back?* She never used to hold back with me. She was always able to say anything to me. *Who does she say everything to now?*

"Something on your mind, Vine?"

"No," she quickly retorted and reached for the handle of her cart before pushing it away from me.

"Vine." She hadn't made much progress in her short strides, so I caught up without a whole lot of effort.

She halted, and this time when she peered over her shoulder to meet my gaze, her eyes were apologetic and held a heavy sadness within their orbs. "I can tell Carrie you aren't able to make it. I'm sure after the way I acted the other night, you'd rather not be around me."

"Was what you said true?" I sucked in a breath while I awaited her reply.

"What part?" Her questioning eyes confused me. She had to know what part I was asking about.

"That you haven't been with anyone since me?" Damn. Burning struck the back of my throat as it became thick with emotion again.

She nodded slowly.

"Is it still true?" Her answer was none of my business, but I couldn't stop myself from asking.

"Does it matter?" Her gaze stayed connected to mine, and her voice never wavered.

Of course it matters. "It's none of my business, and I really have no right asking you that."

"You used to know me better than anyone," she said with confidence, squaring her shoulders and slightly lifting her chin up. "What do you think the answer is?"

I think I would have known if she'd gone home with one of those guys she was hanging out with the other night. I'd like to think I still knew her—maybe she hadn't changed so much from the girl she used to be. Well, except for the whole blindsiding me and breaking my heart thing.

"I think we should stop doing this to one another."

"Okay," she confirmed with a tight nod.

"We were friends way before we were...more than friends." We were so much more than friends. "It's obvious the universe is going to continue to have our paths cross, so we need to find some way to get along, and that means we can't say things that are hurtful or ask questions we don't want the answers to."

"So where do we go from here?" She tilted her head and twisted her lips in confusion. "Do you want us to try to be friends or just be civil with each other?"

"Vine, you were my best friend for over a decade—that's nearly half my life. There's nothing I'd love more than to have you as a friend again."

"But?" she asked cautiously.

"There's no but. We were young and thought we were in love. Everything is so different now that we aren't living in that idealistic version of what we thought our future would be like. The real world is nothing like what we thought it would be." I thought we would be getting married now, and instead, I was engaged to another woman.

"Do you think we can go back to being friends after... everything?" Her eyes widened, and for the first time since she'd been home, I finally saw a sliver of hope. I had seen her anger, frustration, sadness, and vulnerability.

I liked that I still had the power to give her hope.

"I think it would be a shame if we didn't try." I held out my hand for her to grasp.

She dropped her gaze to my hand and stared at my fingers for a beat before slipping her palm against mine. But only she didn't shake my hand by pumping it a few times as I had expected.

She caressed my hand with hers and dragged her thumb over my knuckles. *Shit.*

I hadn't anticipated how her hand would feel against mine. We held hands too many times to recall, and with one touch, those thousands of memories were like flashes through my brain.

I retracted my hand out of her grip, forcing the memories to stop their rapid-fire display in my mind.

"Is your fiancée going to be okay with us being friends?"

Her eyes brightened even though we were no longer in a hand embrace.

Amilyn. She freaked out when I'd just mentioned that Ivy was in town. I hadn't even mentioned that I'd seen Ivy so many additional times. *This is definitely not good.*

"I'll talk with her. We've been together for a long time, and we're engaged. She trusts me." I was babbling, and I hoped Ivy didn't pick up on it. I only babbled when I was bending the truth.

"Maybe she and I should meet...you know, so I can assure her you and I are only going to be friends." The smirk developing on her lips became more evident. She could tell I was uncomfortable speaking with Amilyn about her.

There was no way I would be okay with the two of them meeting. Amilyn already lacked confidence. Being around someone as extroverted as Ivy would only force her back into the shell she used to hide behind when we first met.

I worked for a considerably long time at breaking those walls down, and even though she still kept me somewhat at arm's length, we'd made a lot of progress, and I worried that with one encounter with Ivy, she'd resort back to the shy, introverted girl that barely said two words to me.

She did well in one-on-one situations, but she wasn't into large group settings or anywhere with crowds. Since she preferred to stay close to home, she hadn't ever complained about my going out with my friends without her. She actually encouraged it at times because even though she didn't enjoy going out, she understood that I did.

"You could invite her to tag along when you and I go out with Carrie."

Yeah, right. There was no way Amilyn would agree to that. "She's more of a homebody. She won't want to go."

Ivy's grin grew wider as if she expected me to say that.

"But maybe you can come over one night for pizza and a movie with us."

Her lips fell to a flat line and that smile she had only a moment ago no longer met her eyes.

"Sure, maybe you could invite John, and it could be a double date."

Over my dead body.

And then the giggling started. As much as I missed the sound of her laughter, I knew her response was sprinkled with patronization.

"What's so funny?" I crossed my arms over my chest, attempting to protect my heart from her condescending amusement.

She slowed her breathing down and managed to get her fits of chortles under control.

"You're fooling yourself if you think your fiancée is going to be okay with you being friends with your ex."

I couldn't possibly choose between the two of them. I just got Ivy back in my life. I didn't want to give her up. But she was right; Amilyn was cool with me spending time with my friends, but she was not going to be okay with one of those friends being Ivy.

"I'll figure it out." Because I would.

"I'll try not to get too attached, so when you tell me you can't see me anymore, I won't be devastated."

Her words sliced through me, and I didn't do a very good job of concealing my unhealed wound.

"Dammit, Fletch. I keep saying things that are inappropriate. I didn't mean to upset you. I promised you I wouldn't say things that would hurt you, and I just did...but I didn't mean to." She covered her eyes with her hands and shook her head.

"Vine." I softly let the nickname I gave to her roll off my

tongue, and she pulled her hands away from her eyes, and those big doe eyes wore sorrow just as well as they showed remorse.

"It's going to take us some time to get comfortable with each other again. But I would like to continue to try if you're willing."

"I've missed you, and I would like it if we could be friends again."

She missed me? My heart ached for her for over four years. Hopefully, being friends would be enough.

Chapter 14

Ivy, present day

Carrie: Where are we going tomorrow night?

Me: Thursday's.

Three dots danced across the screen.

Carrie: I just looked it up. Looks like a fun place. What time?

Me: Seven? I can pick you up. Where are you staying?

Carrie: The Treetop Inn. I'll be ready and waiting in the lobby. Just text me when you get here.

Me: Sounds good.

My phone buzzed in my hand, and Carrie's name lit up against the dark background.

"Change your mind already?" I asked when I slid the icon to answer her call.

"I just wanted to ask if there was something between Fletcher and you."

There was so much between us, but I couldn't explain all of that to Carrie. I hadn't seen or heard from her in years. She wouldn't understand.

"We're just friends, Carrie." The truth hurt as I confessed to my old partner in crime.

"I'm only in town for the weekend, and I was thinking about having some fun. Do you think Fletcher would be willing?"

"What kind of fun?" Did she mean drinking, drugs, motorcycle rides? I had no idea. She could be an entirely different person now.

"Like a fling kind of fun."

Nausea plummeted to the pit of my stomach. "He's not like that. And besides, he's engaged."

"What!" she screeched into my ear. "He was flirting with me."

Apparently, Carrie thought every man who flirted with her wanted to take her to bed. "Sorry. You'll have to find another man to have fun with." I was glad Fletcher was engaged at that moment because as much as I didn't want to see him with another woman, I really wouldn't be able to stomach seeing him with Carrie. "But there will be a lot of men at Thursday's tomorrow night, so fingers crossed." I released a faux chuckle, even though relief genuinely flowed through my veins.

"I'm looking forward to it," she said with a little too much cheer in her voice for me to be comfortable. "See you tomorrow."

I decided to make sure she didn't have a little too much to drink and attempt to flirt with Fletcher.

> Me: Is John available to go out with Carrie, you, and me tomorrow?"

> Fletcher: You looking for a date?

> Me: I think Carrie is. LOL

> Fletcher: I'll text him. I'm sure he wouldn't mind spending the evening with a pretty blonde.

> Me: Sorry you're stuck with an average brunette.

> Fletcher: I thought you said you were going.

> Me: ???

> Fletcher: There's nothing just average about you. And I happen to prefer brunettes.

I guess his fiancée was a brunette.

> Me: See you tomorrow.

He sent a thumbs-up emojicon. I could see why Carrie thought he was flirting with her. Because if I hadn't known better, I would have thought his previous text was flirty. But I knew he was engaged to another woman, so he obviously just sent that last text to make me feel better. That's what friends did, and we agreed to try the whole friendship thing.

I just hoped my heart could handle a friendship. With only a few days for his dad to fess up about what happened before I left for college, I questioned if our friendship would be able to handle that fallout.

I texted Carrie when I pulled into the loading and pickup area of The Treetop Inn, and I was quite surprised she actually said she would be right out and meant it. She must have been waiting in the lobby like she said because she was buckled into my car within two minutes of my text.

That would have never happened with my girlfriends in college. We would plan to meet at seven p.m., but we never walked out the door until seven forty-five or eight o'clock.

She surprised me. Just like she surprised me with her comments regarding Fletcher.

"Ivy, you promised me a target-rich environment, but there's hardly anyone here," Carrie said as she slid onto a vinyl-covered stool to the right of me.

"It's still early. Give it some time." I tried my best to reassure her. It was a Saturday night, so I was confident that there would be a large selection of men trickling in soon.

"Shot of whiskey, please," I said as the handsome bartender appeared before me.

He nodded once and smiled broadly at Carrie. "What about you, doll?"

Ick. The doll comment weirded me out. But Carrie got all starry-eyed.

I mean, I thought the guy was reasonably attractive upon initial inspection. He had the bad boy kind of vibe going for him. He was clean-shaven but had long, dirty-blond hair pulled into a hair tie at the nape of his neck. He had a gold hoop in his lower lip and a vertical gold bar in his left eyebrow. I definitely wondered where else he may be pierced. But his hazy gray eyes were small and shady-like.

"I'll have whatever she's having." Carrie fluttered her eyelashes and tilted her head in my direction.

The bartender's brow drew downward in confusion. "Alright. Wouldn't have taken for you the type to shoot whiskey."

Carrie swiveled on her stool and no longer showed interest in the man pouring our drinks.

After a few beats of her ignoring him, he shuffled away to get her shot of whiskey.

"I'm really tired of men that think because I look a certain way that I'm a *type*."

Okay, so there must be a story there. I waited for her shot glass to appear, then I lifted mine in mock salute, and we swallowed our alcohol simultaneously.

"You want to talk about it?" I asked before I flagged down the female bartender and ordered us two beers. I needed to give myself a dose of liquid courage before Fletcher got here.

"I dated a guy in high school that I thought I would marry, and he went away to college and met someone else." Carrie sipped her frosty mug of my favorite lager because since she told the last bartender that she'd just have what I was having, I figured I'd just order for both of us.

"Ouch. When did you break up?" I slid my fingers up and down my mug, chasing the condensation.

"A few weeks ago." She sighed without any sign of anger or regret.

"So you were together in high school and then all of college?" I couldn't possibly have heard her correctly.

"Yep, almost eight years. I went to Florida State, and he

went to Northwestern. He met someone his freshman year and dated her all through college. I had no idea—and I'm assuming he never told her about me either. He decided he wanted to be with her, so he broke up with me." Her gaze drifted off behind me, but when I turned to peer over my shoulder, it didn't appear she was looking at anything in particular. Her blue eyes were full of future, dream-filled days.

"What an ass." I remember when I had dreams of my future. My dreams always included Fletcher, which was probably why I'd been so uncertain of what my plans were now. I couldn't commit to a place to live or a place to work because, deep down, I had a hard time choosing a future that didn't have him in it.

Doing a little self-reflecting daydreaming of my own, I took a long pull of my beer.

"I was in love with him. I had the opportunity to date a lot of men, but I was so blindly in love with him that I never did." There was a hint of defensiveness in her tone.

"Sorry, Carrie, but it sounds like you wasted your love on someone that didn't deserve it." I reached out and touched her arm, and she recoiled slightly.

Her blue eyes cleared from the hazy focus she had moments earlier, and a hint of a smile appeared. "Guys at bars always assumed because I'm confident in my appearance that I was easy. But I've only had sex with one man ever in my life, Ivy."

I could relate to that part, but I wasn't ready to share my story with anyone at this point—not even my childhood best friend. There were too many years that had passed. If she had stayed in Villpointe, she would have been there for my whole relationship with Fletcher, but no one other than our parents were there for every step of our transition from friends to boyfriend slash girlfriend to heartbreak. And I never even told my parents the whole story. Only Fletcher's dad knew the reason why our relationship unraveled.

Julie and I became friends in high school, but she was never friends with Fletcher. They tolerated each other for me, but there was no love lost when we broke up. So, I never confided in her. She was an extremely competitive person, so initially, she fought for her friendship status against her perceived threat—Fletcher. But when he was my boyfriend, her disposition changed. Either she felt like she could no longer compete, or she realized there was no need to anymore because their classifications were different at that time.

The summer I broke up with Fletcher, she was like a kid who won the biggest game of her life. She acted as if she had eliminated the competition. She had no empathy for my feelings of regret and crushing grief. She thought the way to get me over Fletcher was by distraction, which she was extremely good at.

We would go shopping, out to eat, spend the night at each other's houses, watching movies and eating junk food. We drove to the beach on our days off, and we worked at the same restaurant that summer. If I had been just a teenage girl who got her heart broken by a boy, her technique would have been therapeutic. But she didn't know I was the one responsible for breaking my own heart, and no amount of distraction could make me feel better.

"You okay, Ivy?" Carrie's concern dragged me out of the decisions of my past and brought me back to the present.

"Yeah, just thinking about how much I missed having you as a friend."

"Aww, Ivy. You're so sweet." She giggled and sipped her beer.

And then the glass door swung open, and Fletcher's broad frame entered the bar. My eyes couldn't help but drink him in.

"Who. Is. That?" Carrie was stunned to silence because she didn't make any more comments or ask any more questions.

I didn't take notice of who she was referring to because my gaze was glued on the man who destroyed my ability to hold another relationship. I was hoping if we could develop a friendship, I'd be able to move on. Things between us just seemed unfinished. If he truly appeared to be doing okay, then perhaps it would be easier, but I didn't think he'd completely moved on either.

Only the truth would determine how things between us would pan out.

He strode to me with a purpose. His usually light blue eyes appeared darker under the dimly lit restaurant. His T-shirt stretched snugly across his muscular chest, and damn he looked good in worn jeans.

I sank my teeth into my lower lip as my gaze dragged up and down his body. I enjoyed what I saw very much, including his flip-flop-clad feet, because that was just so Fletcher. But he belonged to someone else since I pushed him away.

I swung back around toward the bar and lifted my beer glass to my lips.

"Ivy, the most beautiful man I've ever seen in my life is walking toward us," Carrie whispered as she pushed the blond curls off her shoulders nervously.

"Hello, ladies."

I didn't turn back around. The voice didn't belong to Fletcher, so it was inconsequential to me. I continued to sulk and take swigs of my drink, hoping Fletcher didn't realize how I unabashedly checked him out only a moment ago.

Carrie cleared her throat and crossed her legs.

I rolled my eyes and still didn't turn around.

"Carrie, this is my friend John...and you've already met Ivy." Even though Fletcher wasn't speaking to me, his voice wrapped around me like a warm sweater on a chilly night.

"Hey, Ives."

I waved over my shoulder to John but didn't spin in his direction.

Carrie's giggling had me nearly aspirating my amber ale.

As I coughed and sputtered, a familiar hand tapped the middle of my back.

"You getting choked up over seeing me again, Vine?" His ironic statement had me glaring at him in between my fit of coughs.

"Seriously, you alright?" His whisper to the back of my ear sent a delicious shiver down my spine, and suddenly, his presence was calming, not annoying.

Maybe his aggravating presence was what calmed me— I didn't know. But nonetheless, my breathing turned regular, unlike the short and choppy breaths I had only a moment earlier.

"I'm good, Fletch," I emphasized with a nod.

His own tight nod indicated his acceptance before he slid onto the stool adjacent to me. John had taken up residence on the stool next to Carrie, so the four of us sat alongside each other, but the men were on opposite sides of our foursome line.

I glanced over at the newly formed couple to my left and sighed, realizing their easy conversation and relaxed demeanor. Then I swung my gaze back to my right, where

Fletcher was seated, and recognized our inability to have the same.

I wasn't sure if we would again. As he flagged down the bartender, he gave no indication he was aware of my regretful thoughts regarding our changed and awkward, newish relationship.

"I guess Carrie can become friends with a boy just as easily as you can," Fletcher said as he motioned his head toward our friends sitting on just the other side of us. "I'm a little hurt, though. She seems more interested in John than she is in me. We were the three musketeers back in elementary school."

"Oh, you were her first choice, but I told her you were unavailable."

Fletcher's jaw slacked as his mouth formed an O while his right eyebrow arched upward.

"She's getting over a bad breakup and is looking for a fling."

The confusion that had been so apparent on his face just a moment ago quickly transitioned into a cocky grin.

"Don't get all full of yourself, Fletch. You were just the first man she saw. Clearly, she's not super selective at this point." I gestured with my hand at the couple also. But they were so immersed in conversation, that neither of them noticed.

"I'm not full of myself." He took a pull of his beer and then swiveled on his seat to face me. "I remember when you were full of me."

And for the second time tonight, I choked on my beer. But this time, rather than cough and sputter, I sprayed the bar with a mist of room-temperature ale.

"Jeez, Vine. You held your alcohol a lot better when we

were teenagers," he said as he mockingly wiped liquid with the sleeves of his shirt.

"I can't believe you said that!" I struck him with a fist to his upper arm. Of course, it didn't faze him. His biceps and triceps were as hard as granite. Obviously, he lifted weights and didn't just run his cute ass on the treadmill at the gym.

"What? You used to like me." His playful grin was winning me over.

But I needed to remind myself that he was unavailable. Just as I had informed Carrie, Fletcher Hart was off the market. He was engaged. He was getting married.

That realization, although already there, had a sour taste ascending up my throat. *I shouldn't have ever switched to beer.*

I waved the bartender over, and he began sopping up the beer I spewed across the slick bar with a towel as he chuckled, which made the gold loop in his lower lip dance.

"I guess I should have stuck to whiskey." I smiled at him because, although I had no interest in him, he was friendly and nice, so I shouldn't take my hostility over the suckiness of my life out on him.

"Another shot?" His eyebrows raised, and that bar sparkled under the dim light. Okay, so maybe he was kind of sexy. Unless he said *doll* in the bedroom. *Ewwww.*

"Make it a double on the rocks this time."

The bartender dipped his lips at the corners and nodded his approval at my selection.

"You got someone to drive you home, Vine?" Fletcher's concern-filled voice struck me in a way it shouldn't have. I liked it...too much.

"I know how to get a ride when I need one." I meant my comment as a joke, but the expression Fletch was wearing indicated he didn't appreciate my humor.

"You better not be getting a *ride* from that bartender." His husky yet angered-charged tone actually was a turn-on. He was jealous and some part of me enjoyed that.

Said bartender delivered my drink at the perfect time. "Hey, I'm Ivy, by the way."

His gray eyes brightened, and his cocky smirk softened into a sexy grin. "I'm Cohen."

"Cohen, if a female patron asked you for a *ride*, would you give it to her?" I sipped the freshly poured drink he had placed in front of me.

His gaze bounced from me to Fletcher and then back to me.

"He's just a friend," I clarified. "He's not available to give me a *ride*."

Fletcher's low grumble vibrated the wooden floor and my stool, but I didn't acknowledge it.

"I guess it would depend on the situation." Cohen shifted his stance uncomfortably.

"What if I needed a *ride*?" I shamelessly fluttered my eyelashes.

"Well...I don't get off until two a.m." His voice broke nervously.

"It sounds like you would get off at two-fifteen then."

"That's enough, Ivy." Fletcher's growling comment struck me in the belly and warmed my core.

When I peered over my shoulder at Fletch to flash him a discerning look, Cohen took that opportunity to leave the uncomfortable conversation and shuffled quickly to another patron further away down the bar from us.

"You're a terrible wingman." I huffed out an easy laugh and swallowed more of the briny whiskey.

Fletcher tipped his pint glass up and took an extra-long swallow of his beer.

"I'm not going out with you if you're going to be such a cockblocker." My chuckles unnerved him, which made me only want to tease him more.

"I came here tonight to hang out with you, not help you score with the sleazy bartender." He hissed the words between his teeth.

"You were the one that brought up the sex topic." I shrugged, playing innocent.

"I was not!" Creases deepened across his forehead, and his brow pulled downward.

"You made the comment about me being full of you." Had he forgotten how his comment had me spit my beer all over the counter?

"I meant you used to like me." He shook his head. "That was not a comment about my dick."

"Sorry, I guess my mind automatically went to how your dick filled me."

Chapter 15

Fletcher, present day

Well, now my dick twitched in my jeans. *No.* This is not supposed to happen with her. *Dammit.*

"You can't say things like that...we're supposed to be just friends." My pitch shrilled to a prepubescent adolescent boy.

"Yeah, we shouldn't talk about your dick," she said nonchalantly. "So, can I talk about other men's dicks?"

"No." I shook my head back and forth several times, emphasizing my point. "No dick talk at any time."

"That's probably a good idea. If we talk about a dick, I'll want to see it. And I should just be surprised. I mean, if I talk it up, then I'll have high expectations, and I don't want to be disappointed." She sat and sipped her drink like this conversation didn't affect her at all.

Meanwhile, the thought of her seeing another man's dick had me furious, and the thought of her seeing my dick made me want to march to the bathroom and give her a reminder.

Shit. I gave myself a mental slap as I downed the remainder of my beer in one gulp.

I motioned to the bartender for another.

I wondered if tonight would be challenging after the loud discussion I had with Amilyn earlier this evening. But maybe it was good we got a lot of our feelings out in the open.

I imagined I would be weighed down by guilt and sorrow, but truthfully, it was better that things between us imploded. We'd needed to have that conversation for a while, and the right time had come.

Another beer appeared before me. Cohen didn't stop to chitchat this time. I can't blame the guy. There was no reason to waste his time when there was no way in hell I was going to let him touch Ivy. I'm sure I made those intentions clear.

"So, do you want to talk about your fiancée?" I swore she nearly flinched while asking.

"Nope," I said, popping the *P*.

"Okay. How about work? That's a safe topic, right?"

I wasn't sure if she was asking a question or making a statement.

"Our careers are similar since you're a paramedic, and I work as a nurse in the ER." Her eyes brightened, and I was drawn to the warmth of her.

"Are we going to be able to do this?" Five seconds next to her, and I wanted to touch her. Two minutes, and I wanted to haul her off to the bathroom. And now she wanted to discuss *work*. My mind, body, and heart tugged me in different directions.

I regretted what I asked as soon as I saw the light dim in her eyes. "Fletch, no matter what either of us says, this is awkward as hell. If we're going to be around each other, we're going to need to find some common ground. And I figured work was a good place to start."

"I'm sorry, Vine." I brushed my thumb across her forearm propped against the bar.

Her skin prickled with gooseflesh at my touch. I pretended to ignore how I elicited that response from her, but I filed that into my brain to further explore later.

"I know we agreed to try this whole friendship thing, but I'm still trying to protect my heart. I never thought you'd hurt me like you did, and even though I'd like to believe you would never do that to me again, I'm a little guarded." I blew out a loud breath and stared up at the ceiling for a beat before leveling my gaze back to hers. "Maybe it would help if I knew why you had such a sudden change of heart."

Her eyes widened before a sheen of water covered her chocolate orbs.

"John and I are going to the other side of the bar to dance. We settled up our bill here." Carrie's voice interrupted the intense moment I was sharing with Ivy, but relief pushed her shoulders down into a more relaxed position, and she feigned a smile.

"Okay. Fletch and I will be over in a little bit."

Carrie ignored Ivy's glassy eyes and tossed a wave before she headed to the other end of the bar, where the dance floor was located, with John following closely on her heels.

And then it was just the two of us. Not like it had been four of us anyway. John and Carrie had their own thing going and didn't pay us any attention.

"I know you have a lot of questions, and I want to answer them. But here is not the right place to have that discussion." Her voice shook with unease as empathy shone in her tear-filled eyes. "I promise I'm not avoiding the conversation. I intend to speak to you about everything. But

I want us to have a chance to get to know each other as adults first. Because I wish the girl I used to be would have done things differently, and I don't like her very much. I'm hoping I'll be happier with the choices she makes now as an adult. And quite frankly, it would be nice to like myself again."

Her heart was a fractured mess also. It was so obvious her emotions had control of her, just as mine did over me.

"I work the next two nights, but I'm free Tuesday if that works for you."

What could I say at this point? I'd waited over four years to hear her explanation. What was another few days. "I'll bring tacos."

A hint of a smile tugged at the corners of her lips, and a flicker of hope settled in my chest.

"Should I pick you up, and we drive out to the woods to have the conversation so no one will hear us?"

"Fletch, you used to take me to the woods so we could make out, not talk." She shook her head playfully. "I'm not smuggling booze, and I'm not eating tacos in the woods, even if it is on a Tuesday."

"Come on, Vine. Your parents always had the good stuff and never missed any of the alcohol. I bet their liquor cabinet is still stocked full of everything."

"So just bring the tacos over to my house. My parents are away for a bit."

"Ivy Hatfield. If you have a boy over to your parents' house while they're out of town, it would be scandalous." My attempt at humor had me laughing and her scowling.

She dragged her gaze up and down from my head to my legs and then back up again. "You definitely act juvenile like a boy, but somehow, you have a man's body."

I shouldn't feel the humming throughout my abdomen

and in my boxers right now, but my dick had a mind of its own, and he acknowledged her compliment with a salute.

I shifted my weight on my stool in an attempt to adjust the discomfort quite literally growing behind the zipper of my jeans. My head and my heart were all kinds of confused, but my body reacted to her just like it did when I was a teenager.

"You don't look so bad yourself." I was hoping a little flirting would be harmless. I mean, as long as I don't act on the physiological reaction my dick initiates, I should be fine.

"I never thought I'd live long enough to hear you give me a compliment again."

I hadn't predicted the tears that would begin their descent down her face. But huge, quiet droplets of water slid down her cheeks.

Shit.

"Why are you crying?" I hadn't meant to cause those glistening streams from those chocolate eyes. "I'm going to look like an asshole sitting next to a girl in a bar making her cry."

She laughed as the silent tears continued to fall. At least she wasn't sobbing or wailing, along with the evidence of her crying that I felt compelled to brush away with my thumbs.

She leaned into my touch, and once again, I knew exactly what she needed, and I couldn't deny her anything right now. So I stood and wedged myself between our two bar stools, then wrapped my arms around her shoulders and pulled her into me.

I rubbed the palm of my hand in small circles over her back, and she pressed the side of her face into my chest before slipping her arms around my waist and gently squeezing.

I was in so much trouble. After having a huge fight with Amilyn earlier this evening, I was already wrapped up in another woman's arms, and I felt so much better. *I'm going to need more alcohol.*

Ivy and I joined Carrie and John on the dance floor after I finished half of another beer, and my girl downed quite a few more shots. *My girl?*

She hadn't been my girl in over four years. But who the hell was I fooling? She'd always be my girl. I damn well wouldn't let her belong to anyone else, which was why I was currently dancing with her.

I caught a few men approaching her, but I intervened before either of them could be within five feet of her. I disrupted their attempts to even hope to be close enough to touch her.

With my hands on her hips and her swaying to the music, I realized more than ever that I'd never be able to control my feelings when Ivy Hatfield was involved. I would continue with the facade that her laugh didn't make me the happiest man in the world, that her smile didn't light up the room, and that her body didn't drive me absolutely insane.

She had more curves than she did before she left for college, and I would love nothing more than to explore them without clothes on, but I'm older now too. I'm more mature, and I didn't need to act on my feelings.

We still had a lot to talk about, but I already knew the outcome of our conversation would be the same regardless. I couldn't stay away from her.

When she was away at college, my mind convinced me

the physical distance kept us apart even though my heart was aware I could have easily made the drive to see her at any time.

But now that she was literally living in the same town as me, there was no way I could stay away from her. We had been thrown together on multiple occasions without any instigation on either of our parts.

That's how it had always been with us—ever since the planets aligned and we were on the same bus to school in first grade. Nothing, not even my own free will, could keep us apart.

So when the DJ played a slow song, I welcomed her arms back around my torso. It was as if no time had passed, and we were back at our high school prom.

I brushed the back of her head with my hand while she once again leaned into my chest. She must use the same shampoo she did back in high school because the citrusy, floral scent wafted up from her hair and provided my nostrils with the delicious memory of the many times I held her in my arms and she snuggled into my body heat.

I didn't even feel bad at the reminiscence. I spent countless nights when she first left wishing I could be standing right where I was right now. I pleaded with my brain to recall how she smelled and how her body felt against mine. I begged for one more time to hold her, promising that I would appreciate that moment and commit it to my memory so I could revisit that flash in time anytime I missed her.

"Damn, I missed you, Fletch," she hummed into my shirt.

I pressed my lips against the top of her head unknowingly. It was such a second-nature gesture that I couldn't even feel guilty about it. No wonder Amilyn instantly asked me if I kissed Ivy the moment I admitted to seeing her.

Because apparently, putting my lips on her was as uncomplicated as waving goodbye, nodding in agreement, or shrugging when one didn't know an answer. But somehow, things between us became complicated. The easygoing best friends, soul mates, lovers' relationship was long gone, and I wasn't sure if we could overcome the hurdles of hurt feelings, distance, betrayal, secrets, and broken hearts.

However, I was willing to try. Even one or two years ago, I wouldn't have been interested in having Ivy back in my life, but here on the dance floor of Thursday's, I could no longer imagine my life without Ivy Hatfield again. Time and distance couldn't separate us anymore if we didn't let it.

"Fletch, I think I need to go home." She lifted her hooded lids and peered up at me with that chocolate gaze I adored. "I'm feeling a little too much deja vu. And I don't want to make a false assumption here."

She feels it too. We had an undeniable connection. "I'll take you home, Vine."

"I drove here." Worry creased her brow.

"John drove me. I've only had one and a half beers. I can drive your car home."

She leaned away from our embrace, but her hands were still clinging to my hips loosely. "But how will you get home?"

"I'll just stay at my dad's house. He's with my uncle Jonathan for the weekend. I was actually going to go to his house tomorrow and clean anyway. He's been kind of a mess since my mom died, but he refuses any help from me, so I have to sneak in and tidy up when he's not home."

"Will you drive Carrie back to her hotel?"

"Of course." I had no idea which hotel Carrie was staying in, but it couldn't possibly be too far out of the way.

Ivy released the light hold she kept near the belt loops of my jeans and walked several paces across the dance floor to notify Carrie of the plan. There was some hand waving and soon Ivy, Carrie, and John were heading toward my location at the edge of the dance floor.

"You know, Carrie, I could take you back to your hotel if you want to stay a little longer," John offered when we approached the door to exit the bar where the music wasn't ringing in our ears, and we could actually understand what each other was saying.

Carrie's eyes sought approval from Ivy, with their blue depths pleading for understanding from her friend.

I would love to warn Carrie about John, but if she was truly only looking for a fling, he was probably just as good as any. He was my closest friend, and although he may be a bit of a man whore, he was an overall good guy. He would do anything in the world for me, and he'd never lied to a woman about what he wanted or who he was. He was comfortable with himself and didn't try to be anything he wasn't.

Even though I knew he'd slept with quite a few nurses at the hospital, I'd never heard anyone utter a bad word about him, so at least he hadn't pissed anyone off too badly.

"Carrie, we should have a sleepover tonight like we used to when we were kids." Ivy must have become more intoxicated from the dance floor to the front of the bar because her speech was thick, and she seemed to have forgotten about the arrangements already discussed to take Carrie back to her hotel.

I needed to get her home soon.

Her lids were growing heavier. "You should sleep in

my bed like we used to." She threw her arms around Carrie's neck, and fortunately, she was able to keep herself upright and not topple over when her friend launched her body at her. "Just have John drop you off at my house instead of taking you back to your hotel." It was amazing she could form coherent thoughts with as jumbled as her words were.

Carrie giggled at Ivy's growing drunkenness. "I think you'll be passed out before I even get there."

"I'll leave the key in the usual spot," Ivy whisper-shouted into Carrie's ear while her friend continued to snicker. "Then we'll have breakfast tomorrow."

"Okay, Ivy. That sounds good. I'll see you later." Carrie kissed my girl on the cheek and swung her gaze to me. "You better make sure she gets home okay."

I nodded once. "Of course I will."

Then Carrie leaned close to my ear and cupped her hand so John and Ivy couldn't see or hear her words. "I can't believe you're still just friends. You should make a move at some point, Fletch."

Ivy fell asleep during the car ride to her house. I used the house key attached to the ring containing her car keys to unlock the door, and she sleepily walked up the few stairs onto the front porch of her parents' house after I awakened her.

She didn't speak, just wordlessly kicked off her shoes and proceeded down the hallway to her bedroom.

I had been in her room too many times to count. Sometimes when her parents were home and lots of times when they weren't. We never had sex in her room. That seemed disrespectful somehow. But we had made out like the horny teenagers we were at that time.

I followed her into her room, making sure she would be settled for the night.

However, I was the one that would end up unsettled that night. Because after she plopped her weight onto the mattress of her bed, she whipped the shirt she was wearing over her head and shimmied out of her jeans so quickly I didn't have enough time to give her privacy.

She undressed in front of me like she had a hundred times before, but she was drunk and didn't realize it had been over four years since the last time she had done that.

When she reached around to unclasp her bra, I finally turned and faced the opposite direction. I couldn't willingly look at her naked when she was intoxicated and unaware of what she was doing.

"Fletch, can you grab a nightshirt out of my dresser drawer," her sleepy voice called to me.

I didn't dare peer over my shoulder. I just shuffled my feet toward the dresser, keeping my back to her, and pulled open several drawers until I found a night shirt for her.

If I had my wits about me, I would have realized her pajamas were in the same drawer as they always were. But we were no longer together.

And watching her undress felt extremely intimate. I waited several beats before glancing back at the bed.

When I finally twisted my body back around, Ivy was dressed and lying on top of her covers with her eyes closed.

I lifted her body, pulled the blankets out from under her, and then placed her back down against the sheets.

She flipped over to her side, and I pulled the covers up to her shoulders. Quiet snores already escaped her sleepy respirations, so I kissed the top of her forehead and slipped out of her house.

Chapter 16

Fletcher, earlier present day

"I ran into one of my friends from elementary school yesterday." I tried to keep my tone nonchalant so Amilyn wouldn't suspect anything.

"Oh yeah?" Her voice held genuine interest.

I opened the containers of Chinese food as I attempted casual conversation regarding Ivy and Carrie. "Yeah, I don't think I ever mentioned a girl that lived on my street when I was little. Her name is Carrie."

"No. I don't recall you ever mentioning her." Her posture stiffened as she scooped out sesame chicken onto a plate along with some rice, and once she popped an egg roll out of the bag holding a cluster of them, she headed toward the small table in the dining area adjacent to the living room.

I followed closely behind her, gathering my own food from the different containers on my kitchen counter, and settled in a seat next to her. I hadn't truly prepared for this conversation, but I had effectively procrastinated.

John was picking me up in two hours, and I hadn't told Amilyn I was going out tonight.

"She is in town for a funeral and suggested we get together this evening for a couple of drinks. I invited John to come along so it wouldn't be weird."

"Fletcher, if you want to go out with your friend Carrie, that's fine with me. Thank you for considering my feelings, though." She relaxed somewhat and scooped a healthy portion of rice onto her spoon before placing it in her mouth and chewing carefully.

"Would you like to go also? You would like Carrie." I already knew her response, but I kept my eyes down on my food while I pushed chicken and rice around on my plate with my chopsticks.

Amilyn always used traditional utensils when we ate Chinese food, but I found it fun to use chopsticks.

Ivy was the person who introduced me to chopsticks when we were kids, and although I wasn't good at using them, I had so many funny memories worthy enough to keep me trying to work the sticks together to lift food to my mouth.

"It's not really my thing. I'll hang out at home, and you can stop by afterwards if you want."

We'd had this same discussion over and over again, but I kept asking anyway, hoping there would be a different outcome, even though things hadn't changed in the past two years.

I dropped the wooden sticks on my plate, which didn't make quite the clatter a stainless-steel fork would, but I grabbed her attention, nonetheless.

Her eyes widened initially, but then her brows creased with annoyance. "I'm a homebody. You've always known this about me."

"And I have stayed in with you countless times to watch a movie or eat takeout, but you've never once gone out with me to a bar or restaurant or even to a party at a friend's house." This explosive outburst had been building for a while, and I wasn't sure how much I would be able to hold back.

"I shouldn't have to change for you." Her fiery blue eyes blazed with frustration.

"I never asked for you to change. I love spending time with you, and I would love to share some of the things that I enjoy with you."

"I'm tired after working all day, and I just want to relax." She rolled her eyes as if she didn't just state something completely obvious.

"You don't work every day," I retorted.

Her eyes narrowed. She was becoming angrier by the second. This is a topic we had disagreed about during our entire relationship.

"Of course I don't work every day at my job. But I have to go to the grocery store, clean my house, and get my laundry done on my days off. I'm a grown-up. I don't have the same compulsion you do to go out and consume alcohol." Her aggravation was building, but mine was too.

"You're being unreasonable." I hadn't even spilled the beans that Ivy would be there also, and she was already pissed at me.

"Because I don't want to go hang out in some smelly bar? You're acting like a child." She made a gesture with her hand, dismissing me, and went back to the food on her plate.

I inhaled deeply because the mother lode was about to be spewed from my mouth, and I wanted to do it somewhat tactfully. "Would you go if Ivy was going to be there?"

Her mouth gaped open for a beat before she shoved her plate away and stood abruptly.

"I've been waiting for this to happen ever since you told me she was back in town." The exasperated fury that creased her face intensified, causing her to clench her jaw. "I'm going to make this real easy for you." She angrily pulled the engagement ring off her left finger and tossed it on the table. The gold band that seated one solitary diamond bounced a few times against the wooden surface. "Go be with her. I've listened to you pine over her for long enough. I'm done."

She headed for the door, and I pushed out from the table, scraping the chair's legs over the rough floor, but reached her before she made it to my front door. "So that's it?" I asked while I gripped her upper arm.

"I've never been *it* for you," she snarled. I would have thought most women would have shed at least a few tears if they broke up with their fiancé, but Amilyn stood so close to me I could see the venom in her blue eyes.

"If you weren't, I never would have asked you to marry me. You were the one who never quite committed to this relationship. You've kept me at arm's length ever since we started dating." I needed to understand why the woman next to me was being so cold. She took care of people for a living, but yet, with me, she held no compassion, just frustration and aggravation.

"Well, now there's even more distance—go do whatever you need to do. You're not the type of man I'm looking for."

I released her arm and watched her leave, remaining dumbfounded by her last statement. She didn't look back before she was on the other side of my door, with it latched behind her. Her words struck me with a wave of nausea.

Thankfully, I had only consumed a few bites of food, or I would have been retching up my guts.

I managed to dump the contents of our plates in the

trash can and wash the dishes. I closed up the containers of Chinese food and placed them in the fridge when, truthfully, I would probably just throw it out in a couple of days. That meal would forever remind me of what just happened between Amilyn and me, so if the few morsels I consumed tonight wanted to come back up, eating more of the meal at a later time would most likely have the same results.

After I showered and changed, I sat on my couch and contemplated why the two girls I'd ever thought I loved dumped me so effortlessly. Although, when Ivy broke up with me, she cried and at least acted like she cared about my feelings.

I had no idea why or how I misjudged the situation with Amilyn so inaccurately. I ran over random things she said and events that had occurred throughout the time we spent together and wondered if there had been any clues.

She was unwilling to move in with me or set a date for our wedding. She insisted on keeping her apartment, and we typically only spent time together at her place or mine. She never wanted to take a trip anywhere or go and do *anything*.

She never offered a key to her place, but she had a key to my place and to my dad's. She'd been keeping me at arm's length our entire relationship, but perhaps because I care so much about her, I was never bothered by her distance.

I wanted to be with someone so badly I pushed myself on her, and she never let me in. *Damn.*

I allowed myself to have fun with Ivy, Carrie, and John. We danced and laughed. Ivy drank several shots of whiskey, and I saw the version of her I remembered.

I also saw the grown-up version of her body without intention. And her new curves were quite enticing. I wanted to slide my hands over her skin and see if she still had a silky, smooth feel beneath my fingertips.

But I left her house after tucking her in, and now I lay on the bed at my dad's house, staring up at the ceiling fan rotating around and around, causing a spinning shadow from the light of the streetlamp seeping in through the sheer curtains.

It was a short walk from Ivy's house to my childhood home. I made the stroll between our two homes many times when we were younger, which was another reason I was struck with such nostalgia.

Of course, every time I was near Ivy now, I was hit with thousands of glimpses of our past. Just like the flickers of light floating on the ceiling now, various images of my childhood and teenage years danced through my mind.

The pictures didn't disappear when I closed my eyes either. Nothing made the memories stop flooding my brain. I needed to get closure from the situation that transpired between Ivy and me four years ago, but I needed to figure out what to do about Amilyn also.

I really thought I was all in with Amilyn. She was the one that didn't want to get too close.

I decided moving forward, I would take a similar stance. I would protect my heart next time. Perhaps if I didn't always jump in headfirst, I wouldn't be left with a broken heart. I needed to be smarter the next time around. Thinking with my head was a better alternative than thinking with my heart.

I refused to be like John, however, and think with my dick. I had been so caught up in my own female drama that I hadn't even thought about the fact that I left Carrie at the bar with him. They were getting along fine when Ivy and I were there, so I assumed things continued that way after we left.

I didn't even consume two beers the entire time I was at Thursday's, wanting to make sure Ivy was okay. The last thing I needed was a fistfight, which would have surely ensued if any man in that bar thought he had a right to speak to her. I needed to keep my wits about me to keep a lookout for any men staring a little too intently at her.

Fortunately, with the amount of dancing we did together, I gave the impression she belonged to me, which was exactly the vibe I was looking to send out.

But she didn't actually belong to me. I wondered if the fact that she hadn't slept with anyone since me could possibly mean at least a part of her was still mine.

I was entirely too sober to get out of my head, but I knew all the hiding places for my dad's liquor.

Chapter 17

Ivy, present day

I felt the dip in the mattress behind me sometime in the early hours of the morning, but I didn't look at the time. Carrie must have closed down the bar with John. I had more drinks than I originally planned at the bar. But we were having so much fun I threw back more than a few shots of whiskey.

I hadn't laughed that much or felt so comfortable and relaxed in quite a long time. I remember missing Carrie so much when I was in middle school, but I honestly hadn't even thought about her in years.

I liked the person she'd turned into, and I'm sure if she hadn't moved away, we would have stayed best friends. It was amazing that after so many years had passed, we could just fall back into an easy friendship. There was no awkwardness or loss of conversation.

And now she was asleep in my bed, just like the many sleepovers we had as kids. The reminiscence of those days soon had my lips stretching into a sleepy smile as I leaned over to see the time on my phone.

Eight forty-two. I didn't know what time we should

have breakfast, but I didn't want to wait until it was too late, so I flipped over to my other side to wake my friend.

However, the body lying on top of my covers was entirely too large to belong to Carrie. The olive-green shirt stretched against the muscular back of the sleeping man. The light blond hair was a little longer than when I was in high school, and the urge to run my fingers through it was too tempting.

So I combed the fingers of my right hand through the silky threads. The deep grumble that vibrated clear through to his back didn't deter me. I dragged my nails over the back of his head and swept down toward his neck, causing him to shift his weight.

But then his body stilled, and I removed my hand from the invasion of his soft locks that curled slightly at the ends. I tucked my hand back under the covers and pulled the comforter up to my neck.

"Ivy?" Fletcher questioned, barely above a whisper.

"Yeah, Fletch," I hummed while shutting my eyes. If this was a dream, I didn't want to wake yet.

When he turned over and faced me, the unexpected motion fluttered my eyes open, connecting me to his early morning hazy blue gaze.

"Why am I in your bed?" Worry creased his brow and his day-old stubble danced as his jaw ticked with concern.

"I was actually going to ask you the same thing." I blew out a huff of laughter and tasted my own morning breath. *How much did I have to drink last night?*

"You were shooting whiskey like it was your job, so I drove your car home when you were ready to leave the bar." He scratched his chin, and his gaze shot upward as he searched for the recollection of last night. "I walked to my dad's house after I tucked you in."

"I know I'm going to sound like a hypocrite here, but you don't smell like you should have been driving last night." I giggled and pulled my quilt up over my mouth and nose.

But Fletcher yanked it free from my hand and closed the small amount of distance between us, bringing his face within an inch of mine. "What do I smell like?" he said on a long exhale.

I giggled louder because once he jabbed his finger into my side, I couldn't stop. He was aware of all my ticklish spots. "I have to pee," I hollered in between gasps of air.

He relented the tickling, but his lips remained within a breath of mine.

"You smell like cheap vodka," I said and I swear my mouth almost touched his as I spoke.

"Does it make you wonder if I taste the same way?" The haze had lifted from his blue eyes, and the color darkened with something I'd seen before. Desire.

I swallowed and clenched my legs together, no longer because I had the urge to empty my bladder but because there was a heat pooling there. "Fletch," I murmured on a long sigh.

And then his lips were on mine, his bristly jaw scratching against the skin of my cheeks as he thoroughly tasted, nibbled, and bit my mouth.

I should have pushed him away, but I couldn't. I hadn't realized how much I missed kissing him until that moment when I was swept away in the familiarity of his very essence. His lips always caressed mine, providing me comfort and reassurance. So even though my brain was screaming how wrong this was, my heart and soul were completely invested in how his mouth massaged mine, and I relaxed into him.

I didn't hesitate or worry about morning breath when his tongue pressed against the seam of my lips. He urged my mouth open, and a moan rumbled from his throat when I complied.

I had no resistance or apparently any self-respect when it came to Fletcher Hart. I'd never kissed a taken man before, and I would have thought that went against my morals, but here I was sucking face with an engaged man.

My body reacted without my permission, also. My hips ground just below the waistband of his jeans, and an impressive bulge pressed against my throbbing core.

He leaned over me, and I snaked my arms out from beneath the covers and around his neck, bringing him closer to me. His growing erection could be felt by me through not only his jeans but my thick comforter as well.

Four years, and I'd never felt this kind of chemistry with another man. But a hot second with Fletcher had me shamelessly dry-humping him.

He was the first to break away from our lip-lock, which, if he started it, I figured he had the right to stop it before we got even further carried away.

"Vine," he said near breathless and swiped his thumb across my puffy lips.

I had so many emotions tumbling around in my chest that I couldn't speak. I was disappointed with myself for making out with an engaged man. And I was upset that now Fletcher would think I was that kind of woman.

And I didn't know how I felt about the fact that he kissed me while engaged to another woman. I never expected him to be the cheating type.

"Amilyn and I broke up." He blew out each word as he attempted to slow his rapid respirations.

"What? When?" My voice squeaked with my question.

He used to be so good at knowing what I was thinking I wondered if he could feel and hear all the concerns I had doing somersaults in my mind.

"Last night before I went out with you, John, and Carrie." He rolled onto his back and swiped his hands over his face.

"Did you want to talk about it?" Although I was relieved I hadn't kissed an engaged man just a few seconds ago, I could see Fletcher was struggling.

"I'd really rather not right now." After a long sigh, he flipped onto his back and stared blankly up at the ceiling.

"Was I the reason for your breakup?" I figured his fiancée wasn't happy he would be spending an evening with me even if others were present, so I wasn't surprised. But I felt bad that I contributed to another breakup when his heart was on the line.

"I won't say you were *the* reason because there were several reasons." His body sagged, and his eyes closed for a few beats.

"Maybe you two will get back together." I only offered the reassurance half-heartedly, which I realized was evident in my unfortunate, sarcastic undertone.

Fletcher's eyes popped open, and he twisted his neck so his blue gaze could find me. "Vine, don't say things you don't mean. It's not who you are."

I wanted to apologize for always speaking my mind, but I wasn't sorry. I didn't want the two of them to get back together, but I did feel bad that he got hurt again—especially if I was part of the reason.

"So you just found another woman's bed and landed in it? Is that how you deal with your breakups?" I shook my head and made a tsking sound.

"I honestly don't know why or how I ended up here."

He shifted his body onto its side and propped his arm behind his head, and damn if he didn't look sexy with a day's worth of stubble and his blond mop of hair crazily sticking up in all directions. "But you've always had a way of pulling me to you. When you're upset, I find my way to you. And apparently, when I'm upset, I still find my way to you."

"Yeah, I put a spell on you years ago when I was in my witchcraft phase." I had to lighten the mood and say something ridiculous because I refused to acknowledge his comment otherwise.

"I wouldn't put it past you." His perfectly white teeth peeked out of his recently kissed lips, and I found myself smiling, also. He always did have a calming presence about him even when I was a hot mess. "How about your medieval phase? When you were obsessed with dragons."

"Don't joke about dragons," I said curtly.

"Okay, I can see that wasn't a phase you grew out of." His snickering laugh lifted some of the guilt that had weighed me down for so many years, and I couldn't stop myself from poking my index finger into his exposed armpit.

He flinched and resorted to tickling me on my sides. He was a lot stronger than me, so he was easily able to grip both of my wrists with one hand while jabbing me with his fingertip beneath my ribs.

"Stop! I swear I'll pee on myself." I wheezed in between my screeching fits of laughter.

He released my wrists and ceased the tickling assault. "I'm only stopping because I've seen you actually piss your pants." His devilish grin had me wanting to both smile and punch him.

So when I rolled out of bed to relieve myself, I grabbed my pillow and struck him in the head.

His rumbling chuckles filled my soul with happiness I hadn't experienced...well, in over four years.

He wasn't in my room when I returned from the bathroom after I relieved myself. And although my heart felt empty, I wasn't surprised. I sat on the corner of my bed, reached for my phone plugged into its charging cord on my nightstand, and fired off a text to Carrie.

> Me: Since you didn't make it to my house, I'm hoping you made it back to your hotel okay.

> Carrie: Sorry Ivy. It got to be so late and I didn't want to wake you.

> Me: Are you still able to come to breakfast?

Three dots danced across the screen and then stopped, but no text came through.

Fletcher reappeared at the threshold of my room while I waited for Carrie's response.

"I thought you left," I said, startled that he was still in my house.

"Did you think I would leave without saying goodbye?" He wasted no time taking a spot next to me on my bed, causing my mattress to dip in the corner with his added weight.

"Well, you showed up without saying hello." I shrugged and glanced back down at my phone, but there was still no response from Carrie.

He shook his head and rolled his eyes before leaning his knee against mine. "Sorry about that. I had a lot to drink, and I don't really remember coming over."

"I didn't think you had much to drink at Thursday's."

"I didn't, which was why I offered to drive you home. But apparently, after I walked to my dad's house from here, I hit more than one bottle of his stash hidden there." His shoulders slumped with his confession.

"Does your dad drink a lot?" I had a good idea what the truth was, but I didn't know if Fletcher was aware.

"He has ever since my mom died. He thinks he's hiding it from me, but I'm not stupid." His dejected posture tugged at my heartstrings. "I just don't know how to make it better."

I placed my hand over the top of his and gave it a gentle squeeze, causing his blue gaze to connect to my brown one.

"We have so much to talk about, Fletch." I inhaled and exhaled slowly when my phone pinged with a text notification.

> Carrie: I'm good with breakfast. Just shoot me a text with an address.

> Me: You know my address. Come over to my parents' house and I'll make waffles.

"You're making waffles?" Fletcher said, clearly having looked over my shoulder while I texted.

> Me: I'll invite Fletcher.

I turned my screen toward him so he could more easily read what I had typed out.

His lips curved up into a smile.

"Go shower and brush your teeth. You look like hell." He didn't. He looked like a man I slept with, and I didn't want Carrie to suspect we had done anything when he literally only visited slumberland in my bed.

"You just don't want Carrie to think we've had sex." He

joked, but the situation was so complicated. "Or you don't want her to think we had sex last night?" His eyebrow shot up as his curiosity increased. "Have you told her about us... like about high school us?"

"No, I didn't. She's only in town for a little bit, and our story is too long to explain to someone..."

"Our story isn't over yet." Fletcher quickly cut me off with a hard peck to the mouth, and then he left my room.

And a moment later, the front door opened and closed.

Chapter 18

Ivy, present day

"John didn't want to leave my bed this morning." Carrie's comment caught me off guard, and I nearly choked on the orange juice I was drinking.

At least she didn't say that while I was extracting our food from the waffle maker. I could have given myself a second-degree burn.

After I wiped the counter and stopped sputtering, I didn't respond with any other commentary with words or otherwise before she began speaking again.

"He was very good in bed, which would have made him a good fling, but he was all clingy this morning." She scrunched her nose in disgust.

"I'm back, ladies," Fletcher called from the foyer.

He wasted no time walking into the kitchen and giving Carrie a quick kiss to her cheek before pulling out a stool and sitting next to her.

I felt my cheeks flame with heat as jealousy made me red rather than green with envy. And I poured a little too much batter into the waffle maker in my moment of resentfulness, causing some sizzling and crispy edges.

I reminded myself that I had no reason to feel so possessive because, technically, he didn't belong to me, but also, Carrie was leaving today so I didn't need to be worried. Nothing would happen between Fletcher and her.

I finished the waffles, placed them on three plates, and distributed them to my two friends. I took a seat next to Carrie rather than perching on the stool on the other side of Fletcher.

"Thanks for inviting John out last night," she said to Fletcher around a mouthful of waffles coated with syrup.

He nodded and continued chewing.

"These waffles remind me of your mom, Fletcher." Carrie continued to dip each buttered morsel in a pool of syrup as she spoke. "I loved going there on Saturday mornings. It was one of my best childhood memories. Mrs. Hart's waffles and my two best friends."

I swallowed hard, waiting for Fletcher's reaction. I twisted my head toward him, two seats down from me. He had stopped chewing and stared blankly downward at his plate.

"How is she doing?" Unaware of how this fun breakfast had just become grim, Carrie kept dipping her bites into the maple stickiness and plopping each into her mouth.

After a few beats of uncomfortable silence that I think Carrie was truly oblivious to, I returned my gaze to her. "Fletcher's mom passed away after high school."

Her fork hit the ceramic dish with a clatter, and her hands flew to her mouth.

Her mortification brought Fletcher out of his stupor, and he was quick to reassure her. "It's okay, Carrie. It's been almost four years." The corners of his mouth curled upward slightly, but the smile didn't reach his eyes.

"I am so sorry, Fletcher." After her initial gasp a

moment ago, her soft tone was soothing once she released her hands from her face.

And then her hands were on him. She was brushing her fingertips across the exposed skin on his forearms, and my blood was boiling once again.

"What time is your flight, Carrie?" My tone was harsher than I intended. I wanted to feign calm and collected, but obviously, I missed the mark.

"Not until this afternoon." Although she answered my question, her focus remained fixed on Fletcher.

His blue gaze dropped from her face to his forearm, and then he peered over at me. "I should go so I can let you girls catch up before you have to leave." He slid off his seat, scraped the last few bites of his untouched waffle into the trash can, rinsed off his plate, and loaded it along with his fork into the dishwasher as if he lived here.

The gesture was both comforting and alarming at the same time.

"It was great seeing you," Fletcher said to Carrie as he kissed her cheek. Again.

She jumped off her stool and flung her arms around him, pulling him in close and squeezing him tightly. "I'm so glad I ran into you and Ivy while I was here." She released her embrace and peered up at him before bouncing her blue eyes back to me. "We need to keep in touch. We shouldn't go another decade without seeing each other, okay?"

Fletcher and I both nodded in agreement as she twisted her head back and forth, holding us accountable.

Satisfied with our silent promise, she smiled once again up at Fletcher. "Thanks for coming over for breakfast this morning."

He nodded once more and then headed for the door. *No kiss on the cheek for me.*

"I'll call you later, Ivy." *And no affectionate moniker.* He disappeared down the hall and out the front door without any further acknowledgment of me.

"I can't believe you friend-zoned that fine specimen of masculinity." Carrie *tsked* and shook her head.

I rolled my eyes dramatically. I had zero interest in discussing the nuances of the relationship between Fletcher and me with her, so I went with a swift change of subject. "So, how did things go with your fling? Was it all you thought it would be?"

She smiled and stared past me, off into the distance, with a smile stretched on her face. "He served his purpose."

Although her words said one-night stand, her dreamy expression led me to believe she wanted more. "I have a feeling the one-night thing isn't for you."

Her focus returned to me after a short exhale. "Ivy, I don't even know what is for me. Before last night, I've only ever been with one guy."

I could relate, and although I appreciated her candor and transparency, I wasn't comfortable contributing to the conversation.

"What about you, Ivy?" Her long, perfect eyelashes blinked several times with her curiosity.

"I had a boyfriend in high school that I broke up with before college, and other than a few dates here and there, I haven't found anyone else to keep my interest enough to go further than a polite kiss goodnight." I could offer that much truth.

"Was the boyfriend you had in high school anyone I would know?"

Shit. Time for another change of subject. "Nah. No one you would know." I waved dismissively hoping to cover the blatant lie I just so easily spewed.

We finished eating and drank a few cups of coffee before she told me it was time for her to go. My throat constricted with emotion as I walked her outside to her car.

We had kept the rest of our conversation light during the remainder of breakfast, but I couldn't help but wonder what discussions would have been like had she stayed. *Would she be the one I confided in? How would she have reacted to my breakup with Fletcher?* She probably would have been able to manipulate me into telling her the real reason behind the dissolution of my relationship with him.

Julie was a good friend. She never pressed the cause of our separation. She just kept me well distracted. That had always been her way, and I truly loved her for that. But I know things would have been different with Carrie. She's the sweet one, and Julie is the fun one.

I shouldn't compare the two best girlfriends I had during my childhood, but they were such polar opposites that my mind kept wondering how both of them had been my closest friends—aside from Fletcher.

"Is it weird if I say I'm going to miss you?" Carrie said as she spun around, once reaching the car.

A short, loud laugh escaped my chest. "I was thinking the same thing," I answered while I simultaneously squeezed her for a tight hug.

I released her and noticed the sheen of water covering her blue eyes.

My own unshed tears blurred my vision.

"It's great how we can just pick up like no time has passed, but I wouldn't have worn mascara if I knew I was going to cry," she said, sniffling back her eminent sobbing.

My tears breached the borders of my eyes and slipped down my face. I pushed them away with my fingers but gave up after the first few swipes. There was no point. There was too much water still to roll down my cheeks.

"Well, I better get Aunt Maureen's car back to my uncle's house."

Another bark of laughter interrupted my crying. "I can't believe she was still driving the same car all these years."

The red Cadillac was garage-kept and maintained the same shine as it did when we were in elementary school.

"She loved that car." Carrie sniffled again and carefully patted beneath her lower eyelids, most likely attempting to preserve her carefully applied eyeliner and mascara. "I think we were in first or second grade when Uncle Conway came home with it."

"I remember the smell of the leather interior, and I thought the heated seats were the best," I added, recalling how the three of us thought her aunt Maureen had the coolest car ever.

"She was so sweet to drive you, me, and Fletcher around in it." Her tears were full streams now, and she no longer tried to prevent them from leaving black streaks on her skin. "I've had a great life in Jacksonville. I had friends, a nice house, and great parents. But I miss the life I had when I was a kid here."

"You also had a boyfriend that dumped you." I laughed through my stifled sobs, and she rolled her eyes in response.

"He's securely in my past now. I'm ready to move on."

"It sounds like you did last night. Fling or not, I'm sure you needed to find out what else is out there."

"I had to at least find out if what they say about firemen is true." Her smirk cut through her crying.

"What do *they* say about firemen?" I was suddenly extremely curious. Apparently, I hadn't been privy to the rumors of the first responders.

Her jaw slacked as her mouth gaped in surprise. "They have big *hoses*."

I couldn't believe I was even interested, but I asked anyway. "And?"

"He was *a lot* bigger than Cliff, my last boyfriend." She shrugged and opened the driver's side door, and tossed her purse inside but remained standing outside the car.

She reached over to hug me, and she squeezed me as if it was the last time we were going to see each other.

"You know this isn't goodbye forever, right?" I said into her hair as we continued our embrace.

She pushed out of my hold and grabbed each of my hands in hers. "I'll be ready for dancing anytime you want to visit." Her smile pinched her cheeks, where the dark color of her mascara left significant smudges. "And bring Fletcher. You two seemed comfortable dancing last night. It was almost like you've done it before." She winked and then slid into the seat.

What does she know?

Although stunned at her last comment, I waved as she pulled out of my parents' driveway.

Chapter 19

Ivy, age eighteen

I had waited for eighteen years to go to prom. Dressed in a short, fitted white dress with spaghetti straps and strappy sandals with a chunky heel, I was ready for a night of dancing and fun with my friends.

"Time for a night to remember," Julie screeched as she flung open my bedroom door.

I was still admiring myself in the full-length mirror when she intruded. But that was her way. I learned to lock my bedroom door if I didn't want her barging in. Because to her, an unlocked door was an invitation. I was sure she didn't even knock before entering my house downstairs.

My parents didn't mind. They loved that I had friends who felt comfortable enough to come into my home like they lived here.

Julie tossed a small purse onto my bed, and then stood next to me so our reflections showed in the mirror.

"We look amazing," she said with a tight nod.

I smiled at my friend and twisted to give her a brief hug. Then I stood back to get a better look at her sleeveless, teal-colored dress with a slightly flowy skirt. Her bodice was fitted like mine, but her skirt gave her more wiggle room.

I had practiced dancing in my dress, and thankfully, the dress was short enough that it wasn't all that restrictive, and I could move easily.

Both of us had our hair and makeup done earlier. She had her light brown hair swept up into a French twist updo with some wispy ringlets that framed her face.

My hair was down and curled with a few pins to keep my hair in place to avoid falling in my face.

"Don't your parents want pictures of you and Chip?" I inquired because I knew my mom was going to take tons of pictures of Fletcher and me.

"He's downstairs. My parents already took tons of pictures, but my mom wants pictures of you and me, plus ones with our dates. So she coordinated something with your mom."

I did a mental palm slap to my forehead. I didn't do it for real because I didn't want to mess up my makeup. But after a groan, I left my room with my friend and descended the stairs to the living room.

Fletcher was waiting at the bottom of the stairs, dressed in a black tux and looking as handsome as I'd ever seen him. I was sure to have the best-looking date tonight.

His blue tie accentuated his eyes, and my pulse picked up its pace. He quite literally made my heart skip a beat.

"How long were you waiting at the bottom of the steps for me?" I asked when I approached the landing of the stairs.

He reached for my hand, making my body shiver from the gooseflesh that broke out. "Not long." He leaned into my ear and then whispered. "I just couldn't wait to see you in that dress."

More goose bumps erupted as his low, growly voice tickled my insides.

"One day, I'm going to be waiting for you at the end of a long aisle. You'll be wearing a white dress that day also." I could tell he was smiling by the way his tone softened.

After a quick kiss on my cheek, he continued to hold my hand and guided me to the living room, where he grabbed a plastic container off the coffee table containing a corsage of white roses accented with light-blue wildflowers.

Once he removed the beautiful mini arrangement from its box, he slipped it on my wrist and delivered another peck on my cheek, which I was certain my mom caught on camera because I could hear the telltale click of photos being taken. There were multiple clicks, actually.

My mom broke out her nice camera for the occasion and didn't resort to just taking pictures with her cell phone.

We took more pictures inside and outside. We stood on the porch, then the back deck, and finally, in front of the landscaping in the backyard.

Some pictures were of just Fletcher and me. Then some of them were of me and my two best friends, and of course, there were plenty of us as two couples.

I thought my makeup would crack from all the smiling.

But finally, the photo session was over, and we waved bye to my parents, Julie's parents, and Fletcher's parents. Chip's parents didn't attend so their cameras weren't added into the mix. All of our moms and dads were close, so it would have been awkward if Chip's parents had been there because I was sure the six of them were planning a night of board games and alcohol.

They would all be in bed by nine thirty because none of them were night owls. It was kind of cool, though, that our parents were all friends, just like their kids.

So we waved goodbye to everyone and headed to our cars. We didn't rent a limo like some of our classmates. Chip and Fletcher were each driving their cars. We opted not to ride together as which after-party to attend hadn't been decided yet.

Plus, if Fletcher and I wanted to cut out early, we had that option.

~

The night had been magical. Fletcher and I danced to fast songs and slow ones. We were crowned prom king and queen. Not to brag, but there was really no surprise there. Our town was small, and most of the students had watched our friendship grow into the love it is today.

People apparently ate that stuff up. Not only were we also crowned homecoming king and queen, but we'd been voted couple most likely to marry for the yearbook.

We drove over to Chad Brinkley's house to check out his after-prom party. Julie and Chip wanted to go, so we tagged along.

I had no idea how or why he was able to get his parents to disappear for the night, but they were nowhere to be found. There were probably over a hundred high school seniors there, however.

Some were playing pool or video games in his game room. Some were playing beer pong in his garage. Several were hanging out on his back deck by the pool where the beer kegs were located. And basically, everyone else was scattered throughout his first floor. Chad apparently didn't mind if anyone trashed his parents' house as long as it happened on the bottom level or outside. He had a sign and rope posted that no one was allowed to go upstairs.

I had already seen a few of my classmates hurdle over the rope and disregard his request with their beer in hand, stumbling up the steps.

He had also asked that beer be consumed outside. And although I think most everyone honored his rules, more than a few didn't seem to care.

My parents had taught me to be respectful of other people's property, and I knew Fletcher's parents had the same values.

As we wandered toward the backyard holding hands, Fletcher swept his gaze around, scrutinizing the party scene.

"I haven't seen Julie and Chip yet, have you?" I asked while we dodged empty cups thrown on the grass and bumped shoulders with the number of high schoolers here.

Fletcher shook his head and kept his lips in a tight line.

Once I saw kids that weren't even from our school, let alone our grade, I quirked my eyebrow at Fletcher, and he picked up on my signal loud and clear.

"You ready to get out of here?"

I nodded with a sly smile that twisted my glossy lips into a wide, beaming grin.

I was excited about the next part of our evening. Because as cliché as it sounded, we planned to lose our virginity tonight.

Fletcher and I had combined our money and rented a beachfront hotel room. Since our prom was a Saturday night in May, the price of a hotel room in a resort town increased nearly twofold. I also seriously wondered if they jacked the price up because we were young and they tried to sway us away from their establishment. But we didn't care. We were just happy to be spending the night together.

After we checked in, we each grabbed the bags that we brought and headed to the room overlooking the ocean, again hand in hand. We never seemed to go anywhere with each other without being palm to palm.

Sometimes fingers intertwined, and other times not, but we always reached out for the other's hand whenever we were near one another.

Fletcher flipped the light switch on when we entered our room. The sliding glass door overlooked the water, and the curtains were still open, so we had a view overlooking the Atlantic.

I proceeded to kick my heels off and flip the light switch back off, allowing the room to be illuminated only by the moonlight shining against the calm water.

Typically, the ocean had waves and swells, but tonight, its appearance was as smooth as dark glass. I tugged on Fletcher's hand around the king-size bed and toward the door.

Understanding my hint, he slid it open so we could stand on the balcony and listen to the quiet crashes of the waves against the shore.

I shivered, not anticipating the cool breeze, and Fletcher twirled me so my back was settled against his chest. His hands rubbed up and down the length of my arms in an attempt to warm me up.

He rested his chin against the top of my head, and we stood against each other in comfortable silence for a few minutes, enjoying the moment until I genuinely was too chilly, even with Fletcher's warm fingers massaging against my exposed skin.

I twisted around, breaking his stroking caresses, and peered up at him.

"You want to go inside?" His voice was throaty and apprehensive. *He was nervous.*

"Yeah, to warm up," I reassured him and reached up on pointed toes and delivered a quick peck to his lips before slipping inside again.

He had left the door open while we were on the balcony, so I didn't have to pull on the heavy door to reach the warmth of the inside of the room.

"Do you want to change out of our prom clothes?" I asked once Fletcher had entered back into our room and the door was securely shut once again.

His Adam's apple bobbed as he swallowed. "Sure."

"You can take the bathroom if you want," he offered, and I eyed him curiously, knowing we were planning to see each other naked tonight. Besides, we had seen each other in swimsuits for as long as I could remember.

His apprehension had me thinking he didn't want to do this tonight, which was fine. But I hoped it wasn't because he didn't want to have sex with *me*. I was fine with waiting for however much time he wanted as long as I got to be the first girl he gave himself to.

And I couldn't ever imagine being comfortable enough with another man to do *that* with. His weirdness had me reconsider donning the silk short nightie I purchased for tonight.

Fortunately, I'd also brought a tank top and pajama shorts, unaware of what the etiquette was regarding the whole sleeping together thing. Since neither of us had done this before, I wasn't sure if we put PJs on afterward or if we would stay naked. I figured it was best to be prepared.

So I retreated into the bathroom and wiggled out of my

dress, then hung it up on the back of the door, reminding myself not to forget it was there so I could take it home tomorrow. Once I pulled on my PJs, I brushed my teeth and washed my face before heading back out to the hotel room.

The room didn't have a desk or chair. There was just a king-size bed and one end table. This room was less expensive than other beachfront hotels. Although the balcony and view were spectacular, the room was small and basic.

Fletcher's back was facing my direction when I opened the bathroom door, but he swung around once he heard the hinges squeak.

He wasn't wearing a shirt and had gray sweatpants that hung low on his waist. His chest was without much hair but had a fair amount of muscle for an eighteen-year-old. *Damn, he is hot.*

I crossed the room to where he stood with only a few swift paces and raised up on my toes to reach his soft lips with mine.

He leaned over and wrapped his arms around me, enveloping me in a tight embrace while our kissing intensified.

Our mouths discovered how hungry they were for each other. Soon our teeth were clashing, and our tongues were sliding against one another in messy yet hot, fervent kisses.

Fletcher skimmed his hands down to my ass, and I pressed myself against him, feeling his hardening length against my belly. Warmth flooded my core, and I had a compulsion to clench my legs together, fighting off the tingling sensation developing between them.

My nipples hardened beneath the sheer fabric of my tank top, and I fought the desire to rip the material off.

But once Fletcher's hand roamed beneath the cotton and grazed the bare skin of my back, I moaned into his mouth. His fingertips trailed up higher, pushing the fabric upward as he did.

His delightful torture sent shivers down my spine, but the heat that was generated by his scorching touch had me break free from our kissing to pull the bothersome tank out of the way.

The smirk that tugged at his lips was totally worth my impatience. I didn't want to rush anything, but I wasn't just totally hot for this boy; I was completely and utterly head over heels in love with him.

Seeing the desire swirling in those blue eyes I adored was reassuring. We'd made out plenty of times, but never where clothes were removed. I'm glad he wasn't disappointed.

"Damn, Vine. You're gorgeous." His shyness from earlier retreated, his voice now husky, and his jaw chiseled with confidence.

His tongue peeked out between his teeth as he licked his upper lip as if he was about to ingest a delectable meal. His irises darkened as his gaze settled onto my collarbone, and within half a second, he was licking the side of my neck.

He kissed my right earlobe after his tongue ascended upward to that side of my jaw. He didn't linger there long before his tongue left a wet trail back down my neck to my collarbone. He switched to soft bites and nips to the skin of my collarbone out to my shoulder, and back to the divot in between where my collarbones met.

He peered up at me for only a beat, and then his tongue slid down the length of my sternum.

"I could lick every inch of you." His gravelly tone intensified the heat stirring within my belly and the increasing warmth between my legs had me squirming for relief. "I love the way your skin tastes." His breath cooled my skin but did nothing to squelch the cranked-up temperature everywhere else within me. "I wish ice cream came in your flavor."

Laughing in the throes of passion was probably not good, but I couldn't help it. A burst of loud giggles surged out of me, causing Fletcher to deter from the path he was traveling in between my cleavage.

Deep grooves furrowed above his brow, and his eyes narrowed. His lips dipped at the corners as he stared blankly at my outburst.

"A flavor of ice cream, Fletch? Really?" I continued a series of cackles I couldn't control, and soon I was bent over, bracing my abdomen from the pull at the muscles.

"You think I'm funny?" His arms wrapped around me as I flailed with snickering. "I'll give you something to laugh at." And then his fingers were jabbing at my sides.

He was relentless in his poking, and I became breathless from the embarrassing chortles that led to snorting laughter. "Stop! You have to stop!"

Thankfully, he conceded.

Chapter 20

Fletcher, age eighteen

"I can't make out with you after you've told me to stop, Vine." I slowly blew out each quickened breath after both of us engaged in a fit of laughter.

She made fun of me, and I loved it each and every time. We'd always had that kind of relationship. We were friends for so long, and now we were each other's everything.

She completed the other half of my soul and made my heart happy. I had always recognized her inner beauty, but now, in this hotel room, I was given the chance to admire her body.

The creamy skin of her breasts was on display, with pink, pearled nipples practically begging for my touch.

So I wasted no additional time with the silly giggling we had succumbed to a moment earlier, and I pulled her torso toward me in one swift movement, causing the laughter to die on her lips.

Her dark, wide, doe-like eyes peered up at me, and when she licked her lips, I couldn't stop myself from delving into her mouth with a searing kiss, taking her gasped breath in.

Breathing was essential to life, but this girl was essential to *my* life. We moaned on each other's exhales, and I grazed my finger over the tightened bud of her nipple, causing her to release several mewls.

I was glad I had changed into sweats because even with enough space to lengthen freely, I became painfully hard.

I guided her toward the direction of the bed to give us more room to explore everything about one another.

But as our heated kissing continued, I bumped the back of my calf against the bed frame and fell backward, bringing Ivy's warm body with me.

She grinned happily when she found herself on top of me on the king-size mattress, touching skin to skin. And instead of the giggles I expected as a result of our fall, she murmured appreciation before tracing her fingernail from my breastbone down the entire length of my torso to the elastic waistband of my sweatpants.

We gazed at each other for several beats before her finger breached the barrier and reached beneath the stretchy material to graze her touch against the thickness of my engorged flesh.

I drew in a deep breath as she grasped the shaft of my dick. *Holy hell.* I thought I'd come right in my pants.

I had jerked off to fantasies about her many times. I was a teenage boy, after all, but she had never touched me down there before, and the stimulation was better than I could have imagined.

She stroked tentatively, and I wouldn't have believed that I could become even harder, but I did with every pull she made.

I had to suppress the urge to explode, so I went for some delightful distraction.

I slipped my finger beneath the loose waistband of her tiny-as-hell pajama shorts and found her bare.

My mouth was hungry for her taste again, and I crashed onto her lips with my tongue pressing against the seam, impatiently awaiting access.

She complied, and we resumed kissing each other with unrestrained control. Our tongues slid against each other, our breathing quickened, and our hearts raced.

I found two slick folds as my finger continued its descent into her shorts.

Her breath hitched as I pressed my finger into her tight opening.

I could feel the warmth and wetness of her arousal surrounding my finger, so I added another finger to her tight channel and slowly moved them in sync with piston-like action.

She groaned into my mouth, but I broke free from our clashing teeth and lips, allowing her to release louder sounds of appreciation.

"Oh God, Fletch," she moaned and then murmured other noises that I wasn't sure were words or just noises of approval.

When my mouth latched onto one of her nipples, she arched her back, pushing her breast closer to my face.

I increased the tempo of my fingers, and the friction of her fist sliding up and down my hard length brought me so close to an orgasm I couldn't control my release as she screamed my name and flattened herself on top of me.

"That wasn't how I expected that to go," I admitted sheepishly after we each cleaned up.

We took turns in the bathroom separately, and for some reason, that didn't sit right with me. I went first since I was clearly messier than her, and then she retreated to the bathroom to tend to herself.

I figured we should be okay with seeing each other naked at this point. Yeah, we had never seen each other completely nude before, but maybe that was a hurdle we could get over tonight.

"How do you feel about a shower together?" I asked as hope swirled in my gut.

"You think you can stand how hot I like it?" Her eyes danced with mischief before she let out a tiny squeal and jogged to the bathroom.

I loved the playful nature of our relationship. I only stayed seated on the mattress for another moment before I trailed hurriedly behind her.

She already had the knobs on the spigot turned on, and steam was beginning to form as water rushed out of the faucet into the bathtub.

She sat on the edge of the tub and placed her hand beneath the gush of water spraying out of the spout to test the temperature. She must have been satisfied with the feeling of the water against her skin because she twisted the last knob to initiate the shower's spray.

Without any hesitation, she pulled her tank top off again and slipped out of her pajama shorts and to the other side of the curtain within the blink of an eye.

Seriously, I blinked once, and I thought I missed the striptease show. I followed suit, kicking off my boxers onto the bathroom floor. My sweatpants would need to be washed thoroughly before I could ever wear them again. The load that surged out of me had been a long time coming —figuratively and literally.

I slipped behind the drawn curtain and was greeted with the silhouette of Ivy's backside, devoid of any clothes. The steam hovered around her bare back, and droplets of water clung to her, glistening over her skin.

The smoothness of her creamy complexion trickled with beads of moisture down her back to the slope of her ass and further to her shapely legs.

Damn. No wonder I'd lost control of myself and shot come in my pants. She was the definition of smoking hot.

"You checking out my ass, Fletch?" she said as she turned around, giving me a full-frontal view.

The sight of those taut nipples and her perky breasts had me hard again. My gaze dragged further down her flat abdomen to that sweet haven between her legs.

"My eyes are up here."

I shook my head and met her brown gaze.

She pointed her index finger at the corner of her right eye, and that large, mischievous grin I had seen earlier splayed across her face.

"I love your eyes, I really do," I said as I took the one-and-a-half steps closer to her. "But the rest of your body is so damn distracting." I slid my hands over her arms, down her belly, and around to her ass.

"You're not so bad yourself." And that little minx grabbed my dick again.

"Be careful with that. He gets excited and likes to shoot. He's not confined in here, so you may get caught in the crossfire."

"Then I guess it's good we can readily wash off." Her devilish grin had my dick twitch within her grasp.

"Hopefully, since I got that load out that I've been saving for so long out of the way, I can contain myself as long as needed." Squeezing each firm globe of her ass, I pulled her closer to my soaked body with her hand still in place on my shaft, now as hard as steel.

"We should get out of this shower and get a condom." She finally released her hold and twisted to turn off the knobs controlling the stream of hot water descending on our bodies.

I pushed the curtain open forcefully, causing the metal rings to scrape across the shower rod loudly and reached for a bath towel for each of us.

There were towels stacked on a shelf behind the commode, and I nearly slipped, spanning my arm as far as I could to seize two of the terrycloth sheets.

I swathed one around Ivy's torso and then promptly secured mine around my waist without bothering to wipe off any excess water and dry off adequately before stepping over the ledge of the tub and onto the bathmat beside it.

Ivy tortured me, though. She used her towel to dry off what seemed like every square inch of her body as slowly as possible.

My erection pressed against the material, begging to be free again as I stared at her perfect body like a stalker.

Her silky, smooth skin spanned every curve of her. The slope of her neck, the swell of her breasts, her taut abdomen, her toned arms and legs, the span of her back, and over each glorious round globe of her ass was covered in creamy, soft skin, and I was ready to taste every inch of it.

Once she wrapped the towel around her torso, covering everything from her breasts to her thighs, and secured it by dipping a corner in between her cleavage, she stepped out of the tub and onto the mat next to me.

Her hair was still wet as she peered up at me. The tendrils that fell and stuck to her face gave her an innocence, which made me feel only slightly guilty about what we were about to do.

We moved swiftly from the bathroom to the area of the room next to the bed. I had already ripped open the box of condoms and laid a sleeve of foil packets on the end table hastily before we were kissing again.

Our wet towels still clung to our bodies, and soon, we landed on the bed with me hovering over her. I caressed her skin everywhere that was exposed as our tongues delved into our mouths hungrily.

She reached down between us at the towel tucked into my waist so I wasted no time ripping it off. The damn thing was restrictive. I needed to move.

I found myself rubbing my erection along the terrycloth around her midsection without intention. My hips just wanted to press into her.

She reached between us and wrapped her warm hand around my length again. *She really likes to touch me.* I hope she enjoyed me inside her as much as she seemed to like feeling me against the palm of her hand.

I brushed my fingers along the bottom of her towel and pushed further up her smooth thigh until reaching the semi-bare folds I had seen in the shower only a few moments ago.

"Dammit, Fletch, you're driving me crazy," she murmured as she switched from our deep, passionate kissing to trailing gentle pecks along my jaw, down my neck, and upper chest, keeping a firm grip on my dick.

When she flicked my nipple with her tongue, I ripped the towel off her, and she arched her back, pressing her breasts closer to me.

I drew one pebbled peak into my mouth, eliciting enticing moans from her.

Her fist began sliding up and down the length of my erection, and I switched my attention to her other breast with my tongue, flicking and licking the tightened bundle of tissue while slipping a finger in between the warmth between her legs.

"Fletcher, I need more." Her voice was strained on the end of a groan. "Please," she whimpered.

I added a second finger, and she slid up and down from base to tip, creating a thick coating of wetness on my hand.

"Vine, I need to put on a condom right now," I forced out huskily because I wasn't coming outside her this time.

She released her grip long enough for me to retrieve a foil packet. I carefully ripped it open, unsure how delicate the latex within it was. I had heard of condoms getting punctured and the girl ending up pregnant.

Plus, condoms weren't one hundred percent effective against unwanted pregnancy anyway, so I wanted to be extra careful. But seeing as we had been planning this night for a while, Ivy went to her doctor two months ago and had been on the pill.

Again, we wanted to take every precaution we could. We both wanted this. But we wanted to be responsible. We had plans to go to college and get married afterward.

There was plenty of time for us to have babies. But not right now. So I carefully unrolled the latex down my shaft and squeezed the tip just like the instructions said while the thoughts of pregnancy prevention rolled through my mind.

As I dragged my gaze up from its concentration on my correct placement, I met the hot chocolate gaze of Ivy staring at me with swollen lips and a mess of semi-wet hair with flushed skin as she lay on her back on the bed.

I crawled over her, and she reached between us, guiding my dick to her opening.

I couldn't have stopped myself from pushing into her if I tried. I had been dreaming about being inside her for so long. The fact that I was so close to experiencing the feel of her warmth enveloping me was overpowering my ability to remain patient.

I certainly didn't want to hurt her, but she felt so good. I pushed some more.

Ivy's moans encouraged me to penetrate further. And then I met resistance.

Ivy's eyes shot open, and I stopped my dick's forward movement.

"You okay?" I asked, hoping to God she said yes because this felt way too good to be over already.

"Just keep going," she urged, although fret filled her doe eyes.

"Vine, I can't if it's going to hurt you." I remained half inside her, propped up on my arms so I didn't crush her with my weight, peering over her.

"It will only hurt for a second, I swear." The apprehension eased within the contours of her face, and the lines around her eyes softened as her voice pleaded.

I pushed again, harder than before, and the barrier that had been in place was no longer preventing me from stretching her further. "You okay?"

She shook her head up and down while she sucked in her lower lip and sank her teeth into it.

"I'm going to move back and forth, okay?"

She drew in a deep breath as I slid out and pushed back in with easy thrusts.

"Hmmmm." She squeezed her eyes shut and reached around to grab each of my ass cheeks. She pulled me closer to her, and I swear she seemed to be drawing me further into her.

Once I was seated all the way inside, I moved slow and easy, trying to get her used to me.

"You've got to move faster, Fletch. I'm dying over here." Her teasing tone drove me to thrust deeper and harder.

"Fuck, Vine, you feel so good."

"Damn. I had no idea sex would feel like this." Her heart rate kicked up, and I could see each beat pulse at the side of her neck.

I continued the piston-like action within her, pumping into her welcoming channel over and over again, but as soon as her inner walls were squeezing me, a tightening developed in my balls, and I knew I would explode again.

"Oh God!" she huffed out at the tail end of a grunt, causing me to spill my load into the condom.

I pulled her close to me, seated as far as possible inside her as we both shuddered with our releases.

Chapter 21

Fletcher, present day

The dancing Ivy and I did yesterday had me revisit the last time we danced the night away in a daydreaming episode I fell into while I was picking up trash at my dad's house. And unfortunately, my mind went back to later that night following prom also.

For chrissake. I hadn't even been broken up with Amilyn for twenty-four hours, and I was already thinking about sleeping with another girl.

Not a girl. A woman. Ivy transformed from the eighteen-year-old girl I last saw into a beautiful twenty-two-year-old woman. I was foolish to think I'd ever get over her.

It was harder to stop thinking about her now that she was back than when she was gone. I had thought I wouldn't survive back then when she left.

I wondered how long she was planning to stay in the area now that she had graduated college. She had mentioned at the gym that she wasn't sure what she would be doing after the summer.

Maybe I could convince her to stay. Maybe she would

love her job and want to stay. Maybe she would remember she loved me and want to stay.

Maybe she would break my heart again. Maybe she would leave again even if I begged her to stay.

No. I wouldn't be begging her to stay this time. If she wanted to go, I'd turn and run in the opposite direction. My heart and soul wouldn't be intact, but at least I would maintain my dignity and go about life without pleading for a girl to want me as much as I wanted her.

Because one thing was certain. I still wanted her. I never stopped wanting her.

I was so totally screwed. *How in the hell am I supposed to protect my heart?*

I'd never done anything half-assed, so I needed to tie up loose ends and proceed full force like I only knew how to do when it came to Ivy Hatfield.

So that's how I found myself back at Amilyn's place.

I knew she would be home. She was off today, and she rarely left the house, so seeing her car in the parking lot wasn't a surprise.

It was a surprise that she didn't answer the door when I knocked, however. I could hear rustling behind the door—because she didn't live in the most expensive apartment housing, the door wasn't heavy-duty.

I knew she was home, and she was in her living room.

I knocked again, more forcefully this time.

Something didn't seem right, and worry tugged at my gut.

Dammit. Why hadn't she given me a key? "Amilyn! Amilyn!" I shouted with each thump my fist struck against the wood door.

A gust of air greeted me as the wooden entryway

opened inward to reveal Amilyn with a head full of messy blond hair and... *her pajamas?*

"Are you feeling okay?" I asked as I pushed past her into the tiny apartment.

"Fletcher, I think we've said everything we needed to say to each other." She kept the door ajar and gestured toward the opening. "You should go."

"What's going on with you?" I was perplexed at her attire. It was well after noon, and she looked like she had just gotten out of bed. This was not typical behavior for her unless she was upset or feeling under the weather.

"What are you doing here?" Obviously realizing I wasn't going out the door until we had a conversation, she pushed it shut and crossed her arms over her breasts.

The oversized T-shirt she wore with *Girls Just Want to Have Fun* faded on the front of the thin cotton didn't do much to conceal her hardened nipples. She was the type of girl that wore a bra almost all day, every day, even though she didn't go to many places.

I narrowed my gaze, taking in her rumpled appearance. And as I surveyed her from the sleepwear she chose downward, I noticed she was only wearing one sock.

As I continued to ascertain the oddness of her attire, a soft, rustling sound came through the thin wall. And it wasn't a sound from the apartment above or the adjoining wall next door. This noise was in *her* apartment.

"Is someone in your bathroom, Amilyn?" I quirked my eyebrow upward and tilted my head, trying to listen more intently.

"No." She wasn't telling the truth, but she appeared nonchalant, keeping her arms crossed close to her body.

"Why are you lying to me?" Worry was now tossed

aside, and annoyance took over. She knew I didn't like games, and clearly, she wasn't being upfront with me.

"There's no one in there, Fletch." A huff of frustration blew out her mouth between pursed lips.

I took two steps nearer to the bathroom, which put me within reaching distance of the top of the trim framing the door, and I grabbed the key I had placed up there.

"Either tell me who's in the bathroom, or I'm going to open the door with the key..." Before I finished my threat, Amilyn lunged at me and tried to retrieve the key. I held the old, molded piece of brass high in the air as she jumped upward, still attempting to grab it from within my grasp.

I kicked at the door during our mild tussle of keep away. "I'm going to force entry one way or another on this door. So you may want to consider showing yourself now before that door comes off the hinges."

A loud click proceeded the door opening only a sliver.

I shoved the door open with my foot. It would have been better if I had been wearing boots instead of flip-flops, but regardless, it was still effective.

The door plunged inward, and a man wearing a short buzz haircut and only appeared to be nineteen or twenty stood next to the commode in nothing but a pair of boxer shorts.

"Who the hell are you?" My harsh tone roared with anger.

Amilyn rushed into the small room, apparently in an attempt to protect the slim, mysterious man.

"It's not what it looks like, Fletcher." She extended her arm and held up one hand.

"What is it then?" My gaze bounced between my ex and the man with coffee-colored skin and more muscles on his chest than I originally noticed lining his thin frame.

The young man swallowed and then detached his dark gaze from me and mouthed the words *it's okay* to Amilyn and swung his leg around where she stood to regain footing between her and me.

"I'm sorry, sir." His soulful eyes did indeed hold sorrow within their brown orbs. But *sir?* Seriously? "My name's Mateo," he said and jutted a hand in my direction.

I glanced at his hand suspended in the air but made no effort to exchange pleasantries. Instead, I clenched my hands into tight fists at my sides.

Mateo withdrew his hand, and I couldn't settle the fury flowing through my veins. "Is he the reason we broke up?" I gritted my teeth before hissing out my next question. "Were you fucking him while we were together?"

"God, no." She shuffled in front of him. Apparently, they were going to take turns facing me head-on. "Mateo and I dated in high school."

"I enlisted right after graduation, and I'm home on leave for the next couple of weeks."

I rolled my eyes at this shitstorm of obvious infidelity right in front of me.

"I never cheated on you, Fletcher." Her blue eyes were focused on me, but her fingers laced with his, demonstrating their united front. "Mateo called me last night. You and I had broken up."

My facial muscles tightened at her too-convenient explanation. As if I was going to believe she didn't get together with him until we broke up less than twenty-four hours ago.

Even if her flimsy excuse for having a man in her house so soon after we ended our engagement was true, I'm glad I shed myself from her.

"I invited Mateo over, and...well, things happened." She shrugged sheepishly.

"Things happened?" How in the world she expected me to believe this preposterous story was beyond my comprehension. I guess she took me for a fool.

"I swear, Fletcher, I didn't know we would end up in bed together." Her shrill voice grated my nerves even further.

"I'm sure Mateo here knew that's what was going to happen. It's called a booty call, Amilyn." My exhaled warm air exited my nose forcefully since my jaw was clenched tight. So, my nostrils were probably flaring by that point.

"Sir, Ami and I have a very long history—" I launched one of my fists toward his jaw, but he somehow seemed to dodge it, and I was left swinging into the empty space.

"Stop calling me fucking sir!" This little shit may know how to avoid a punch to the face, but he wasn't that many years younger than me to call me sir like I was someone's grandpa.

"I'm sorry, si..." He clipped the last word before finishing his thought.

"And stop apologizing for banging my fiancée."

"Ex-fiancée," Amilyn corrected with finality in her tone.

That was, after all, why I came over in the first place. I was looking for closure. My heart wasn't here. I thought it had been at one time, but this whole scene just gave me an additional convincing reason to rid myself of her.

"I didn't come over for a reconciliation, but I did feel bad about how things ended between us." Amilyn and Mateo still huddled next to each other in the bathroom while I maintained a stance two steps away securely in the door's threshold. "But I see you've moved on rather easily, so I guess I didn't have anything to feel badly about. You didn't act like you cared last night, and you clearly don't act like you care now." I shook my head, unable to fathom how things between us unraveled completely in less than a day. "Have a nice life, Amilyn."

And I turned on my heel, leaving behind my ex and the man who supposedly was her ex but her hookup for the night. As I opened the door to the outside, I found myself thinking about the next chapter of my life. And once I slammed the door shut, I was certain I had closed the door to my past, not to be revisited.

I wish Ivy didn't have to work the next two nights because I ached to tell her about what I had just witnessed.

It didn't take long for her to be the person I wanted to go to for everything. The past four years seemed to have evaporated because she was again the one I wanted to run to with good news, bad news, and weird shit.

She could so easily resume that role in my life. I needed to hear her out. I just hoped her explanation had more validity than what I had just witnessed in Amilyn's house.

I was angry at first regarding her indiscretion, but it only took a few moments of reflection to realize maybe this was how things were supposed to go.

I had a clean break, and I could move forward with a clear conscience.

Maybe that was screwed up, considering I was engaged to another woman yesterday, and now I planned on pursuing someone else. But Ivy had always been my heart. My mind may have once thought I could build a life with somebody other than her, but my heart wasn't in it.

The Amilyn and Mateo Show just got my mind on board with my heart. Because no matter what Ivy had to say to me, it had to be more believable than what my most recent ex had to say.

Chapter 22

Ivy, age eighteen

The graduation ceremony was long, but like any ceremony during our school career, my saving grace had always been being able to sit next to my boyfriend for the duration. Since his last name was Hart and mine was Hatfield, we'd been bound together by the rules of the alphabet since forever.

Even before he was my boyfriend, he was my best friend, and we had the fortunate surnames to be seated side by side at all field trips, spelling bees, classroom arrangements, picture days, and random school programs and events.

Not only could we be found next to each other at school, but we had been inseparable for over a decade. We were together every day, not just during time for classes, but at our homes also. Unless one of us was sick or out of town, we saw each other every day.

I was glad we had decided to attend the same college. I knew we were young and so many things could still change, but I couldn't imagine not seeing him every day.

He's the first person I wanted to see every day and the

last person I wanted to talk to every night. No matter how much time we spent together, we never seemed to tire of each other's company. We never ran out of things to say, but we were comfortable just cuddling and watching a movie in silence also.

And as we grinned goofily at each other and tossed our caps in the air, we got to start the next chapter of our lives. College would definitely have its set of challenges, but I looked forward to going through all of them with Fletcher.

He was my confidant and my go-to for everything in life. As long as I had him with me, I could get through anything. We'd talked about getting married one day, but we agreed we would like to wait until after college and after we'd established our careers.

"Ivy, dear." Mrs. Hart's sweet voice cut through my nostalgic memories and my daydreams about the future.

I blinked to regain my presence and turned in her direction.

"We want to get pictures of you two outside." She waved me toward the exit door, away from the sea of high school graduates that had filed out of the convention center.

"Come on, Vine," Fletcher said, grabbing my hand and leading me through the door.

We squeezed through the exit along with everyone else, and it was just as crowded outside as it was inside. With everyone snapping pictures of their graduates, it was difficult to sidestep and avoid photobombing someone else's memory.

When our families agreed on a suitable spot to capture the moment sufficiently, we held our diplomas in their leather-bound binding and smiled happily, wearing our gowns and the caps we retrieved from the floor near our seats.

Julie snagged me from Fletcher long enough to grab some bestie selfies. We promised to see each other at the party later that evening, and then both the Hart and Hatfield families left the convention center and headed to Fletcher's parents' house for a lovely lunch prepared by his mom.

She appeared tired, but she shooed me away every time I offered to help her in the kitchen.

Fletcher and I continued to see each other at least for a little bit every day for the next couple of weeks. We were both busy with work. He was working long days at a local construction company, and I was working as a waitress at a beach restaurant with a thirty-minute commute.

With plans to attend Grandview University in North Carolina in only a couple of months, we wanted to work as much as possible now and save as much as we could before we left for school.

While walking to Fletcher's house on a random Thursday night at the beginning of July, Fletcher's dad opened the door to their home and stepped out onto the porch as I was walking up the stone path, startling me.

I gasped and held a hand over my heart. "Mr. Hart, you scared me." It was after ten o'clock at night, and I had plans to sneak into Fletcher's bedroom like I had done before, not for sex, but just to cuddle while we slept.

"It's late, Ivy," he said without contention in his voice. Instead, his tone was wobbly, as was his gait. *Is he drunk?*

"I'm sorry. I was just going to pop over and see Fletch for a minute and then head home. We can sit outside so we don't bother you or his mom," I offered, hoping to cover the fact that we slept in each other's bedrooms on the regular and slipped out early in the morning before our parents awakened for the day.

"I actually wanted to speak to you in private."

Ivy: Not going to be able to make it over tonight. I'm really tired. I'll see you tomorrow though. Love you.

Fletcher: I'll miss you sleeping next to me, but I understand. Let me know when you get home tomorrow night and I'll climb into your window since it will be late. Love you more.

The next day, I felt ill during my entire double shift. Nausea swarmed within my empty stomach. I didn't dare introduce any food to the empty pit of swirling anxiety just waiting to make a projectile splash out of my gut onto the floor of the restaurant.

Thankfully, Julie was off this weekend since she was on vacation with her family. She would have seen my fret, and although she wouldn't have pressed me on the reason for my angst, she would still try to reassure me that everything would be alright.

And everything was not going to be alright. I probably would have either fallen into a hug with her and confessed the whole story, or I would have given her the cold shoulder she didn't deserve.

Because even though I was incredibly sad by the things

Fletcher's dad said to me last night, I was equally just as angry. My chronological age of eighteen gave me the right to vote and buy lottery tickets, but it did not give me the ability to adequately deal with big adult things.

Maybe I wouldn't be so distraught if I thought I had a choice in how to proceed moving forward.

Twenty-four hours wasn't long enough to prepare for seeing Fletcher walk down the stretch of road between his house and mine. I texted him after I got home and showered.

I could tell the instant he saw me because his pace increased from a leisurely stroll to a jog. "What are you doing outside?" he whispered.

It was after ten o'clock at night, and typically, he would have slipped in through the unlocked window in my bedroom, but I was seated on the grass where he usually hoisted himself up.

"Let's go for a walk," I said, raising to my full height and reaching for his hand.

"You okay, Vine?" He accepted my hand and intertwined our fingers without a moment's hesitation.

"We need to talk, and I don't want my parents to overhear."

He swiveled his head and eyed me suspiciously, scrunching his nose and furrowing his brow.

I wasn't sure I could go through with this plan. But I was a tough girl, and just like the heroines in great love stories, I would do anything for the man I loved. So I mustered up courage I didn't think I owned and decided I had to be brave.

"Let's go to the woods." This wasn't just any place. This was a specific place Fletcher and I had beyond our neighborhood.

"You want to walk there?" Confusion marred his gorgeous face, and I realized this was only the beginning of the upheaval yet to come.

"Yeah." I smiled weakly at him. "Is that okay?" I didn't want to be trapped in a car with him. I needed the open space.

He shrugged, and without any additional questions, he fell in step with me at his side, our fingers still laced together.

This was him. He would follow me anywhere without a second guess. He was my other half, my ride-or-die, my best friend, and the love of my life. Although our lives were less than a couple of decades apiece, I couldn't foresee loving anyone else like I loved Fletcher Hart.

We had always stood by each other, and I knew he was not going to understand what I was about to do, but I had to believe I was doing the right thing, or I'd never get through this.

"I love you, Fletch," I said on a long exhale.

"I love you more." He had his response out before I drew in my next breath.

He always said he loved me more, but I loved him so much that I was willing to give up my own happiness. Supposedly, that's what great heroines do. They put themselves through heartbreak to save their men. And although Fletcher may not see our upcoming conversation for what it was, I was about to save him. I prayed that one day, he'd forgive me and realize I did what was best at the time.

"Are you really going to make me wait until we get to the woods, or are you going to share what's running through your head while we walk?" He stared ahead without twisting in my direction, but he did swing our joined hands back and forth like we did as kids.

I barely had any memories of my childhood without him included in those reminiscent pieces of my brain. "I've been thinking about how a lot of things will change when we go to college."

"Are you nervous, Vine?" His snickering laugh reinforced my concern that I was going to blindside him. "We haven't even left yet, and you're homesick already." He shook his head, and although I didn't actually see his blue orbs, I envisioned a dizzying eye roll.

"I'm not worried about being homesick, Fletch." I halted on the sidewalk in front of Miss Miller's house, causing him to stop abruptly as well. "I'm looking forward to spreading my wings."

"I get it, babe." He reached for my other hand and pulled me into his chest, leaving a soft kiss on the top of my head. "It's hard to leave high school and our friends behind, but we'll meet new people and have so many new adventures together."

Together.

I twisted my hands free, flattened my palms against his firm chest and attempted to push him away from me.

Although stunned, my shove didn't cause him to budge at all.

I drew in a deep breath and seethed it out through pursed lips. This was frustrating and unnerving. "No, Fletch. Not together."

"What do you mean, not together?" His confusion returned in deep grooves across his forehead.

"I don't want a boyfriend going into college." I couldn't force my gaze directly to his blue topaz eyes because they have always had a bewildering power over me, so I kept my focus downward at his chin.

"What's going on, Vine?"

I had feared his voice would tremble or his breath would hitch, but I only heard the concern in his words. He was worried about me.

I swallowed the raw bile burning the interior of my throat, along with the tears that wanted to surface, and steadied my breathing. "Fletch, I'm sorry." Regardless of holding back unshed waterworks, my vision clouded all the same. "I want to break up."

The concern he had previously worn in the creases of his face became more pronounced as hurt flashed in his eyes. "If this is a joke, it's *not* funny." His husky voice hitched with an infliction of pain.

We had never spoken of breaking up. We had only ever talked about forever. But I needed to temporarily pause our relationship for him. I had to keep reminding myself that I was doing this for him.

"It's not a joke."

Chapter 23

Fletcher, present day

I couldn't stay away from her. I didn't even make a stop at home before heading back to Ivy. Since we both worked the next two days, I needed to see her today. Being close to her was what I needed, and now that she was back in town, my reality could include being wrapped in her arms.

It was too easy to be drawn back into the old us. I didn't know why we didn't work out years ago, and I didn't know why I thought I'd ever be able to get over her. She said we needed to talk, but as far as I was concerned, nothing she could tell me would change how I felt about her.

I had loved her forever, and I knew I would love her always. Even though things may be difficult to navigate past the previous hurt, as long as we were together, we could lean on each other.

Going through my mom's illness and death were some of the worst times of my life, and I wished I had her to lean on then. I knew she tried to reach out to me, but my missing her was displaced with anger. I was alone and so incredibly sad. I was stuck in an in-between spot of longing for her to hold me and wanting as much distance between us as possible.

Of course, the majority of love stories wrote of a strong male who protected his woman with his strength and loving arms, but in our love story, we were there for each other. Ivy would protect me and love me if needed, just like I'd do the same for her.

Just like that first day of school over a decade and a half ago when she pulled me close and sheltered me under her wing. I could depend on her through thick and thin for my entire childhood until when I needed her most.

However, that went both ways. If she had reached out to me and needed something during that time, I wouldn't have been able to be a person she could depend on either. The emotional torment I went through when I lost Ivy and then my mom was suffocating.

Many of those days were a blur. I moved through that moment in time like wading through a mud pit. I trudged forward without a destination, but somehow, I kept going. Although there were a string of days, months, and years, I still considered it only one moment in time. It was like one bad day that lasted for thirteen months. The hours and minutes ticked by. The sun rose and set, and stars filled the night sky on repeat many times but looking back, it was still only a moment—a long moment, but a moment, nonetheless.

Once I shifted my truck into park and shut off the engine, I slid out onto the paved driveway of her parents' house with my flip-flop-clad feet and jogged up the few stairs to the porch.

And although I raised my fist to knock on the door, I thought better of it and twisted the knob. Knocking on that door was a formality that didn't exist to me for my entire childhood and early adulthood.

So now that I was older, I could have considered it good manners to knock, but Ivy and I were way past showing proper etiquette.

"Ivy," I called as I pushed the wooden door open and stepped into the foyer.

I leaned my weight against it to shut the door but didn't latch the lock in place.

"Fletch?" She peered her head out from the entryway of the living room and smiled.

I could feel my face cracking into a grin in response to the warm welcome she gave me, with just a show of her teeth peeking in between perfect pink lips.

"I thought you were going to call me." Her brows knitted together, and her gaze narrowed suspiciously.

I ate up the last few paces between the two of us as my flip-flops noisily struck the hardwood floor with each step I stomped down the hallway to her.

I wrapped my arms around her waist and swung her around, causing her to squeal from the surprise lifting and twirling.

Her hands reached for my neck to steady herself before I let her bare feet return to the floor.

But I didn't release my hold around her. I nuzzled my nose against the crook of her neck and her damp hair smelled of citrus, which was exactly how I remembered her scent to be still wet from the shower.

How many times have I inhaled the fragrance of her hair? Too many times for the scent of lemon and orange to be forgotten.

Her hand rubbed against the back of my head in a comforting, gentle motion. "You okay?"

"I am now," I murmured into her hair before my lips grazed the side of her neck.

A wistful moan emitted from her throat, signaling me that she was receptive to my nuzzling.

I delivered several light kisses along her neck, up to her jaw, and eventually to her lips.

"Fletch, what are you doing?" she asked but hummed approval.

"I'm kissing you." I huffed in between the trail of kisses I continued to brush her face with.

"I think we should talk." Her words should have halted my delivery of affection, but she didn't sound convincing enough to mean she truly wanted me to stop.

So I did what I thought she wanted. I focused on her mouth and kissed her like I wanted to—like I needed to.

I nibbled and tasted her lips for several moments before I pressed my tongue against the seam of her mouth.

She willingly allowed me access, and soon, our tongues were sliding over each other's.

She tasted like toothpaste. She must have just brushed her teeth before her shower. "I've missed you so damn much."

Her hand glided to my chest and pressed against me, attempting to put a stop to the best kissing session I could remember since she and I were teenagers.

I didn't want to stop. I needed to taste her—to hold her, to feel her.

But a sniffle from her slowed my aggressive assault on her mouth.

I returned to lighter pecks against her lips and peered up at her chocolate, glassy eyes that held a world of guilt and regret.

"Baby. What's wrong?" I asked as I skated my fingers along the angle of her jaw, caressing her face.

"I'm so sorry. I made some bad choices, and I regret what I did. I need to make a confession, and I know you're going to be upset and the last thing in the world I want to do is give you more heartache."

I threaded our fingers together and pressed soft kisses against her knuckles before peering back up at her. "I think it's time to get everything out in the open."

I nodded and swallowed hard. I feigned courage I didn't really have. I truly believed she couldn't say anything to change my mind about her, but whatever she was holding back had obviously changed her.

She didn't use to have any trouble sharing what was on her mind with me. But now her brown eyes held defeat and worry within their shining orbs. I didn't think she had appeared so heartbroken since Carrie moved away the summer before middle school.

And even then, her emotions raged with anger, not utter dejection.

But here, standing in her childhood home, her toned body tensed within my hold. She was frightened, and I needed to be brave enough for both of us. Her reaction terrified me too. But I loved this woman. I loved the girl from years ago, and now I loved the person standing before me.

"I think we should sit down," she whispered and broke her hold with one of her hands but kept her fingers locked with mine of her other hand as she led me to the couch.

It's never good when someone says, "I think we should sit down," but I'd honestly go anywhere with her at this point. She wouldn't need to pull me there, either. I'd follow her willingly.

No sooner did our butts hit the cushions of the sofa, and tears slipped down Ivy's face.

"Vine, baby, don't cry." I choked down my own emotion and brushed the water off her cheeks with my thumb.

She clutched her hold on my hand tighter as those golden-brown eyes shed tear after tear.

Despite the obvious difficulty this conversation would hold, she held her gaze with mine.

There were a lot of people who would stare anywhere else to avoid dealing with the situation head-on. But my girl was brave. She had more courage than I ever did.

"I don't want to hurt you any more than I already have." She hiccupped.

I brushed wet strands of her hair behind her ear while keeping my gaze locked with hers. I would be strong for her.

"It's been four years, and we've found our way back to each other."

Her sobs grew louder with my statement.

"Because we'll *always* find our way back to each other. Time and distance won't ever change that," I said.

She retracted the hand from its hold with mine and swiped her face from the cascading salty water sliding down her face.

But the moment her gaze drifted from mine, I pulled her into me, embracing her hard.

As her body shook, her shuddering cries filled her living room.

She hadn't even told me anything, and I was already wrecked.

"You deserve to hear the truth, and I'm just a mess." Her words were sputtered in between quick breaths.

I rubbed circles over her back and held her until her crying slowed.

"I'm so sorry, Fletcher." She sniffled into my shoulder.

"It's okay…"

She pushed me away abruptly before I could finish my placating thought.

"No, it's not okay!" Her voice elevated several decibels, and fury narrowed her eyes as her shoulders stiffened.

Angry Ivy was good. I didn't like grief-filled Ivy.

"I hurt you, and I destroyed us!" She hopped up from the couch and stood to her full height while I remained seated.

I've seen her outbursts before. She paced and gestured with her hands. This was only giving me a glimpse of memories with her. Fortunately, her anger was never directed at me, but I always stayed by her, watching her outrage.

"I was naïve and…and… I could strangle your dad!" She shoved fingers through her hair in frustration as she paced the throw rug covering the hardwood floors.

This wasn't the first time she'd mentioned my dad since she's been back home. *What does he have to do with our breakup?*

"Vine, what happened with my father?" His role in whatever transpired all those years ago needed to be explained *now*. He had resorted to drinking after my mom died and hasn't really been there for me since she's been gone.

I'd taken to being there for him though. I cleaned his house and cut his lawn. I purchased groceries for him every week and made sure my uncle Jonathan got him out of the house regularly.

She turned on her heel, and her chocolate gaze once again connected with mine. "He told me to break up with you, and I foolishly listened."

I sat stunned at her declaration while she still stood in the middle of the living room.

"I'm so damn sorry, Fletch." Her shoulders slumped forward, and her head dropped down as her larger-than-life persona deflated along with my hope that what she had to say wouldn't damage my life any more than it had already.

I shook my head several times in denial. What she said didn't make any sense to me. This was crazy. My dad had no motive for the dissolution of my relationship with the love of my life. He had no reason to wish heartbreak on me. "Why would my dad want us to break up?" And why would she listen to him?

"Because he knew your mom was dying, and unless we broke up, you would have gone away to school with me."

I was thankful for my seated position because a woozy feeling rushed over me, causing my mind to go hazy, and my vision became blurry. My head squeezed like a vise, being tightened to excruciating pain.

"He wanted you to stay home with your mom." Her words wavered like twisting a volume knob up and down. "He said if I took you away from your mom, you'd regret it for the rest of your life."

Nausea swirled within my gut, and bile threatened to creep up my throat, so I swallowed hard again.

"He said if given a choice, you'd pick me...so I needed to eliminate the choice."

"W-w-why didn't you tell me?" I still couldn't believe what I was hearing. "We used to tell each other everything." I choked back the lump of nausea that would transition to vomit if left to its own accord.

"He convinced me I was being selfish if I didn't do this and keep the reason from you." Her gaze dropped to our joined hands.

Her words punched me in the gut.

"I loved you so much. I would have done anything for you." She sighed a long breath of frustration as she continued her downward gaze. "I thought I was doing the best thing for you at the time."

This couldn't be true. None of this made sense.

"He said if I loved you, I should set you free, and when you came back, you'd be mine forever." When she lifted her chin, and her eyes peered back up at me, sad tears spilled over onto her cheeks again.

"I was already going to be yours forever," I whispered, still racked with disbelief.

"I shouldn't have listened, but I didn't know what to do, and I didn't feel like I could talk about it with anyone." She finally sat next to me and grabbed my hand. "I didn't want to do it, Fletch, but I didn't want to keep you away from your mom either."

"So you're saying my dad knew this all along and never told me?" There had to be some miscommunication between my father and her.

"I would have explained everything to you, but I never had the opportunity to speak with you. I thought maybe your father would have said something to you after your mom died, but the last time I saw him, he admitted he hadn't." Sad streams of water slid down her face, and typically, I would have been only thinking about comforting her, but my affectionate side took a back burner to the chaotic emotions churning within my chest.

I yanked my hand out of her hold, my heart reeling from this conversation. "Why didn't you tell me before now?"

"I told your dad it was best to hear it from him, but if he didn't tell you, I would." Her doe eyes blinked out several large, crocodile-size tears, and once again, I was overcome by my wounded spirit.

"When did you see my dad?" We had spent so much time together over the past several days that I couldn't figure out a time when she would have had time to have a heart-to-heart with him.

"The day after I went to Thursday's with Julie."

Chapter 24

Fletcher, age eighteen

Stage four ovarian cancer.

I'd have to Google that later when I had more of my wits about me. But right now, all I know is it's more or less a death sentence for my mom.

My parents told me my mother was dying this afternoon, and the only person I wanted to be with right now broke up with me three days ago. I couldn't remember a three day stretch of time where we didn't speak to each other.

I didn't know what the protocol was for something like this. *Can you stay friends with an ex-girlfriend?* We didn't discuss the specifics of where our relationship would go after the termination of our romantic connection.

Can I still call her? Or do we continue our standoff with no communication of any kind?

We would be attending the same college in less than two months, so we could still run into each other on campus. We were friends for so many years. Even though we were no longer labeled as boyfriend and girlfriend, it didn't mean we couldn't go back to a friendship.

Me: Can you come over? I need you.

Vine: I don't know if that's a good idea.

Me: Please. I know we're not together anymore. But I need my best friend.

Vine: It's too hard.

Me: Why?

Three dots danced across the screen and then stopped without coming through as a message.

Me: If I have to beg, I will.

Two minutes went by without a reply from her.

Me: I won't try to convince you to give me another chance. I promise. I just need a friend.

Another three minutes and no response.

Me: I got some really bad news and I don't have anyone I feel comfortable enough around to talk to about this.

After five minutes, I left my bedroom and climbed into the shower to wash away the stress from the day.

I turned up the water temperature to scalding and allowed the wet pellets to prick the heat against my skin, hoping to have the pain cause me to forget what had happened over the past few days.

I didn't even know Ivy anymore. She was someone different now. She used to be my protector, and now she was the one to hurt me. I couldn't have misjudged over ten years of friendship.

I scrubbed my body with soap, lathered my hair with shampoo, and stayed in the shower, rinsing myself off until the water turned cold.

Feeling dejected, I grabbed a towel and wrapped it around my waist before returning to my bedroom.

When I pushed the door open, my beautiful ex-girlfriend lay on my bed, propped on her forearms, on her belly with her legs crossed and kicked up behind her.

As soon as my gaze met hers, she sat upright and scooted to the foot of the bed.

I clicked the door latch into place when I shut it behind me and switched the knob to the lock position.

Her dark hair was straightened and only hung to her shoulders, but she was just as gorgeous as ever.

"Your hair is different." *I haven't seen or heard from her in three days and that's the line I led with?* I gave myself a mental forehead slap.

"I'm trying something new."

Yeah. She was trying something new, alright. Out with the old and in with the new. The novelty of our relationship had run out, and she needed a change. I was sure the alterations wouldn't stop with a new hairdo. She would probably want different clothes and different friends also.

I gave a curt nod and turned to open a drawer and retrieve a clean shirt and boxers. I slipped on the shirt first, and after unwrapping the towel around my waist, I tossed it into my hamper.

I kept my back to her as I pulled my underwear on, which was ridiculous because she had seen me naked many, many times. But our relationship had shifted to something I didn't even recognize anymore.

The same could be said about her also. Her changes didn't end with her weird behavior, her disregard for me and my feelings, and her hair. I didn't know her anymore.

So once I had myself covered appropriately by my standards, because truthfully I was still standing in my bedroom wearing boxer briefs with a girl on my bed, I twisted to face her direction and leaned against my dresser.

"Thanks for coming over." I wanted to unleash the conflicting emotions at war within my chest, but I had asked her to see me and she had complied, so I didn't want to discredit that.

"You said you needed me." Things weren't the same as they used to be, so her comment actually stung more than it should.

"I appreciate it, considering you gutted me with your breakup a few days ago." I couldn't stop the words from leaving my mouth. I was angry and hurt, and unfortunately, she was within my line of fire at that moment. "But regardless of what you did, you are still my best friend, and I need you right now."

Her throat bobbed up and down as her lips fell to a flat line, and she shifted her weight on my mattress.

"My parents just told me my mom has ovarian cancer, and she's probably not going to live another year." I hadn't cried since hearing the news, but saying them out loud to my person had emotion clogging my throat.

"I'm sorry, Fletch." For hearing such devastating news, she seemed to be keeping herself together extraordinarily well. Her emotionless stare was suspicious.

"They want me to stay home and spend this last year with them." I wanted to hear her advice. I wasn't thinking clearly and I valued her opinion, but I didn't expect her to spew out her recommendation so quickly.

"You should. We aren't together anymore, so it's for the best." Her pursed lips and stern expression portrayed an unsympathetic image that was so unlike her.

How can she be so nonchalant about this? "Seriously, Vine? We've been talking about going to Grandview University together for four years."

"Yeah, but things change, Fletch." She shrugged—freaking shrugged like this was no big deal. But it was a big deal. This was huge, and she seemed like she couldn't care less.

"So that's it? We broke up, and you're planning to go off to college while I stay back here with my dying mother?"

"Yep." She even popped the *P* without a hint of hesitation or reluctance.

I let out a hoot of sardonic laughter. "I don't know you at all anymore, *Ivy*."

At least she visibly flinched as I spat out her given name. "I just don't think it's a good idea to be away from your mom while this is going on. And since we aren't boyfriend and girlfriend anymore, you don't need to worry about me."

"I love you. That hasn't changed for me in the last three days. I will always worry about you. I will always want to be with you. That's never going to change, no matter where you are or what our relationship status is. You've been my best friend since first grade. I've spent my entire school years being with you. I'll miss you like hell, and I'll never stop wishing for the day that we can be together again. If you only want to be friends, I'll take whatever I can get because I need you in my life, Vine. I can't go through this without you." Getting my feelings out in the open had me eager to feel her body against mine, so I took the two long strides in my bare feet to her, still seated on the edge of my bed, and bounced onto the mattress next to her.

I gripped her hips and pulled her into me. I slid my arms around her waist to embrace her, but she squirmed within my grasp and pushed out of my hold.

"Fletcher, don't do this," she pleaded as she twisted and shoved away from me until she was standing, leaving me sitting on my bed alone. "You need to stay home with your mom, and there isn't an *us* anymore. I'll go to college and maybe find someone else."

"Is that what you want?" When I questioned her intentions, I didn't see the disdain I assumed I would.

Her coffee-colored orbs glistened with unshed tears.

"Vine, you can try to find someone else, but you'll always belong to me." Unfortunate tears burned in my throat and pricked at the back of my eyes. Unable to contain them, water flowed freely down my face, causing my vision to blur.

But when the other part of my soul stood and walked out the door, I was able to see my life would never be the same with utmost clarity.

Chapter 25

Ivy, present day

"I saw your dad at the liquor store. We were both looking to drown our sorrows, I suppose." I left out the part about how I was scornful and threatening to his father. He didn't need to hear that right now.

"You're saying my dad has known all this time why you broke my heart, and he never thought it was important to divulge that information?" Fletcher shook his head multiple times, drenched in his denial. "I bawled my eyes out and begged you to give me some comfort after finding out about my mom, and you were an ice queen to me. I told myself there was something so fundamentally wrong then. I knew that wasn't you. But I was so confused and swimming in a mixture of sadness, despair, and hopelessness, I couldn't think straight."

Not only had my heart been ripped apart four years ago, but it was also being shredded again, bit by bit. "I'm so sorry. I wish I had made a different choice. I wish I could go back and tell your dad to fuck off."

He released a small chuckle, and that little bit of laughter had me breathing a little easier.

"If I could go back to that time, I never would have left you. I would have stayed with you and gone to college here."

Fletcher rose to his feet and paced the floor, apparently trading places with me. He kept his head hung low and stared at the floor as he shuffled in his flip-flops.

I sat motionless, tracking his movements with my eyes.

He stomped his feet in frustration and eventually kicked his shoes off, obviously tired of listening to their incessant clapping with each step.

He raked his fingers through his hair as he swiveled back and forth along the same ten-foot track he kept pacing across the living room in front of the couch.

Unsure of what I should do, I waited patiently for him to settle his ongoing aggravation.

When he stopped his infuriation-filled pacing, his light blue gaze connected with mine. "My dad knew I wouldn't be strong enough to say no to being with you. It's no secret that you have always been my kryptonite. I was powerless with regards to you. I always wanted to be in your orbit." He once again filled the vacant spot on the sofa next to me and clasped my hands within the grips of his. "He was worried I wouldn't have a choice—that I would be sucked into the world of Ivy, unable to break free. So he made it impossible for me to have any other option."

"I would have understood if you told me you needed to stay home and be with your mom," I whispered with a large gulp of air.

"Of course, you would have." A slight smile tugged at the corners of his mouth. "He wasn't worried you wouldn't let me go." His fingers rubbed across my knuckles in a soothing motion, and the smile reached his eyes. "He was worried I wouldn't leave you. You were always the leader, and I was always the hopeless puppy dog that followed you everywhere."

"That's not true." I swallowed as I pushed the words out, fending off a sob. "We were partners. We always stood by each other."

He leaned into me, and I reflexively stretched in the opposite direction.

A rumble of laughter echoed in the empty room. "Apparently, we aren't on the same page now." He settled back into the cushion with a huff of indignation.

"So many things have changed." I hiccupped when the sob freed itself. "We can't go back to the way things were. We're different people now."

"Are we?" His nose scrunched as his gaze narrowed with inquiry.

"I know I'm not the same since all that went down. I turned my back on you under the misrepresentation that was what was best for you, but all the while I destroyed us instead." I sniffled the whimpered cries pulling at my chest.

"My father destroyed us. We were invincible together, but apart, we were vanquished." He leaned in once more, and this time, I didn't flinch. He embraced me, and I melted into the strength of his strong arms.

"I thought your avoidance of my calls and dismissal of my texts was to pay me back for hurting you so badly that summer." My words were broken with my quick breaths during my full-on weeping session. "I didn't realize I was saying goodbye to you for four years when I ruined us."

"Vine, I'm here now," he said, smoothing out my wet hair on the back of my head before kissing my temple. "We can rebuild us. We don't need to start over because we already have a strong foundation."

"How will you ever be able to trust me again?" I sniveled, once again pushing out of his hold.

"Are you worried *I* won't be able to trust you again, or are you worried you won't be able to trust *me* again?" Damn him and his perception regarding me. His head tilted, and his assessing gaze narrowed. "I've hit the nail on the head, haven't I?"

Obviously, I had no poker face. Or maybe he still had the uncanny ability to read me.

"Your tells are showing." His gaze dropped to my hands stacked in my lap, which I twisted repeatedly.

I unthreaded my fingers and placed them at my sides. "Maybe we should just be friends." Four years ago, I would have wanted what he was offering, or really any time before he was engaged to another woman.

His face paled, and the slight smile he had been wearing dropped off his beautiful face and his lips flattened into a thin line as disappointment infused his once-hopeful expression.

Releasing a loud whoosh of air, he flopped himself against the pillows on the back of the couch, resting his head against the top and staring toward the ceiling.

"Your parents came to my mom's funeral," he whispered while still gazing upward. "I thought you would come." Another exhausted breath released from his chest. "I looked for you in the endless sea of people. But you weren't there." He turned his head, and those enticing blue eyes flickered with flashes of sadness. "You weren't with your parents or any of our friends. I needed you, and you didn't show up for me."

My nose dripped with snot as my tears increased with intensity, and my throat restricted, thick with emotion. "I thought you didn't want me there, and I didn't want to make anything harder on you."

He sat up quickly, causing me to flinch as I simultaneously squeaked a small yelp.

"Vine, I know my anger got tossed in your direction, and I'm so sorry. I was hurt and upset. And I can't promise that my misery wouldn't have shown up that day if you had been there, but I can assure you, I would have cried and yelled but then fell into your arms because I wanted you there."

"But..." I started, trying to unnecessarily defend my actions.

"I wished you had seen through my unanswered texts and realized I needed you."

His words gutted me. How had I become so unsure of his feelings? Of course, he needed me. I wanted to be there for him, but I thought my presence would have caused him more pain rather than comfort.

Nausea swayed within my gut as I continued to choke back more sobs. My breathing quickened as bile crept up my throat, and my head began to spin with the painful memories. I bent at the waist and wrapped my arms around my middle as I drew in deep breaths, attempting to fend off the blackness closing in.

"Vine, baby, slow down your breathing." His hand once again rubbed comforting circles on my back as my heart squeezed within my chest painfully. "You're hyperventilating. Please focus on my voice."

I earnestly tried to push out my regret and listen to the deep baritone of his words.

"Tell me three things you see in the room."

With my gaze focused downward, I said, "My pink socks."

His small chuckle eased the pressure behind my ribs.

"My parents' hardwood floor." I mentally counted one, two, and...I still needed a third item. "Your adorable feet."

His palm, which had been settled against the cotton of my shirt on my back, slid to the side of my waist, and his hand pulled at my arm.

I inhaled slowly and released the breath easily before raising my head from where it had been perched onto my knees only a moment earlier.

My watery vision blurred the silhouette of his form, but I threw my body in his direction regardless. "There were so many times during college that I wished I could talk to you. Sometimes, it was just to report something silly that happened, and sometimes, when I was upset about something." My pulse still thrummed hard against my breastbone, but at least my breathing regulated its rhythm. "And then I would remember how I broke your heart, recognizing that having my own heart fractured was probably my atonement."

"If you only want to be friends, I won't lie and say that I want to settle for that, but I need you back in my life, and if that's all we're ever meant to be, I guess I'll have to learn to accept it." A weak smile tipped one corner of his mouth upward.

"I feel so guilty for how I hurt you. And you were going to marry another woman. I literally pushed you into someone else's arms." I returned to standing and pushed my fingers through my drying hair in frustration. "I foolishly thought you would commit to staying home with your mom, and once your dad or I explained what we did, you and I would get back together. I'm so pissed at myself...and I'm furious with your dad."

Fletcher stood again, and I quickly released my tangled

locks and held up a hand, urging him to keep his distance from me.

"I know I shouldn't be upset with your dad over this, but I can't help it. The decision was ultimately mine, so I have no right to hold anyone else accountable for my own actions."

My socked feet shuffled across the wood floor as the unsettled feeling urged me to move.

"If I thought there was a chance you would come back, I *never* would have looked in another woman's direction." Ignoring my plea for some personal space, his bare feet shuffled along the floor, keeping pace with the back-and-forth movement of my feet.

I halted my steps, and the moment my gaze connected with his sorrowful, blue eyes like pools of rain from a storm that blew through town, his lips whispered, "I never stopped loving you."

I needed more air. The room spun, and a loud shriek proceeded more waterworks. My legs didn't want to keep me upright any longer, and I began to sink downward, hoping for a soft landing.

Fletcher's strong arms wrapped around my middle and hoisted me back into a standing position, but I didn't think my feet touched the ground. He was holding me suspended in the air, pressed up against his body.

He was warm and familiar, and I missed his touch fiercely. Even with his added weight and harder muscles than when we were teenagers, my body molded to his, acknowledging how well acquainted I once was being held by him.

Reflexive to those memories, I snaked my arms around his neck and sank my face onto the top of his shoulder. And without thinking, I also lifted my legs and squeezed them around his waist.

Sweet and gentle kisses brushed against the side of my head, and his large hand stroked my hair. I inhaled the scent of him that I had missed so much.

"I had no idea you were hurting as badly as I was. I thought you were out there living your best life while I was here suffering alone."

I wailed louder, causing hot tears and probably snot to wet his shirt. I was a blubbering mess. I was once strong and confident. But this situation turned me into a weak, insecure heap of vulnerability.

"I was trying to be strong for you. I kept attempting to convince myself that although my soul was tortured without you, it was best for you. I tried to be selfless, but I missed you so much," I sobbed, soaking his shoulder more.

"Oh, Vine. I'm so sorry, baby," he murmured into my ear while still holding my weight up.

I lifted my head and peered into those denim-colored eyes that pierced through the watery haze I viewed through.

"I wished for so many days that you would forgive me and give me another chance." I sniffled and wavered my tone. "And I promised that if I was ever given the reprieve, I'd never squander the opportunity. I swore I would never let you go again."

"You don't still feel that way?" Disappointment flattened his initially optimistic affect.

"Are you willing to forgive me and give me another chance?" Tears halted their descent, and hope swelled within my chest.

"There's nothing to forgive. Having you in my arms again is what I've wanted all along. I want *you* to give *me* another chance." A slight grin drew his lips into a sexy curl upward. "I'm sorry I didn't answer your texts or your calls." His hands slid down from my waist and palmed each globe of my ass.

I thought the gesture was sexual until he hitched me upward. I must have slipped from his grip.

He kept his hands planted in place, though. "I thought about blocking your number, but I couldn't completely eliminate your ability to reach me."

"But you never responded to any of my messages." I blinked away my tears of disbelief. My legs were still wrapped around Fletcher's waist, and his hands were on my butt.

"I typed out a million messages to you, but I either erased them before I hit send or I kept them in draft form... sometimes for days." His face approached mine slowly, probably assessing if I was going to pull away.

I wasn't going to lean back. In fact, I moved closer in his direction.

When his lips touched mine, we both released a small moan, like tasting the first spoonful of ice cream. His mouth gently kissed mine. I parted my lips to deepen our kiss, and blasts of memories struck me. The taste of him. The soft probing he did with his tongue.

I scraped my nail along his scalp as I combed my fingers through his hair, and although I was consumed with our kissing, I didn't miss the fact that we were moving.

Fletcher was carrying me across the room. I still clung to him, not caring where he was taking me one bit. I would go anywhere with him now.

I would have gone anywhere with him as kids, and even during these past horrific four years, I would have gone anywhere with him if he asked.

I never stopped loving him, but I was sure he hated me.

My thoughts were interrupted when Fletcher lowered us to the sofa.

Lying on my back, I released the grasp of my legs but kept my arms wrapped around his neck.

He hovered over me, with each of his arms caging me in between them.

He tasted delicious. Not like any food or tang of something sweet or savory, but something exclusive to him. I missed his taste because he was my favorite flavor. I could kiss, lick, suck, and taste him for hours and never tire of his essence.

His erection pressed against my pubic bone. He was clearly turned on, and I pressed my hips upward into him.

We moaned in unison again.

Without breaking our kiss, our shirts were tugged, and although we broke our lip-lock long enough to toss the cotton material over our heads, our mouths fused again and became more frantic. We nipped at each other, sucked, and our teeth struck in the chaos.

Fletcher slid his hands behind my back, and knowing he was looking for a hook on my bra and also aware that he wasn't going to find one on the tight sports bra I had on, I whispered into his mouth, "Let me sit up so I can take it off."

He halted the kissing and leaned back onto his haunches.

I took in his red, swollen lips and his messy hair as I crisscrossed my arms to lift off my bra. But as my gaze drifted down to his defined pecs, an image caught my attention.

"What is that?" Not only did he not have this chiseled chest in high school, but his body also used to be ink-free.

He didn't peer down; he knew what I was asking, so he stared blankly at me.

Across the left side of his chest, covering his entire pectoral muscle, was an illustration of a heart with a vine of ivy wrapped around the red-colored shape. "When did you get that?" I probed softly.

"After my mom died."

I hiccupped a small gasp. "But that was more than a year after we broke up."

He shrugged. "You left your mark on my heart. You might as well leave your mark on my skin also."

The heated intensity of a moment earlier vanished just like that. The passion that fueled our kissing evaporated.

I sat before him in my bra while he still straddled me for several quiet beats.

Our gazes stayed locked for that long moment.

"Fletch..."

Before I could begin speaking my thoughts, he climbed off the sofa and retrieved his shirt from the floor.

He pushed his head and arms into his tee while walking out of my living room.

Chapter 26

Fletcher, present day

I didn't even bother to relocate my vehicle. I pounded down the sidewalk to my dad's house on foot from the Hatfield house, leaving my truck in the driveway. Ivy's approaching steps stomped quickly behind me.

"Fletcher," her voice called.

I continue my determined path without peering over my shoulder.

"Fletch," she called again.

But I didn't stop. I needed to see my dad.

"Don't leave me, please," she cried, and my senses finally came to me, so I halted my paces and swung around to face her.

"I'm *not* leaving you. Ever." I ate up those few feet of distance between us and cupped her jaw with my hands.

I noticed her shirt was back in place, but she wasn't wearing any shoes in my brief appraisal of her before my lips crashed into hers again for a hard but fleeting kiss.

"I'm with you now and always."

She placed her small hands over mine that still rested against her cheeks. But her chocolate gaze shook with fear.

"You believe me, right?" I searched her eyes, but the apprehension was still there. "Vine?" Brushing my thumbs against the soft skin of her face, I attempted to reassure her. "I promise you can trust me, okay?"

She nodded once and drew in a deep breath.

"I'm going to see my dad for a little bit."

"I want to go with you," she said as her hands slid down to my wrists and forearms, tracing back and forth with her fingertips.

I kissed her forehead and then quickly on the lips. "Go slip your shoes on and meet me there."

She nodded again, but the dread that had stretched across her face was now replaced with courage and possibility. She was still my Vine.

After her lips tipped upward into an optimistic smile, she turned on her heel, and I swear she skipped back toward her parents' house. *Damn, I love that girl.*

"Dad?" I called as I unlocked my dad's house with my key and pushed the heavy door inward.

He always kept the house locked, unlike Ivy, who left her door unlatched nearly all the time. Hopefully, she put the deadbolt in place when she was gone or sleeping. But I'd have to confirm that tidbit of information later.

Cabinet doors shut, and glass clinked as I walked toward the kitchen.

My dad had his back to me when I entered. His middle-aged body leaned over the sink while he reached in, pulled out multiple glasses, and placed them into the dishwasher.

"Sorry, Son. I didn't know you were coming over. I

would have cleaned up a bit." His voice was unsteady, but so was his gait most days.

I honestly didn't know what he meant by the cleaning comment. I saw how unkempt his house was on the regular. I always assumed he knew I cleaned his house and cut his grass when he was gone. I'd seen his mess many times.

"Dad, don't worry about cleaning up," I said as I removed the two glasses from his hands. I didn't bother to put them in the dishwasher. I just sat the tumblers on the counter and shut the door to the appliance. "I need to talk to you."

My father turned to face me and leaned his frail body against the counter. I swore he used to be six inches taller, but these days, he walked hunched over. And his clothes hung from his body now because he'd lost a considerable amount of weight also.

He didn't look anything like the man he was before my mom died. His hair was always disheveled, and he had perpetual stubble on his face. He dressed every day, but I had no idea how often he showered.

But what was worse than his appearance was that I'd ignored the reason for his change. I'd disregarded his ongoing mourning. I guess I thought he would eventually stop grieving and missing my mom.

"What do you have on your mind?" Although he stood before me a wounded man, he still cared about me. I could see that in the concern etched on his face.

"I spoke with Ivy."

His eyes widened slightly, but only for a fraction of a second. "Oh yeah? How's she doing?"

"Not so good, actually." I waited for another subtle clue that he realized where this conversation was going, but when I didn't get any indication, I continued. "She misses me, Dad. And you took her away from me."

"What are you talking about?" He played the surprised person well, but I recognized his nervous twitch. His teeth clenched, and he ground them, causing a tic in the muscle movement of his jaw.

I left the door ajar when I entered the house a few minutes ago, and I could hear the soft sound of it swinging out farther and light footsteps down the hall.

My father was only in his mid-sixties, but his hearing wasn't what it used to be. He didn't flinch at the noises of another visitor.

"It's a little late for her to tell you that. Don't you think? You're engaged to another woman." A short chuckle escaped his raspy throat.

"I broke up with Amilyn."

Now, the flabbergasted expression of wide eyes and gaping jaw was genuine.

"I want to be with Ivy. I've always wanted to be with her, and you took her away from me."

"But what about Amilyn?"

"She was merely a placeholder until the love of my life returned."

"But you love Ami." His brow furrowed with confusion.

"How can I love her when my heart belongs to someone else?" Frustration festered within my chest, and I gritted my own teeth—probably a habit I picked up from him. "You told Ivy to break up with me."

"I didn't tell her to break up with you." My dad waved dismissively and snorted out a nervous laugh.

"You sure as hell did." Ivy finally decided to make an appearance after holding her post inside the hallway for a while.

"Ivy," he whispered with a hint of contempt.

"Mr. Hart, he knows. The jig is up. I gave you the opportunity to tell him the truth, and you didn't. So now he's caught up on everything." My brave woman stood self-assured with her arms crossed over her chest and her feet apart in a confident stance.

I liked this version of Ivy. This was the girl I fell in love with in first grade, and I'd loved every day since. Of course, she could cry on my shoulder and show me her vulnerability, but my woman was a badass. And I loved it when I got to see her in her true form.

My dad peered over at me, obviously awaiting my reaction regarding her appearance in his home, but I was still in awe of her strength, so I was too caught up in her presence to respond to my dad's expression.

"Fletcher, I don't know what she's told you, but..."

"Give it up, Dad," I grumbled. "Don't try to lie your way out of this. If you don't admit the truth, then I'll walk out that door and never return."

Tears glistened the globes of his blue eyes and his gait wobbled as he shifted his weight uncomfortably from one leg to the other. "I knew you would want to be with your mother during her final days, so I helped make that happen."

"You helped make that happen?" I echoed angrily.

"I thought you would stay home for the rest of her days, and then you would get back together with Ivy." His gaze swung to Ivy and then bounced back to me. "I figured you would follow her to college after... the end."

I crossed my arms around my chest, and Ivy shuffled her feet in my direction until she stood alongside me.

He nodded in acknowledgment of our united front.

"So why didn't you tell me what happened after Mom died?"

Ivy's hand brushed against my forearm. Her touch could always calm me, and in this instance, I was able to relax my arms at my sides.

She took the opportunity to thread her fingers with mine, and as furious as I had been when I stomped into my dad's house, I recognized that I was where I wanted to be. We were back together, and although I missed these past four years with her, I had her with me now.

My dad's throat bobbed up and down as he contemplated his response. "Because I didn't want you to leave also."

I truly had empathy for my dad, but I couldn't believe he was so selfish. Ivy sacrificed selflessly. She gave me up because that's what was best for me, but ultimately, my dad couldn't do the same.

"Why didn't you tell Fletcher I left so he would have that time with his mom?" I would have assumed Ivy would have irritation in her tone, but she maintained her composure. "I could have come home and gone to college. I only stayed away because I thought he hated me."

I swung my head quickly and addressed her statement. "I never hated you."

Her gaze met mine, and I realized there was so much new we needed to learn about each other.

"I missed you," I mouthed to her, all but forgetting that my dad was even in the same room as us.

"I missed you too." Her brown eyes were soft and loving but transitioned to dark and fiery when she twisted her neck to shoot my dad a warning glare. "We stayed apart because of you, but that will never happen again."

"I'm glad you two have found your way back to each

other." My father narrowed his pale blue eyes, and I swear there was some contempt still evident there.

"What the hell, Dad? Why don't you want Ivy and I to be together? Don't you want me to be happy?" Maybe misery really did love company.

"Being with someone for so long leads to unimaginable heartache. I don't want that for you." His shaky voice broke with emotion.

"I already had the heartache. And for the record, I will take as many days with Ivy as I can. You took away my choice. And who I love and who I want to be with is my choice, Dad." My mom's death shattered and splintered my dad's heart into a million pieces, and although I truly felt sorry for him, I was angry with him at this moment, and the rage was easier to find right now instead of empathy.

"I thought if you found someone else, you wouldn't miss Ivy. Because you were lost without her. You've loved that girl since we moved here, back when you were in first grade. And the guilt I had over your heartache has kept me up at night for years. I know it was wrong to keep you away from her, but..."

"But you did anyway. Obviously, the guilt didn't drive you to tell the truth." Ivy's tone was harsh, and I still didn't have it in me to be upset with how she spoke to my father because she only said what I was feeling.

My dad's gaze left mine and shifted to Ivy. "I couldn't tell him because I didn't think he would ever forgive me. I had already lost my wife. She was my other half...I didn't want to lose my son. He's the only piece of my heart left." Tears escaped the confines of my dad's eyes, and that did hit me in the feels.

I'd never seen my dad cry. And now assessing my old man's frail body and frumpy attire, I saw a shell of the man that he once was. He drank himself into a drunken stupor most days. I had always assumed it was over my mom, but maybe some of the guilt that was weighed down on his shoulders drove him to the overconsumption of alcohol also.

And before I could hug my old man myself, Ivy's arms were around my dad, shedding her own tears.

Chapter 27

Ivy, present day

My mom always planned her calls with me around four o'clock in the afternoon since I could be sleeping at any hour, day or night. So I wasn't surprised by her phone call, even though she typically only called me once a week or once every ten days or so.

She would call before my dad got home. She anticipated he would arrive home a little after five o'clock, but my father had been working late most nights, so she was probably a little lonely, which had prompted this call only five days since her previous call.

"I'm so happy you reconnected with Julie and Carrie," my mom said after I recounted my texts with my old neighbor and time spent with my high school best friend. It was good to hear the voice of one of my parents after my emotional day with Fletcher and his dad.

"Any more run-ins with Fletcher?" She asked me this same question every time she called me.

"No, Mom." I shouldn't lie to my mother, but I wasn't ready to admit that I'd seen him, talked with him, held hands with him, kissed him, slept in bed with him, and confronted his dad with him.

I'd catch her up eventually. Maybe after he and I got back together, or *if* we got back together. I wasn't even sure what that would look like. How did a couple get back together after a tragedy and years apart?

I was pretty sure we were friends again, but anything more than that was still a bit fuzzy.

"Well, I'm sure your paths will cross again, and each time, it will be easier." Her voice was wistful. "And who knows, maybe you'll become friends again, just like you have with Carrie and Julie. When you've been friends with someone for so long, once you talk again, it's as if no time has passed."

I giggled a few times, playing along. "Give Dad a hug and kiss for me. I can't wait until I see you both."

We exchanged our goodbyes and ended our call. My mom and I weren't super close like some daughters and mothers, but our relationship was exactly what I wanted. I could go to her for advice, and she'd give her opinion. But she didn't get upset if I figured things out for myself. She'd never been a helicopter mom. She'd always encouraged me to find my own way and fostered my independence.

I loved being on my own, but I knew she was always there if I needed her. I was grateful to have my mom in my life, and I felt terrible that Fletcher didn't have his.

My dad was always busy with work when I was growing up, but he was always there for me if I needed him. He always came to my home soccer games even if he had to miss the ones at other schools. He told me once that he was glad I had a boy as a friend because he felt better knowing that someone was looking out for me even if he wasn't around.

I think Fletcher and I were twelve at the time, so before the shift in our relationship from friends to more. Our friendship still remained the foundation of our relationship even after romantic feelings became involved.

Maybe we'd be able to have a good friendship again, but I was sure it wouldn't be the same as it was back when we were twelve.

Because even if he and I were friends again, it wouldn't ever be like the friendships I had with Carrie and Julie. And not just because I'd had sex with Fletcher, but because he was deeply rooted into the fibers of my being.

It felt normal to text each other again, even if it was just a quick hello or funny meme. But I probably wasn't ready to talk about our future yet. I wasn't sure how to define our relationship at present, which made it difficult to look too far ahead.

It'd been three days since his dad's emotional breakdown in the kitchen of his childhood home. I had to work the past few nights, but he and I both had tonight off. We hadn't made official plans for this evening with each other even though we had exchanged several texts the past couple of days.

I wasn't sure if we could avoid a conversation about our future if we got together tonight, but I was willing to take the risk because I missed him.

I was tired of missing him. He said he would always show up if I needed him, and right now, I felt like I needed him. Even though that's ludicrous and pathetic, I fired off a text to Fletcher anyway.

> Me: You still like Chinese food?

I expected a text back right away, but after a few

minutes of no reply, I jumped into the shower. And when I got out twenty minutes later there still weren't any new messages on my phone.

> Me: Was thinking we could get together tonight for dinner and a movie at my parents' house?

I tossed my phone on the couch after no response again after a few minutes. I couldn't believe how ridiculous I was acting. I didn't need Fletcher to come over if I wanted Chinese takeout and an evening of watching television in my sweats.

So I retrieved my cell from its resting place on the sofa and scrolled through the screens of restaurants until I found the number to my favorite place. I was pleased to see the establishment was still in business four years later.

I had just pressed the *call* button when a knock at my front door had me ending the call.

I didn't see a car on the street, but a familiar truck was parked in my driveway, so a grateful smile pinched my cheeks. Because my evening just got so much better.

"Hey, Fletch," I said as I swung the door open. I didn't bother peering through the peephole. His vehicle gave away his surprise.

He held up a brown paper bag and wore a mischievous grin. "I had them throw in extra chopsticks in case we decide to have a good old-fashioned chopstick fight like we used to."

I stepped out of the path to the living room so he could enter.

"So I assume the answer was yes?" I asked as we traveled down the short hallway toward the kitchen.

"Huh?" Fletcher asked, raising a single eyebrow.

"I asked if you still liked Chinese food." My intent was meant to be playful, but he slumped his shoulders forward as he placed the large bag on the island resting in the middle of the room.

"I need a happy memory associated with Chinese food." He braced his arms on the counter with his back toward me as he spoke, but I still heard his comment.

"Did you have a bad experience with Chinese food before?"

"You could say that." A loud exhale followed his brief explanation.

"Did it make you barf or something?"

A throaty chuckle left him, and he finally swung around and leaned against the island, meeting his blue gaze with my brown one. "I need a pinky swear."

I couldn't remember the last time either one of us uttered those words. When either of us needed to share a secret, we would call for a pinky swear, which would issue to the other complete and total confidentiality. Neither of us could utter a word to anyone.

I folded my fingers down and held up my right hand with only the pinky standing.

"Amilyn and I broke up while eating Chinese food, and I swore I'd never eat it again." A somewhat shy smile tugged at his lips as if he were embarrassed to tell me the story.

I briefly placed my hand over my mouth before rolling my eyes. "Seriously, Fletch? You were going to let a woman take away Chinese food from your consumption eligibility list?"

His laughter rang happily into our space, and it was a sound so familiar that I longed to hear it over and over again. "What the hell does that even mean?"

I shrugged.

"I'm here with the food, aren't I?" He gave a light shove to my shoulder, bringing a smile to my face and a flutter of giddiness to my heart.

"I'm just saying no man will ever be able to take away sesame chicken from me." I pointed a finger toward the center of my chest, and Fletcher lifted the bag from the island and took a few paces out of the kitchen.

"You know I'll tackle you over that," I called after him.

"You go ahead and try," he yelled back.

"I've already got the number to the *Duck & Dragon* on my phone. I'll just order my own."

His footsteps halted, and he turned on his heel with the paper bag still in hand.

"I told you no man is keeping sesame chicken away from me."

And then it was his turn to roll his eyes.

I didn't care. I was winning whatever this banter thing was going on between us. "There is sesame chicken in there, right?"

"And vegetable lo mein. And extra egg rolls because you always used to eat more than one. I grabbed plenty of spicy mustard because I know you love it. And I ordered steamed rice *and* fried rice because you and I could never compromise. Steamed rice for you and fried rice for me."

I nodded once but stood, mouth gaping, frozen in my spot. He remembered.

"I wasn't sure if you had chopsticks or not, so I picked some up."

Damn. I missed him. I missed this. I missed having someone know me so well. I missed having someone in my life that I held so many memories with.

"Thanks." Freaking tears stung my eyes, and that burn

traveled up my throat, forcing me to swallow it down before a sob fest began over Chinese food.

Only a few steps were between us, which Fletcher closed within half a second. He slid the bag back onto the island, and soon, I was engulfed by his strong arms in a warm embrace.

I released an unintentional sigh—or was it a moan? As I pressed the side of my face against his chest, I didn't care what kind of muffled sound came from me. I was just elated to be back where I've wanted to be for so long.

"Let's eat before the food gets cold."

I wrapped my arms around his waist and squeezed for a fraction of a second before stepping out of his welcoming hug. Because even though I'd been staying in my parents' house for a few weeks now, I just now felt like I was home.

After food was consumed and settled in our bellies, we parked our butts on the couch in front of the television. I handed the remote to Fletcher, and his eyebrows shot up.

When he held his hands up in surrender, I couldn't help but laugh at his typical antics that I had all but forgotten about.

"Don't point that thing at me." His blue eyes were still wide with surprise. "Is it loaded?"

"I was offering to give you control of the viewing selection, but now I don't think you deserve it," I said, stifling my giggling.

"You're the one that made the *I watch what I want at my house, and you watch what you want at your house* rule." He lowered his hands as he shrugged.

"You don't forget anything," I said, shaking my head.

"Not when it comes to you." His sapphire eyes softened to pensive, and my insides turned to mush.

His rebuttal would probably sound cheesy to another woman, but I'd known Fletcher since I was a little girl. He was sincere and loyal. And caused my heart to kick up its rate. And my breath to hitch. I still loved him.

"Fletch..."

"I know you're not ready for something more than friendship, and I swear I get it. But please understand that what we've had is still here." He waved his finger in the air, alternating between pointing at himself and me. "I won't push you for more than you're able to give, but I'll continue to remind you about us any chance I get."

"Okay."

"Okay?" Fletcher narrowed his gaze with uncertainty.

"I'm not saying I'm ready for us to try dating again. But I'm saying that I'm open to that as a possibility someday."

"Does this weekend work for you?" His eyebrows waggled playfully as his sexy smirk flirted with me.

"I said *someday*, not *Saturday*."

"So Sunday, then?"

"You're incorrigible." I picked up a pillow from the sofa and heaved it toward his head.

Of course, he effectively dodged it from connecting with the side of his face. "Come on. You know you're dying to go to the carnival with me again, and there's only one more weekend that it's in town."

Chapter 28

Fletcher, age seventeen, summer after junior year of high school

My idea of a date wasn't a carnival, but Ivy wanted to go. We'd gone to the carnival every year for as long as I could remember, so I guess this year shouldn't be any different.

Maybe I'd kiss her at the top of the Ferris wheel. That would be something we hadn't done before. I thought I was too old to play the games there, and the rides were mediocre at best.

But anytime I was with my best friend, we had a good time. Although Ivy had been my girlfriend for a year and a half, she'd been my friend for ten years. And truly my best friend just as long.

I had quite a few good friends on my soccer team, but Ivy was by far my closest friend.

The guys had given me crap a time or two when I chose to spend time with my girlfriend over them, but I didn't care.

We weren't one of those couples that'd forgotten we had other friends. When she spent time with her girlfriends, I spent time with my guys.

Sometimes, we still met up as a group, and even though we might arrive with other people, we always found our way to each other.

Like at the bonfires at Jericho Walker's farm or at Rider Conklin's house parties. I'd head out to the edge of town with a bunch of my friends to Jericho's and after we'd had a beer or two, the pack of girls seemed to always find us.

I wasn't complaining. I enjoyed being found by my favorite brunette.

Most of us ended up crashing in his barn, or at least the ones that had been drinking did. Ivy typically chose to stay sober so she could drive girls back who didn't want to stay the night.

But every so often, one of the other girls would volunteer for that job, and Ivy would stay with the group overnight. We didn't typically sleep much. We stayed by the fire until we got sleepy and then headed to the barn with our sleeping bags in tow. But even once bags were rolled out, we all still stayed up talking.

The parties at Rider Conklin's house were quite different. His parents went away almost every other weekend, and he would invite several of us over. We usually drank a little more because if you went to Rider's house, you weren't going home until morning.

He took everyone's keys upon arrival. At first, I thought the reason had to do with concern for our safety, but now that I'd been to many of his parties, I thought part of the reason had to do with the next day's cleanup.

He handed everyone's keys back once the house was put back together and the evidence (aka trash) was removed. Although Rider didn't just get rid of glass bottles and plastic cups. He wanted the house *clean*—like cleaner than when we'd arrived.

So, we would scrub the bathroom and kitchen and vacuum the carpet. Paul Riggleman had bathroom duty one weekend, and he kept puking in the toilet and had to clean it over and over. I felt bad for the guy, but not bad enough to clean up his vomit.

It was hard to imagine we'd actually be seniors after the summer. Only one more year until college and all the freedom that came with it. I'd miss my friends and my soccer team, but Ivy would be with me always, and she was truly all I needed.

I'd make a lot of new friends, and she would, too, but we'd stay friends forever because I planned on marrying her one day.

So if she wanted to go to the carnival, I'd go to the carnival. In fact, I'd go anywhere with her.

And when I picked her up from her house, and she jumped into my car wearing the prettiest smile I've ever seen, I couldn't believe I was even dreading the outing.

She had a baseball cap on and wore her hair in twin braids. The tight cotton shirt clung to her breasts, and the denim shorts showed off her tan.

The bright yellow top she had on provided a contrast against her bronzed skin, and those shorts revealed her toned legs.

"Hi," she said brightly, shutting the car door, and after fastening her seat belt, she threaded her fingers through mine.

"Hi." My vocal response was brief because I wanted my lips on hers as soon as she climbed into my vehicle, so I leaned across the console between us and pressed a chaste kiss to her mouth.

"So, are you ready for the itinerary?" she asked while rooting around in her purse with her unbound hand. "Aha!"

Her gaze had dropped to her lap while she scoured the bottom of her leather bag for a small, lined sheet of notebook paper folded several times.

"Hit me with it." I exhaled as I turned back onto the road in front of her house.

And well...she hit me with it, alright. But rather than only having the paper swat at my upper arm, a hand smacked at my bicep.

I shook my head at her humor. She enjoyed taking my words and twisting them into some literal high jinks.

"Cotton candy, funnel cake, caramel popcorn, and... corn dogs if you must."

"The corn dogs are my favorite. You know I can't go to the carnival and not have one." I pushed my lower lip out, making a ridiculous pouty face, causing a sweet giggle to escape her.

Her laughter was worth a hundred corn dogs.

"Merry mixer, Tilt-A-Whirl, carousel, and Ferris wheel." She settled her laughing and continued with a list of the same rides we go on every year.

"It's amazing we haven't barfed on each of those rides with the amount of junk food we consume."

She only offered a smirk and a shoulder shrug to my comment, which was essentially a true blessing. "And, of course as many games as we can fit in."

"Why is it you still find the same excitement in the carnival as we did when we were nine?" I asked while keeping my eyes focused on the road.

"It's tradition, Fletch. How can you *not* be excited about our tradition? We've been going to the carnival together since forever. Even after college, when we're married, we still need to go to the carnival every year. It's bad luck to break tradition."

I swung my gaze to her momentarily before bouncing it back to the highway, catching a glimpse of her silky legs crossed, revealing a mile of smooth skin.

"And when we have kids, we'll bring them to the carnival."

I swallowed hard at her declaration of our future together and tried to maintain my concentration on driving us safely.

We had spoken about getting married one day, but I couldn't remember if we were being serious or not. I certainly hoped she was being truthful now. I would marry her this second if it was legal. I want to be with her for all her adventures, new and old.

A grin tugged at the corners of my mouth, and suddenly, I couldn't imagine anywhere else I wanted to be at that moment.

We ate too much junk food, and I questioned my decision of a second corn dog after we got on the Tilt-A-Whirl. But I managed to keep my stomach contents in place even with the turning and twisting of our car during the ride.

I was thankful we got that ride out of the way because once confident I could keep the crap I had consumed down, I was ready to get on that Ferris wheel. Barfing on my girl-friend during the ascent was not an option.

We waited in line for the Ferris wheel for what seemed like forever. Not that I minded. We talked while we waited for our turn. No matter how much time we spent together, we never ran out of things to talk about.

Sure, we could sit in comfortable silence also. We didn't feel the need to fill every moment with useless conversation, but we enjoyed talking about everything, anything, and nothing at all. When you were with the right person, you could be relaxed and content no matter whether you had something to say or not.

Once the ride attendant gestured it was our turn to load the seat, we stepped up onto the platform, and Ivy moved forward into the car. The seat was large enough to hold four people, but we would be the only two to occupy the metal bench.

I slid into the middle of the cart close to Ivy, and the carnival employee latched our bar in place and shut the door to the car. The Ferris wheel began turning but had several stops while other cars unloaded and reloaded.

The ride halted at the top, and we stared out to the coastline. The sun was still high in the sky, and a glow was cast over the water, causing it to shimmer with sparkles of green, blue, and gray streaks.

"I'm glad neither of us is scared of heights because we would miss out on this amazing view," Ivy said as she squeezed my hand.

"Even if I was afraid, I'd still get on this ride if you wanted to do this because I want whatever you want."

She twisted her head, and her chocolate eyes left their position, staring at the horizon to penetrate my heart and soul with the depths of their gaze. Flecks of gold spoked the chestnut-colored background.

"Damn, I love you so much." My chest constricted with overwhelming emotion, and I sucked in a shallow breath.

"I love you too, Fletch."

And then her lips were on mine, and I moaned against her mouth.

I didn't need to initiate the kiss at the top of the Ferris

wheel because Ivy was so in tune with me. She and I were always on the same page.

Her lips were soft, and I teased my tongue against the seam of their supple fullness.

She complied with my unspoken request and opened her mouth, allowing me access to her welcoming warmth that my tongue happily delved into.

Her taste intoxicated me. A mixture of cotton candy and caramel reminded me of her sweetness, but as she grabbed the back of my head and deepened the kiss, I was reminded of her toughness as well.

I loved both sides of her. Our kissing became more intense and remorseless. Our teeth clashed numerous times, and the gentle swipes of our tongues became more aggressive. The subtle nips at our lips were now biting with need.

Of course, my dick hardened with the increasing hunger I had.

She was just as eager with unrelenting desire as her hands took to roaming over my back and eventually under the cotton of my shirt, gliding against the skin along my spine.

Our breathing quickened, and my pulse thundered loudly in my ears.

Our car jerked unexpectedly, and we broke from our searing kissing session.

Ivy cracked a grin, and giggling erupted from her, causing me to laugh as well.

I wrapped my arm around her, and she settled into my side, placing her head against my shoulder.

My erection eventually softened after a few adjustments on my part, and I enjoyed the ride with my girlfriend, who happened to also be my best friend and my whole world.

We were on our fifth or sixth game by the time I got to my favorite one. There was something so gratifying about throwing a dart at a balloon and hearing the pop.

Ivy and I always did well at that kind of game because my parents have a dartboard in our garage, and we'd been playing ever since the adults in our lives believed we wouldn't be seriously injured throwing sharp objects.

"That's three for me, Fletch," Ivy said after the result of her third throw ended in a resounding bang.

"You still have two more throws, Vine." I smirked and handed a five-dollar bill to the game attendant.

She'd already won a prize because three out of five wins.

"Can we have a shootout?" she asked the employee with a surge of excitement.

He merely shrugged, and we proceeded to throw one for one, each piercing inflated latex two additional times.

I stared at my last three darts that lay on the counter and selected the red one for my third throw.

Ivy strummed her fingernails against the wooden surface of the booth.

I swung an annoyed glare at her, and she retreated her hand.

The first balloon cracked loudly with my first throw, and I peered over my shoulder at her wide smile.

I chose the blue dart for my next turn and burst another balloon.

"That's four for you and five for me." Her tone was both mocking and comforting as well.

"I'm aware. Thanks for the score check." I was only satirical in my response.

When my green dart struck a balloon with my last

throw, my heart rate pulsed faster than when I had been on the Ferris wheel earlier. Losing to your girlfriend at anything was a shot to one's masculinity, regardless if she was a total badass and the best person I knew.

"That's five for me too, Vine." The grin that broke free wasn't meant to be smug. It was an expression of my relief.

"I saw it with my own eyes." Her voice was laced with exasperation this time.

"You didn't have confidence in my skills, did you?"

She slowly lifted her shoulders, and her nose crinkled.

"I haven't seen anyone as good as you two at this game all season," the attendant said, and when I glanced at him, his mouth gaped.

"If we combine our wins, what do we get?" I asked the employee, who appeared no older than us, but I was fairly certain he didn't go to our school. Maybe he was a college student.

The kid dressed in a yellow-and-purple striped shirt pointed to a large, cream-colored bear hanging from the back of the booth.

I twisted to Ivy, and she adamantly shook her head.

"That bear can't come home with us. He won't fit in the car."

"Come on, Vine. That bear is big because my love for you is big also."

I wore her down with my declaration, and that fuzzy stuffed bear sat in my back seat until we got back to her house.

I carried it into her bedroom at her request, with her guiding me down the hall as I couldn't see around the large animal.

After I flung him into the corner of her room, where he

landed squarely with a soft thud, she reached for my hands and stood on her tiptoes to give me a chaste kiss on my mouth. "My love for you is big also."

Junior year, we were all about the I love yous. We said it so effortlessly. Now, I wondered if or when the next time we'd be able to say those three words to each other.

Chapter 29

Ivy, present day

I had no idea the carnival after junior year would be the last time Fletcher and I went together. I used to be so incredibly excited to attend the town tradition, and until Fletcher mentioned it a few days ago, I hadn't realized I almost missed it again.

Since I stayed in North Carolina every summer, I didn't have the opportunity to attend the carnival anyway. As I recalled, Fletcher didn't like the carnival as much as I did. So I supposed he made the suggestion for me.

He didn't realize I had avoided any fair that had a semblance of a carnival for the past five years because the memory was painful.

Even though the last carnival I went to with Fletcher was a wonderful time, the thought of ever going to another one always left my stomach twisted in knots, and not from the queasiness of stuffing our faces with junk food. Because, like so many other memories that were linked to Fletcher, the thoughts reminded me of what I lost. Well, not so much lost as gave up.

Although the choice was mine, and I'd convinced

myself it was the best thing for Fletcher, I had so many doubts. The biggest doubt occurred when he wouldn't answer my texts or calls.

I was lonely and wanted so badly to be with him. That fresh hurt never decreased, even though it was supposed to lessen over time. But time went on, and so did the pain.

Pain could manifest in a lot of forms, such as sadness and depression, but also anger and frustration. I chose to channel my pain into resentment and irritation, basically forcing me to pretend I never met Fletcher Hart.

But now, all the memories were rushing back, and unfortunately, the old feelings were presenting themselves also. The unrelenting desire and undying love were wreaking havoc within me. He'd taken up residence in my heart for as long as I could remember. Now that we're in each other's lives again, it felt like he was only away on vacation, but he was home again.

Because somehow, I couldn't think of home without equating his presence also. That's why I never came back to my house while I went to college. Home wouldn't feel like home without him.

I convinced myself that I was only visiting for the summer, refusing to believe I was *home*. Now, being here genuinely felt like home, however.

I wasn't sure how to navigate all our baggage, old feelings, and time lost.

He was engaged to another woman. He couldn't possibly be ready to be with someone else, even if that someone was me. I didn't know how long he was with his fiancée, but I didn't want to be some kind of rebound relationship.

I would love nothing more than for us to be together again, but the timing was wrong.

Then again, the timing was wrong years ago.

When is the time going to be right for us?

"Hey," I said as I opened the door when Fletcher arrived.

He knocked and waited for me to let him in. I preferred the days better when he only half-assed pretended to knock before swinging the door open himself.

"You didn't need to stay outside until I answered." I stepped aside so he could set foot inside, but he remained rooted in his spot on the porch, standing on my parents' welcome mat.

"I'm picking you up to take you on a date." His perfect white teeth peeked out from his growing smile. "It wouldn't be appropriate for me to let myself into your house. That would be something someone that is only a friend might do."

I could feel my eyes roll. "We went to the carnival together for over a decade, as friends, and then...uh, more." I coughed to clear my throat somewhat, but mostly to erase the words I had just thrown out into the universe.

"So we'll go to carnival today as friends, and then one day we can be more." His rough hands gripped my waist and pulled me from my spot at the door threshold onto the porch, with my chest slamming into him, surprising me enough to squeak out a gasp.

I peered up at his whisker-covered jaw, and he tilted his head down, connecting his sparkling blue gaze with mine.

"Vine, I'm not letting you go anywhere again unless you take me with you. I love being your friend, but we've always been meant to be more."

My tongue refused to move and produce words in

response. I wanted to agree with him, but my brain refused to allow me to speak.

My heart accelerated its pace, and there was no doubt that organ wasn't on the same page as the one in my head.

I hadn't even thought about the logistics of resuming a platonic friendship with a man I had been intimate with. I certainly couldn't forget the big feelings I continued to carry for him. And I couldn't ignore how my core heated with just his mere proximity.

"Have you always been such a flirt?" I shook my head in an attempt to shake free the thoughts bouncing around in my mind.

"Flirt?" His head tilted slightly as confusion caused an eyebrow to quirk upward. "I thought I was being sweet."

"Well, knock it off." I waved my hand dramatically.

"Then how will I win you back?" His thumbs brushed over the knuckles of my fingers still clasped within his hands.

"Jeez, Fletch." I pulled away from his grasp and side-stepped a few times. "You just broke up with your fiancée."

"So?" Damn, he wore the perplexed expression well. The bewilderment in his eyes almost had me believing he was truly clueless.

"I'm not going to be some rebound fling for you." The fun, friendly afternoon carnival date wasn't going to go the way I pictured it after that declaration.

"Vine, you could *never* be just a fling for me." His eyes flashed with hurt as if I offended him with my comment.

"Fletcher, you were going to marry another woman." I didn't mean for my frustration to sound so obvious, but I couldn't stop the jealousy vibrating through my veins.

"I'm so sorry." He swiveled on his heel and threaded his fingers together before bracing them behind his head.

Staring off into the distance from the side of my porch, I only had his backside to look at. "If I thought for a split second that you would come back to me, I would never have considered dating anyone else."

"It's not a good time. You'd just be setting yourself up for disappointment. You can't just jump from one relationship to another."

"Seriously, Ivy?" His heated blue glare swung at me.

And just like any time he used my birth name, a little stab struck my heart.

"You think I'm jumping from one relationship to another?" Anger meshed with the pain in his tone. "What I had with you...what I *have* with you can't be compared to anything else. If you want to do this song and dance, fine."

He hopped off the few steps from the porch and headed toward the driveway. He wore sneakers on his feet today instead of his trademark flip-flops, so there was no flapping of the soles against the walkway. He took purposeful yet quiet paces.

"What song and dance?" I called after him, seeking an answer for his last declaration.

"The one where we pretend we don't know what we mean to each other." He opened the door to his truck and was about to step into it and away from me.

"I love you," I mumbled.

That halted his progress in leaving me alone at my parents' house.

His gaze once again found mine as disbelief grooved deep lines into his forehead. "What did you say?"

A stone statue would have been able to move easier on its own than I did at that moment.

Thankfully, he elected to help me out of my frozen stupor. "Did you say you love me?"

I shrugged sheepishly, still unable to utter another sound.

Then those sneakered feet stomped at me, still standing on the wooden planks of the porch of my childhood home. I expected his lips to crash onto my mouth, but his strong arms wrapped around me, and he swung me around in a circle, dizzying me with the muddied waters of my confession.

"I never stopped loving you, Vine," he murmured into the crook of my neck once my feet were once again planted on the porch. "I know we can't jump back to how things used to be. And I'm sorry I've made you doubt how I feel about you." His lips pressed against the same spot gently with a brief peck. "I know you love me. I don't question that now that I know what you did for me, but I know it's going to take a while for you to realize I feel the same way about you." His hands gripped my shoulders, and he pulled away slightly to meet my teary gaze. "I fell in love with you the first time I met you on that school bus, and I've never stopped. I will love you forever, even if we never get back together."

Dammit, the ridges of my lower eyelids could only hold back the waterworks for so long, and now salty rivers streaked down the sides of my face. Apparently, I hadn't shed enough tears over Fletcher Hart.

"Come on," he said as he reached for my hand. "Let's go back inside and talk."

I allowed myself to be guided by him, following his silhouette through my blurry vision.

When he reached the couch, he sat and pulled me into his lap, but I quickly scooted off him and onto the cushion of the sofa next to him.

His eyes widened, and his lips pursed in disappointment.

"I'm going to tell you something you probably don't want to hear because you can't be left with questions about us if we're going to move forward." His hand found mine, and he interlaced our fingers.

If he admitted he was about to tell me something I didn't want to hear, I absolutely believed I wouldn't want to listen to whatever he was about to dole out. My whole body tensed, bracing for impact.

"We didn't used to keep secrets from each other, and I'm sorry I didn't allow you to tell me yours."

Was he crazy? I kept a secret from him. He didn't need to believe me. He could have brushed off my truth as a lie. We'd been apart for over four years.

"But I don't want to keep anything from you. So I'm going to satisfy your curiosity." After a brief pause, he continued. "I'm going to talk about my relationship with Amilyn."

I shook my head. "No, Fletch. Please don't." I found myself pulling my hand away, but my effort was only counter measured by him pulling against my force.

Was this some kind of penance for what I did? Hadn't I suffered enough? Apparently not because he forced words out despite my protests.

"She was my mom's nursing assistant. When my mom got really bad, my dad hired a hospice home care company, and Amilyn was sent to my house to take care of my mom."

I attempted to muffle the sobs attempting to break free while my tears continued their descent down my face.

Fletcher's thumb chased the water sliding down my cheeks and brushed it off my skin.

"She took good care of my mom and was so kind to my dad."

I shut my eyes as if not seeing him speak would silence his words. I didn't want to think of another woman in his parents' house. I didn't want to think of another woman in his life. I should have been there...not anyone else.

"After my mom was gone, so was Amilyn. She didn't come to the funeral."

"I'm sorry I didn't..." I choked out before his finger was against my lips.

"It's okay, Vine. If I had told you I wanted you there, I know you would have been." His mouth tugged slightly at the corners. "I didn't see Amilyn for over a year after my mom died, but we randomly ran into each other at a grocery store..."

"Please, Fletch...please stop." My shaking voice whined. "I can't take it."

A deep sigh exited his body, and he leaned in to softly kiss my saturated cheek.

"Okay."

"Okay?" I blinked.

"I'm not trying to hurt you. I just don't want to have any more secrets between us."

"I just can't listen to how I pushed you into the arms of another woman." I hiccupped with each syllable.

"You didn't push me towards someone else. I've always wanted you. I was lonely. I missed you. I missed my mom." Water gathered within his eyes, and my heart gained additional fissures from hurt.

"I never stopped loving you." My blubbering barely allowed me to mumble the words.

"And Amilyn knew I never stopped loving you. That's

probably why she never wanted to commit to a wedding date. I'm honestly surprised she agreed to an engagement."

"What?" Although my crying hadn't stopped, I was interested in hearing more now.

"I was trying to force something that was never going to work out. She and I were never meant to be together. You and I are."

"You weren't making that stuff up when I heard you talking to your dad?" My disbelief was obviously apparent on my face since Fletcher offered that sympathetic grin I could melt for.

"I know you think I need some time to get over Amilyn, but I'm telling you, I don't. I just need to be with you. I've always just needed to be with you."

"But people with talk," I huffed.

"Will talk about what?"

"That you dumped your fiancée and ran back into my arms." My crying had slowed to just a trickle compared to the torrential downpouring from only moments ago.

"Ivy Hatfield never gave a damn what anyone said before. Are you saying she does now?"

I sniffled, and a snort of a laugh rushed out with an exhaled breath. "It's going to take me some time being with you again. I've wanted this for so long that I'm just over-whelmed right now."

"It's okay. I can live with that. I just can't live without you anymore."

Chapter 30

Fletcher, present day

We ditched the carnival idea and went out for drinks and appetizers, which was more like a date than junk food and rides. And neither of us had been chagrined during our outing. No one seemed to pay us any mind at all.

Our town seemed small on most days, but we could blend in with the scenery if we wanted. We sat at the bar among the locals at Tara's Tavern. After a few beers, mozzarella cheese sticks, and chicken fingers, we were ready to leave the bar and spend some quiet time together, so we walked down the length of Main Street, holding hands and peering into shop windows.

Ivy convinced me to go into the jewelry store she used to visit when we were in school. She loved the crystals, beads, silver bracelets, charms, homemade pendants, rings, and necklaces. I frequented the store when we were younger, and I wanted to impress her.

She received a few gifts from me that were purchased at this store, and I guess she was still a fan. I took mental notes of things she eyed carefully, and after several passes around the store, she told me she was ready to go.

I drove her home and dropped her off with only a short kiss on her porch. She didn't invite me in, and I didn't press the issue.

Since we had agreed to a second date for Wednesday, I felt satisfied enough that she wanted to see me again in a few days.

We texted and talked on the phone the next few days when we weren't working, and by the time Wednesday arrived, I couldn't wait to see her again.

I had texted her before I left my house, but I didn't wait for a response before I headed over. Since this evening was technically a first date of sorts, I decided to dress up a little for the occasion.

It was still summer in Maryland, so I didn't go crazy and wear a sports jacket or a suit, but I did select some khaki slacks that weren't wrinkled and paired them with a short-sleeve button-down shirt. I even wore some casual, brown leather shoes instead of the flip-flops I preferred to wear this time of year.

I rang the doorbell with a bouquet of flowers in hand when I arrived at her parents' house. After almost a minute of no answer, I pressed the buzzer again.

And after another couple of minutes, I no longer cared about the whole date etiquette. She had said I didn't need to wait for her to answer, so I impatiently twisted the knob and pushed the door open.

"Vine?" I called as I entered the living room.

Her car was parked in the driveway, so there wasn't a concern that she wasn't home. I was more concerned that she was home but didn't hear me knock for some reason.

We had agreed to go out at six o'clock, and it was a few minutes after six by this point, so I didn't think she would be in the shower. And because I'd known her nearly all my life, I was well acquainted with her idiosyncrasies. And one of her quirks has always been the necessity to select her outfit at least a day in advance.

I climbed the stairs after dropping the flowers on the surface of the coffee table in her living room and surveying the empty kitchen.

"Vine," I called again.

I heard some movement coming from the direction of her room, but when I swung open the unlocked door, my gaze swept the room, and she wasn't in the bedroom, but the light was on in the adjoining bathroom.

"You okay?" I asked while knocking softly.

But she didn't answer. Well, she didn't answer with conventional means. The sounds of retching and gagging came from the other side of the door.

"Vine, I'm coming in." I wasn't sure what she was going to look like when I found her, so I felt like it was important to let her know I was entering. I didn't give her a chance to refuse my entry, but I figured I'd at least warn her so she could be away from the back of the door.

I twisted the knob, and the damn thing was locked.

Sure, she leaves the front door open to whatever tres-passer may be passing by, but she locks the bathroom door in a house with no one else in it.

I dug into my pocket and retrieved my key ring, where I keep an extra interior doorknob emergency key for incidents just like this. As firemen, we didn't always need to bust a door in with brute force.

I wouldn't hesitate to bust this door down if I didn't have this alternative, though. So I inserted the long, thin metal rod into the knob and twisted, freeing it from its latch.

Ivy had her head lying against her arms propped on the toilet.

"Vine, I'm here." I lowered myself next to her onto the cool tile floor where she was stooped over the opening of the commode in a pretty light-blue sundress with her hair hanging over her shoulders in brown waves.

Her body began heaving, and I instinctively grabbed her hair while she expelled more contents into the bowl with an unfortunate splash.

The skin on the back of her neck was clammy against my hand.

"Fletch," she grumbled.

"Yes, baby. What can I do for you?" I spoke softly and rubbed circles over her back while I retained a grasp of her hair with my other hand.

"I have a migraine." She cried quietly with her explanation. "I have medicine for it in my nightstand."

I pressed a small kiss on her forehead and returned to her bedroom. There were a few amber-colored bottles with prescription labels. One read *take at onset of headache,* and another read *take as needed for vomiting.*

Gripping the cup next to the toothbrush at the bathroom sink and filling it with some water from the faucet, I handed the cup and one tablet from each bottle onto her hand.

She sipped the water and swallowed down the pills.

Her face was flushed, and her dull, brown eyes were hooded with exhaustion.

"Do you think you can get up from the floor?" I asked while she still clung to the side of the toilet as if she might fall over in her weakened state.

She nodded and attempted to push herself to a standing position, but I slid my arms around her back and beneath her legs and lifted her into a bridal carry.

She didn't hesitate to wrap her arms around my neck and squeeze close.

The stench of fresh vomit wafted to my nostrils, and I realized she had barfed on her pretty dress. I took care to lay her carefully on her bed before I began to undress her.

I slipped the thin straps off her shoulders and unbuttoned the front of the top so I could slide it down the length of her body, leaving her in a strapless bra and some flesh-colored lacey panties.

"Baby, I'm going to grab something else for you to put on."

She nodded with her head against the pillow, and I opened the drawers in her dresser until I found a cotton T-shirt and a pair of pajama shorts.

Before I could help her, she was unhooking the clasp on the back of her bra and wiggling out of her panties. My brain and my heart ignored her naked body and focused on getting her dressed and beneath the covers. But my dick could only think of one thing once her breasts were exposed and her underwear wasn't covering her.

Even though I had seen her naked many times before, I hadn't seen her without clothes on in an exceptionally long time. And her body was curvier. Her breasts were fuller, her hips slightly wider, and I loved every inch of the changes.

Thankfully, the control my brain had trumped my dick's compulsions and kept me from acting like a horny teenager.

I helped her pull the shirt on over her head and slipped each of her legs into the shorts before shimmying them up her legs.

Then I took the sundress she had been wearing and

rinsed the vomit soaked into the fabric out in the sink in the bathroom and wet a washcloth to use on her face.

"I want to take a shower," she whispered when I returned next to her bed.

I sat next to her, sinking into the mattress, and wiped the warm cloth over her face. "I think you need to rest a while before trying to shower."

"I ruined our date, Fletch." Her eyelids fluttered closed, and her voice trailed off.

I rubbed my hand across her forehead and over the crown of her head. "We can go out anytime. I'm not going anywhere."

~

Ivy, senior year of high school

"Mom, Fletcher is going to be here any minute,and I can't stop barfing my brains out." I managed to get the sentence out before the next wave of nausea struck with an unrelenting force.

I abandoned my mom in the hallway and fled to the bathroom to discharge my stomach's digested food for the fifth time.

It was our two-year anniversary, and I hadn't even been able to quit retching long enough to get dressed. I should have texted Fletcher not to bother coming over, but unfortunately, I hadn't been able to pause my vomiting to even locate my phone.

Once I finally convinced myself there was no more contents in my gut, I relinquished the embrace I had with the porcelain commode and slid down to the floor. The tile cooled my heated skin.

The thermometer I attempted to use didn't register a fever, but that was before the upchuck festival. I was convinced I rocked a high temperature now as I pressed the back of my hand to my forehead.

I was planning to push myself up to a standing position after only a few moments of recovery time splayed out on the bathroom floor, but at some point, I must have shut my eyes. Because I opened them when I heard my name.

"Jesus, Ivy. Are you alright?" Panic filled Fletcher's booming voice.

"Am I dead?" My head was pounding with his loud shrill his concern.

"Damn, Vine. You're alive, but you scared *me* half to death."

My eyes fought to focus on my worried boyfriend. "You called me Ivy. You haven't done that since I was fourteen. I figured I was either dead or you were upset with me," I whispered while he squatted on the floor next to me. "Since I'm not dead, you must be upset with me. I'm sorry I'm sick. I don't think I can make it to dinner."

"I'm not upset with you." He crossed his legs and lifted my head into his lap. "I'm sorry you're sick, too, but not because we were supposed to go to dinner. But because I don't like seeing you hurt." His fingers raked through my hair, and as his nails scraped gently across my scalp, my eyes drifted shut again.

"Vine, let's get you to bed first. And then you can go back to sleep."

I moaned my discord but accepted his assistance in standing, hobbled toward my bedroom, and flopped onto my covers with my bare feet still in contact with the floor. My face welcomed the mattress against my cheek regardless.

Fletcher peeled back the bedspread and aided me under the blanket. When he sat next to me, I finally took in the sight of him.

He was dressed in black slacks, a dark blue pressed shirt, and a tie that had a design with silver, black, and navy swirls. Damn, he was handsome.

"You look so good, and I'm a mess. Our anniversary is ruined."

"It's just dinner." His hand swept my hair behind my ear, and he stroked against the crown of my head again. His soft touch lulled my eyes to shut again. "It's no big deal. We'll eat all of our dinners together soon enough...at the dining hall, in our dorm rooms, or out somewhere together. I'm not going anywhere."

Chapter 31

Ivy, present day

I officially suck as a dinner date. I barfed my way out of our two-year anniversary dinner and our first date of whatever we were now.

Fletcher's soft snores and easy respirations whispered in my quiet bedroom, so I attempted to move off my bed without much motion or noise to get that shower I desperately wanted.

I eased myself out from beneath the covers and swung my legs over the side of the bed without him seeming to notice, so I scooted off the mattress and onto my feet to stand. I stood for a few beats, watching his sleeping form before shuffling to my bathroom.

And again, trying to be as inaudible as possible, I cracked open the door to my adjoining bathroom and slid inside without any movement from him.

Being an only child meant I had a bathroom all to myself. I heard many tales of sharing the space with a sibling when I was in high school. I had to share a bathroom several times in college, and I longed to return to having my own area again.

My bathroom at home joined both my bedroom and my dad's office in jack-and-jill fashion. But I kept the door that adjoined his office locked at all times, so he didn't really have access to it unless he entered through my bedroom. Besides, it was well understood the bathroom was solely mine.

Although I had free rein over the counter space, cabinets, and drawers, I still kept the area neat and tidy. Truthfully, that was probably why it drove me crazy to share. Other girls left hair products, curling irons, and hygiene crap everywhere.

I twisted the handles of the tub to adjust the water temperature and slipped out of my clothes before switching to the shower setting.

I pulled the shower curtain shut after I stepped over the side of the tub and into the welcomed hot spray. As much as soaking in a tub relaxes one's mind, the hot spray of a shower relaxes one's body. And after a migraine, my whole body was tense.

I lathered shampoo into my hair and washed my body in the steam-filled, calm, and serene space.

"Vine." Fletcher's voice cut through my tranquil time and startled me into a squeaking gasp.

The curtain was shoved back with a force that had the rings scrape loudly across the length of the rod.

"Jesus, Fletch. You scared me." I placed a hand over my upper chest but didn't think to cover my breasts because I was too alarmed at his unexpected appearance and hadn't realized I was completely naked until he stood before me, staring at my nude form for several seconds.

I retracted the curtain shut with the same force as he had used to open it.

"Sorry, Vine," he huffed. "Shit. I thought you were hurt when you screamed."

"Nope. I'm good." I did my best to sound nonchalant, but having his gaze peruse me had my pulse rate kick into overdrive. I left my hand in place over my heart, willing it to slow down with its pounding behind my ribs.

"How's your headache?"

"Uh...it's gone." I had all but forgotten about the reason our evening took a turn.

"Okay...I'll leave you to finish your shower. I'll be downstairs."

The door that I had never heard open shut with a click, and I was left in my own space again.

I used the extra adrenaline from my startled response to hurriedly finish washing and rinsing off. I wrapped myself in a towel before returning to my room, where I selected a different shirt and shorts to change into.

I twisted my wet hair into a single braid and secured it with a tie before heading downstairs and praying Fletcher was still there.

As I descended the stairs, I heard noise from the television, and knowing I hadn't turned the device on, I released a sigh of relief at his presence.

"Hey," I said with another attempt of nonchalance upon entering the living room.

Fletcher twisted his neck, and his blue gaze slammed into mine. "Hey." He stood as I walked the few paces to the couch where he had been seated. "Sorry about busting in on your shower."

"It's alright." I was over feeling uncomfortable about everything Fletcher-related. We had seen each other naked hundreds of times. We had showered together a few times also. This shouldn't be awkward, but yet here we were, stunned and silent.

We stood only two feet apart for half a minute without words, just breathing and blinking. Actually, I wasn't even sure if I was breathing. I may have held my breath the whole thirty seconds.

"So, should I go shower now?"

I quirked my eyebrow and narrowed my gaze. "Um, sure?"

Picking up on my confusion, he added, "That way, you can walk in on me naked, and then we'll be even."

A loud chortle flew out of my mouth unexpectantly, causing me to clasp my hands over my mouth.

"I know we've seen each other naked before, but it's been a long time, and we've both...changed." His brows knitted together as if pained or apprehensive to deliver identical thoughts I had in verbal form.

And again, another laugh broke free, and I released my palms from their covering over my lips. "You can't plan when I'm going to see you naked, Fletch. There needs to be spontaneity. Just surprise me sometime."

A grin tugged at his mouth, and a full smile stretched across his face slowly.

"I've seen that smirk before. Don't surprise me tonight, okay?" I couldn't help myself from giggling. He still had a way of getting a laugh out of me in an otherwise uncomfortable situation.

"It's already after nine o'clock. Tomorrow is only a few hours away." He actually waggled his eyebrows, which only intensified my laughter.

"I told you it's not a surprise if I know it's coming." I huffed out words in between the fits of hysteria.

"Pretty sure you always knew if I was coming."

And the laughter died on my lips.

But he took my sudden change of demeanor in stride and merely shrugged. "I'm starving. You feel like going to Scott's Diner?"

Thankful for the change of subject, I nodded wordlessly.

"Great. Let's go." And with a wave indicating I should follow him, I grabbed my keys and purse and did just that, kicking my flip-flops on as I shut the door behind me.

Fletcher drove to the restaurant, and I hopped out of his truck before he could do the chivalrous thing and open my door for me.

The deep furrow of his brow indicated his displeasure at my prompt exit of the vehicle. But when he held out an outstretched hand, I eagerly accepted it, loving the feel of our palms pressed together.

He relaxed his posture as we walked together, hands joined, toward the restaurant. When he pulled the door open for me, I attempted to withdraw from his grip so I could enter the diner easily. But he refused to release his grasp and dragged me through the door with him, tandem style, to allow us entrance.

I continued to hold his hand while we waited for the hostess and the walk to our table, only finally breaking free when we scooted into a booth. We sat opposite each other on separate vinyl benches, but after the hostess deposited two sets of silverware rolled up in napkins and two menus, I slid out of my side of the booth.

"You going to the bathroom already?" The lines around his eyes creased with his full smile.

"No." I gestured with a shooing motion, indicating for him to scoot further into the bench and then I slid in next to him.

"You're planning to eat food off my plate, aren't you?" he asked, still sporting his playful grin.

"Of course," I admitted but stared at the menu as I spoke.

"Well, just so you know, I'm getting breakfast for dinner," I heard him say but kept my gaze on the laminated meal selections.

"Obviously." I huffed the end of the word with a laugh.

"I'm thinking about pancakes or waffles."

I craned my neck with a quick twist to meet his gaze. "We could have just stayed home, and I could have made pancakes or waffles for us." He had always said my pancakes and waffles were better than he could buy anywhere.

"Nah, I like showing you off. It gives other men hope." He winked and dropped his gaze back to the menu in front of him.

"Huh?" I had no idea what breakfast food had to do with showing me off.

"If someone as beautiful as you is with a guy like me, other men can believe the same good fortune could happen to them also."

"You're laying it on a little thick, aren't you, Hart?" I quirked a brow and shook my head at his unfiltered flirting.

"I'm speaking from my heart, Hatfield." His shoulder playfully shoved at mine, and I adored how easy the banter and teasing were to relax back into like a broken-in pair of shoes. They may look different, less new and shiny, but comfortable, nonetheless.

Neither of us was ready for the night to end after the

good food and perfect dinner conversation. We talked about everything, anything, and nothing. We never ran out of topics to discuss or things to say. I hadn't felt that good about a date since I was with Fletcher all those years ago.

I dated a few boys in college, but nothing ever serious. None of the relationships ever lasted long enough for me to be truly comfortable, yet never feeling truly comfortable was always the reason I ended each of the budding relationships before they could ever turn serious.

I should have known all those years that no one was ever going to come close to comparing to my easy-going relationship with Fletcher. I guess that's what was different with dating someone you'd been friends with forever. There were no secrets. There wasn't any tidbit of information I was worried he might find out about me. There was no need to hide my idiosyncrasies.

Because only Fletcher knew everything about me. He kept all my secrets, was well acquainted with my quirks, and loved me anyway. I could be strong and vulnerable with him without fear of judgment.

And the more time I spent with him now, the more I realized that the bond we shared was still there.

So when he drove me back to my parents' house, I invited him in to watch a movie.

Chapter 32

Ivy, present day

"My parents have Netflix if you want to scroll through and pick a movie." I handed the remote over to Fletcher after we entered the living room.

"You've tried to pawn the remote off to me twice now." He raised a scrutinizing eyebrow. "Should I prepare for the apocalypse now?"

I blinked hard a few times, willing myself to absorb the reality and believe the most perfect man was truly standing in my parents' living room. The only man I've ever loved was, in fact, teasing me a few feet away, wearing a hopeful grin. This was the moment I had wished for.

Raw emotion clogged my throat, and tears pricked the back of my eyes.

Fletcher's blue eyes widened as his dumbfounded expression washed over the chiseled features of his face. "Vine, baby." He quickly ate up the few paces to reach me and grasped my cool hands with his warm ones.

His thumbs brushed rhythmically over my knuckles, and I riveted into his touch, feeling my eyes flutter shut momentarily.

"You okay?" His comforting whisper had my lips tilt upward into a slight smirk as scattered droplets of tears fell down my face.

I nodded and blurted out my truth before I could get cold feet. "I've just missed you, and I'm taking a moment to soak up this moment." The skin across my cheeks tightened as my happiness stretched my smile. "I've loved you for as long as I can remember." Snot leaked from my nose, and I sniffled in an attempt to keep it from dripping. "I never stopped being in love with you, but I thought you didn't love me anymore, and now you're here." Tears, sobs, snot, and all parts of ugly crying ensued.

He pulled our joined hands up to his lips and brushed kisses over our intertwined fingers. "Just like I told you when we were in ninth grade. You're my vine. You're wrapped around everything in my life. You're wrapped around my heart."

"Are you just saying that because I'm crying?" I chuckled through the sniffles.

"Yes."

My laughter shook within my chest, and I felt lighter than I had in so many years. "You gave me that same line when I cried before."

He leaned in closer, and this time, his mouth meshed with mine with gentle pressure.

I relaxed into his closeness and moaned my satisfaction against his lips, which made him part them, and my tongue swept inside instinctively.

His kiss was exactly how I remembered. He was Fletcher. My most familiar, comforting place of warmth and happiness.

I broke the tangle of our fingers and slid my hands along

his waist, and pushed the shirt up his back so I could trace lines up and down his skin with my nails.

His large hands moved to each side of my jaw, and the gentle nibbling and stroking our lips and teeth had been doing became rougher and messy.

Fletcher groaned with satisfaction at the increased intensity, so I tugged at the back of his shirt, and his grip relocated to his shoulders to grab the cotton material and bring it over his head, breaking our kiss momentarily with the removal of the T-shirt.

When his lips touched me again, they skated across my jaw and down the side of my neck to my collarbone.

I lifted my blouse over my head to allow him easier access, even though my shirt had a scoop neckline. I wanted more exposed skin for his trail of kisses.

Our erratic breathing had us break free for a few heated seconds to resituate ourselves.

His gaze lasered in on my chest as I stood mere inches away from him in just a bra from the waist up.

I took my time appreciating his chest during his perusal. As I surveyed his defined pecs and rippled abs, that blur of color captured my attention.

I focused on the artwork of ink that covered his left upper chest as my vision cleared from the tears I had shed a few moments earlier.

Right over his pec was that drawing of a bright red heart with a green vine wrapped around the middle. "Fletch..."

His chin dipped down, and his eyes examined the area where my gaze fell.

"That's an ivy vine." If I had any doubt about how much this man loved me, there were no longer any questions about his feelings for me. "And it's wrapped around a heart."

I reached out to touch it, effectively breaking his stare at his tattoo. Tracing the outline with the tip of my finger, I watched his skin flinch at my light strokes. And when I flinted my gaze from the ink to his eyes, those blue eyes burned with heated desire.

I recognized that look. Just like I remembered his kisses, I could recall with amazing clarity that glare he wielded when he wanted me. His regard drew me in with a magnetic force, attracting my body to his.

Before I took time to realize what was happening, we were once again fervently and thoroughly tasting and caressing each other's mouths. But this time, we didn't stop when our pulse pounded fast, or our breathing quickened.

His hands gripped my denim-clad ass, and I could feel the outline of his erection against my lower belly. The temperature in the living room seemed to increase several degrees, and I couldn't stand there any longer, so I stepped backward, leading Fletcher toward the staircase.

I grasped the railing once we reached the stairs and took a tentative step upward. I stood a step above his spot on the ground, causing him to break the fusion of our mouths once again.

And after a rapid breath, he leaned down, and his shoulder met my waist before lifting me.

I squealed from the unexpected fireman's carry.

He ascended the stairs two at a time until he reached my bedroom. And after twisting the knob and pushing the door open, I was dropped onto my mattress, causing my body to bounce gently.

He straddled me and hovered over my body in a hasty move that had me gasp at his swiftness.

"Tell me more about the tattoo," I urged in between my short huffs of breath.

"The heart represents Momma Hart and, well, I think you know who represents the string of leaves." His smoldering look would have typically scorched my core, but a small giggle escaped at his explanation.

"I'm a string of leaves?" I attempted to stifle additional peals of laughter, but just like the first time we were at this level of intimacy, I couldn't seem to help myself.

"Yes, you're *my* string of leaves. You. Are. Mine."

The laughter died on my lips.

"No matter how far apart we've been in distance, there has always been a string that has kept us bound to each other. That string is anchored around my heart, and each one of those leaves is a memory I hold dear to my heart."

"Fletcher, I don't know what to say." I dreamed of those words. I wished for so many days that we would run into each other again and he would confess his undying love for me. He didn't tell me but rather permanently inked it on his body.

I traced the outline of the image again and delivered a kiss over the brightly colored picture of a heart, which covered his actual, living, beating organ.

I kissed the area repeatedly before traveling across his chest, tickling my nose with the dusting of blond hair as I went. After I had sufficiently covered the skin over his pectorals, I allowed myself to lick at a nipple.

He still held himself over me, and although he flinched at the contact, he caught himself before crushing me with his weight. Not that I would have minded. I was willing to be smothered by his body in my bed, preferably naked, though.

I fumbled with the button of his slacks and managed to release it so I could more easily slide down his zipper. The moment my hand touched his impressive erection through the cotton of his boxer briefs, his lips were on me.

He kissed my mouth hungrily and needy before trailing off to the side of my jaw and across my upper chest.

I reached around and released the clasp of my bra, and rather than slowly pulling my arms through, Fletcher grabbed the material. The elastic held on to my elbow for a moment as he tried to extricate the undergarment, and the thing flew across the room like a rubber band.

Normally, I would have laughed at the hilarity of my bra slingshot, but his warm mouth was on a nipple next, and I had inhaled a huge intake of air from the unexpected pleasure.

Heat crept through my core and in between my legs. I leaned into him as his tongue circled and teased the erect peak. He used his finger to flick the pebbled tissue of my other breast, and I couldn't help the memories that flooded me of years ago when he explored my body, learning everything I enjoyed.

He obviously never forgot how much I adored the attention he spent on my breasts, but I needed more of him.

I continued to stroke up and down his length over his underwear, but when I slipped my hand beneath the fabric, a deep, feral moan erupted from his throat.

"Fuck, Vine. You're going to make me come in my pants again, just like that time as a teenager." His growling voice had me shimmying out of my shorts and panties because *Ohmigod, yes!*

Fletcher grabbed my clothes and forcefully yanked them down the length of my legs before tossing the items somewhere in my room.

"It's your turn now, Fletch. It's time for you to be naked."

"Yes, ma'am." He stood only long enough to remove his slacks and fitted boxer briefs before jumping back on the bed and bracing himself over me again.

I stared downward from his broad chest to the muscles of his abdomen and legs. He was bigger and stronger everywhere, so when I saw the size of his erection, I wasn't surprised. He was never small by any means, but he was a boy before, and now, *every* part of him was a man.

"I didn't bring a condom, so I can't come inside of you."

"Look in the usual place."

He pulled open the drawer of the nightstand that was within his reach and retrieved a strip of condoms.

"They're new. They're not our leftovers from before."

A sexy smirk curled at his lips before he ripped off a packet and tossed the rest back into the open drawer. "I hope this is enough for the night because I plan to use every one of those."

A giggle escaped my lips. "Just remember it's been a long time for me."

"Oh, I plan to take my time and savor every moment each time I'm inside of you. But it's been quite some time for me as well. So I'll try my best not to go all savage on you."

My widened eyes gave away my swirling thoughts. *He just broke up with his fiancée. Maybe he thinks going a week without sex is a drought.*

He grabbed the sides of my face, forcing my focus back to him instead of letting my thoughts carry my gaze out somewhere other than right here, right now.

"Look at me, Ivy."

Our gazes locked just like they always could whenever we were within a short distance from each other.

"I haven't had sex in over six months, so I'm going to try

my best not to lose control, but I can't promise once I'm inside you that I won't explode at that very instant."

A flirty grin swept across my lips. He was just as sexy as ever, all corded muscles, broad chest, strong arms, and powerful legs. The stubble that would have taken him a couple of days to grow before, now grazed his jaw after less than twenty-four hours from his last shave.

His mouth was on mine in half a second, his tongue delving in with urgent fervor. I was swept up in his all-consuming kiss, but when his finger teased along the inside of my thigh, I couldn't help reaching for his thick erection.

He jolted back away from me. "I'm not going to come before you do." His husky voice whispered harshly into my ear.

His fingers continued walking a path toward the apex of my thighs until he swept in between my feminine folds.

An appreciative groan was elicited from the back of my throat.

His own moan vibrated from his chest following my approval. "Damn, Vine. You're so wet."

A finger plunged into me. Despite my channel being slick with my arousal, the deep penetration had me gasp a quick intake of air. Although unexpected, I succumbed to the welcome intrusion within half a second.

By the time a second finger filled more space, I was relaxed, and after he pumped in and out a few times, I was thrusting my hips in sync with his rhythm.

His thumb gently massaged circles around my clit while his fingers angled upward, striking a spot that had me clutching to the comforter anchoring me in place because I thought I might float above the bed into a cloud of ecstasy.

When my vision blurred and a warm sensation tickled

the base of my spine, I knew I was close to climax. "God, Fletch."

"Oh, you like that, Vine?" He pistoned faster and rubbed harder against that tight bundle of nerves, and when he bit one of my nipples, I fell off the cliff as wave after wave of my orgasm convulsed throughout my lower body.

Once my form stopped shuddering from blissful after-shocks, he withdrew his hand from in between my legs, and although I lay sated, I reached for his erection, nonetheless.

Even in a restful state, I wanted him. I needed him inside me.

I grasped the base of his shaft and glided my hand up and down his thickness, drawing out more gravelly moans from him. Once I slid my thumb over the tip of the swollen head and swirled the leaking fluid around, he was ripping the foil packet with his teeth.

I retracted my hand so he could sheath himself but then gripped his erection again to guide him to my entrance.

He pushed in slowly, inch by delicious inch until he was fully seated, and then he stilled.

I writhed beneath him, willing him to move. "Fletch, I need you to..."

"I've wanted to be here again for so many years, and I'm afraid if I move, it will be over quickly, and I'm not ready for this to be over."

I bucked my hips upward and then pushed myself back onto the mattress, causing him to withdraw slightly.

He plunged back into me, striking the back wall of my aching womb.

"God, yes," I ground out in between my teeth, hissing as I spoke.

He pulled out again and drove in a few more times, picking up speed with each motion. "I won't last long, baby.

You feel too good, and it's been too much time since I've been with you."

My channel began to pulse around him. I was so close, and the buildup to my orgasm thrummed inside me with each stroke inside me.

Explosions of stars burst behind my eyes, and surges of heat rolled through my core when I felt his release within me.

We rode out our climaxes together, enjoying each ripple of pleasure. And after panting and moaning each other's names multiple times, rather than collapsing, he still held his weight off me and kept his place deep within me.

"Damn. I've missed you." He huffed each word out in between erratic breaths. "Sorry if that was rushed. But I plan to take my time with you each time from now on."

Chapter 33

Fletcher, present day

After the number of times we made love last night, I couldn't believe I awakened so early. The woman I gave my heart to in first grade and had resided there ever since was snuggled into my chest with her long brown tresses creating a curtain over her face.

I leaned down and pressed a kiss to the top of her head, causing those waves of hair to get caught in the short hairs of my chest as she wriggled beneath the covers. My arms remained wrapped around her naked body pulled in close to me.

I didn't want this feeling I had of nostalgia and love to ever go away. She was my past and future, and this very instant, she was my present also. I was never going to let go of her *ever* again.

The sun began to peek out after hours of us getting reacquainted with each other. I explored and worshiped every inch of her many times before we finally gave in to exhausted sleep.

But now I was awake, and although I would have loved

to stay put with her perfect, warm body molded to mine, I needed to relieve my bladder, so I slid my arms out of the embrace.

She squirmed with disappointment.

"I'll be right back," I whispered in her ear and went to the adjoining bathroom to relieve myself.

When I returned, she was in a cocoon of blankets up to her neck.

I located my discarded articles of clothing strewn all over her room and managed to find all the items needed to dress myself after deciding to pick up coffee and breakfast sandwiches for us. Even though I let her know I'd be back, I scribbled a note and left it for her on the kitchen table in case she awakened before I returned.

We had just patronized Scott's Diner the previous evening, but the restaurant was close by, and they offered takeout.

The line for takeout was long, and I wished I had mobile ordered prior to arriving, but I hoped it wouldn't take too much time before I could be back with Ivy.

There were about seven or eight people ahead of me when a petite blond woman got into line behind me, informing me the wonderful, cozy bubble I was in this morning was about to burst.

"Fletcher." Her voice was stern with her call. She wasn't just trying to get my attention. She was demanding for me to listen to her.

I swiveled on my heel to address her, not wanting to have her continue calling my name and look like an asshat for ignoring her.

Whatever she had to say to me couldn't hurt me anymore. I was with the woman I was meant to be with now.

"I'm so sorry."

"We don't need to do this, Amilyn. Everything worked out the way it was supposed to." I had no desire to rehash the nuances of our failed relationship.

She shook her head several times and inhaled a deep inspiration of air. "I should have broken up with you months and months ago."

Unsure where she was going with this, I wasn't sure standing in line for takeout was the most appropriate place to have this discussion, so I shuffled a few sidesteps to allow others to move ahead.

"You're a good guy, and I couldn't for the life of me figure out why I couldn't just love you the way you needed. I thought I was an idiot for not reciprocating your feelings. But I just didn't have the ability. I know now it's because we were never meant to be together long-term. I'm meant to be with Mateo, and you're meant to be with Ivy."

"So why didn't you end things?" Dumbfounded, I stood in disbelief.

"I tried pushing you away, but you were always so understanding. You are seriously the nicest man I've ever met, and Ivy is one lucky woman. You and I," she said as she pointed her index finger back and forth between us. "We just didn't have the thing."

"The thing?"

"You know the thing where you can't live without the other person." She hushed her voice and grabbed my upper arm to pull me further away from the onlookers. "You were mourning your mom's death and missing Ivy when we got together. We needed each other for a short while and got what we needed at that time."

"It was good for quite some time. I'm not sure when things changed. I tried really hard to make you happy." I recalled all the times I would bend to try to accommodate her. "I was a damn good boyfriend."

"Yes, you were. But you weren't the one for me."

My jaw slacked, and I quirked an eyebrow. Now that Ivy and I were back together, I knew Amilyn and I were never meant to be each other's forever, but I did everything possible to make this woman believe I was the one for her.

She dropped her head and lowered her voice before whispering additional conversation. "You were very good to me. But I was never into you. I thought I must have been crazy that I wasn't interested in such a good-looking, sweet, kind man like you. I couldn't break up with you. I didn't have it in me to break your heart. I tried pushing you away so you would see the hints, but you stayed. Even after we hadn't had sex in forever, you still didn't give up on me." Her blue gaze slowly lifted and met mine. "I just couldn't break things off with you when you were holding on so desperately."

"Desperate?" I chortled exaggeratedly. "I cared about you. I was loyal, not desperate." I swung my gaze around the busy restaurant and honed my sight back to her. "What are you doing here anyway? Shouldn't you still be in your sex cocoon at your apartment?"

"You're awful full of hate for someone that has gotten back together with the love of his life."

She had me there. There wasn't any reason for me to hold on to things in the past anymore. I wasn't upset about how things were handled after high school any longer. Everything has worked out the way it was supposed to.

"Mateo is my Ivy. We dated all through high school, and he left after graduation."

"If he was so important to you, why didn't I ever hear

about him? In fact, why didn't you ever share *anything* about yourself with me? We were together for years, for chrissake." I wasn't really angry, and definitely not jealous. Now, I just felt like my relationship with Amilyn lasted longer than it should have, and it was possible that I could have been back with Ivy earlier if I hadn't tried to force this relationship to work.

"It appeared you had given up on Ivy, but I guess I never gave up hope on Mateo. I was lonely at times, and you were at the right place at the right time." She shrugged. *Freaking shrugged.* Like our relationship was just a hobby to pass her time. "I'm getting married to him while he's on leave, and then I'm going to Virginia with him."

I shook my head in disbelief. "You're crazy. It's only been a hot second since you were engaged to me. You couldn't even commit to a wedding date with me after months and months, and you're going to jump into a marriage with someone else in a few days." Apparently, I didn't know this woman at all.

"And what if we had gotten married? Then what would have happened?"

Damn. I thought about Ivy back at her parents' house in her bed. Amilyn was right. Our relationship was over a long time ago, and she should be with whoever she wants. She was there when I needed someone, but we both should have moved on a long time ago.

So, as difficult as it was not to hold some disdain, I lifted my lips into some semblance of a smile. "Well, good luck to you. I hope you find your happiness." It was becoming clearer with every interaction I had with her, that even as hard as I tried, I was never going to make her happy. Maybe someone else could.

I stepped back in line, and rather than fall into the spot behind me, she headed for the exit and walked out of the restaurant.

~

I used the key that was still kept in its usual spot under a rock that had a plate with the house number adhered to it.

The house remained quiet when I entered, so I toed off my shoes and softly padded across the floor and up the stairs back to her bedroom.

The damn door squeaked when I pushed it open, which caused her to stir slightly. I placed the bag containing our breakfast sandwiches and two cups of coffee on the dresser, pulled my shirt over my head, and shucked my pants off before sliding back under the covers with her.

She moaned sleepily when I wrapped my arms around her chest as I attempted to spoon her, but she flipped over to face me.

Her eyes fluttered open, and a smile tugged at her perfect pink lips. She was utterly stunning, even first thing in the morning, and I couldn't keep myself from pressing my mouth against hers.

Another moan escaped her, and my dick twitched beneath the cotton of my boxer briefs. She was still naked beneath the sheets. So, of course, my body was going to react to her presence.

Although, I hadn't expected such a quick boner, considering how many times we had sex just hours ago.

Plus, I imagined she was sore this morning. I willed my erection to relax and pulled away from her with massive reluctance. "I brought food and coffee."

"One of the things I love about you." She dropped a

chaste kiss to my nose, and I happily slid out of bed to retrieve the breakfast I had purchased.

I handed her a cup of coffee seated in the cardboard holder I was given at the restaurant and set the bag down on top of her bedspread. I placed my coffee on the night-stand next to the bed and slid back beneath the covers next to her.

I reached into the bag and handed her a foil-wrapped sandwich and a couple napkins. She used the cardboard holder as a tray to hold both her drink and sandwich.

"I could get used to this, Fletch." Her tone was playful, but I needed her to understand my intentions were long-term and not just for some fast fun.

"I'm never leaving again, Vine." I twisted my head, and my blue gaze connected with her brown one.

Her smile widened, causing small wrinkles at the corners of her eyes to form. "Well, I'm never letting go."

I squeezed her hand and nodded, suddenly choked with emotion. I distracted myself with the wrapper of my sand-wich because having her back was something I wanted but didn't think would happen.

A loud ping of her phone disrupted my sappy, sedi-mental state.

She sat her sandwich on the tray and leaned across me to reach her phone on the end table.

I should have retrieved the device for her, but I was awestruck by the sight of her full, supple breasts spilling out from the bed covers as she stretched.

Her nipples tightened as they brushed against the dusting of hair on my chest, and my dick stood at attention again. At least I was beneath the comforter, so it wasn't so apparent.

She was focused on her phone anyway. "Julie wants to

go out tonight." Her gaze darted up from the screen and over to me. "You up for it?"

"Oh, I'm up for it." I waggled my eyebrows, and her gaze dropped to between my legs.

She giggled and typed away on her phone before pushing her tray of coffee and food, along with her phone, over to the nightstand. Wearing a mischievous smile, she swung her leg over my abdomen and straddled me, pushing the covers down.

"I told her my boyfriend and I were free."

I could feel my smile widen at her proclamation. She was claiming me as hers, and when she rocked her hips against my throbbing erection, my boxers dampened. I wasn't sure if it was from my arousal or hers, but I needed to get them out of the way sooner rather than later.

We sat up in bed after our lovemaking and snuggled naked, sipping our coffees.

"And to think, the week after high school graduation, we were thinking how nice it would be when I wouldn't have to sneak you into my room, but here we are having sex in my childhood bedroom at my parents' house." The lightness in her tone was felt deep within my soul.

"You should move in with me...I *want* you to move in with me." We shouldn't be apart any longer.

"Just like that?"

"Yes, just like that. I want you to stay in our hometown, and I want you to live with me." We had talked about the present, but we hadn't spoken much about the future.

"I have a job here, and there's this cute fireman I kind of love in this town, so I think I could get on board with that idea." She leaned over to kiss me chastely on the lips, and her bright smile made my heart perform a happy dance within my chest. "My mom will be calling today around four, so I'll tell her then."

I'd spoken to Mrs. Hatfield numerous times over the years. I had no doubt she would be ecstatic about our rekindled relationship.

Epilogue

Ivy, one year later

My parents returned home after nearly a five-week hiatus. Even though I told them about Fletcher and me, which they were thrilled about, they insisted on having the two of us over for dinner a few nights after they returned.

I explained the situation surrounding my breakup with Fletcher because I hadn't shared the story with anyone back then.

I moved in with Fletcher within a week of their return home. It was better for me to permanently stay over at his house than to ultimately spend every night there anyway. I had trouble sleeping without his warm body lying next to me. And we were a little too old for Fletcher to sneak into my bedroom every night and too disrespectful to have him parade into my bedroom at night right in front of my parents.

It would have also been awkward for me to pack a bag each night and confess to my mom and dad that I was going to stay at his house. So, it was best for all parties involved for me to move in with him.

His dad went into an inpatient detox with the help of his uncle Jonathan. He could never be gone for more than two or three days before because if he was away from alcohol longer than that, he would have seizures. He needed to be monitored during the detox phase of recovery. He was currently attending AA meetings and doing well.

Only six months after moving in together, Fletcher asked me to marry him. Of course, I said yes. I had dreamed of being his wife since forever, so getting married to him would make a dream come true.

And today, just over a year after he asked me to marry him, it was finally the day I'd been waiting my whole life for.

I asked Carrie and Julie to be my bridesmaids, and they agreed to wear the periwinkle-colored dresses that were actually very flattering, considering all the attention was supposed to be on me—the bride. I would have asked Aunt Charlotte to be a bridesmaid as well, but she has her hands full with my one-year-old little cousin, Tucker. I decided to have my cousin Harper, Aunt Charlotte's eight-year-old daughter, be the flower girl, though.

She had to be a part of the wedding since her entrance into the world was the first day Fletcher kissed me and the day our relationship transitioned from friendship to so much more.

Fletcher selected John, obviously, and Matt, another paramedic from his firehouse, to be groomsmen.

Carrie volunteered to be paired up with John, and I would love for something to develop there. Maybe that would get her back home to Maryland on a more permanent basis.

"You look gorgeous," Julie said before delivering an air kiss to avoid messing up her lipstick or my makeup as the processional music began and she started her walk down the aisle.

Carrie fell in line behind her after giving me a quick wave and smile, and after I heard the church full of *awwws*, I knew my cousin had thrown the flower pedals down the aisle for my dad and me next.

"You ready?" my father asked, wearing his black tux and a tie that matched the dark blue of my mother's dress.

"I hope Fletcher and I will be as happy as you and Mom," I said as I hooked my arm around his.

"I knew from the moment that boy asked for permission to be your boyfriend that he would be the one to ask for my permission to marry you." He patted my hand that was draped onto his forearm. "He is the only man I would ever trust to take care of you."

"I don't need anyone to take care of me, Dad." I shook my head and laughed happily.

"Oh, I know, sweetheart. And Fletcher is the only one I can imagine able to handle that fact."

After another giggle of agreement released from my overjoyed heart, I headed down the aisle of the church with my father at my side toward the man I'd loved forever and would be with for the rest of my life.

THE END

To hear more about my other books, click here to sign up for my newsletter and receive a FREE book.

Gratitudes

B: This has been a tough year and you continue to be at the top of the list of people I'm grateful to have in my life. You have stood by me through all the good times and the challenging times including my latest health scare. I have been beyond blessed to have you be my partner in life.

Sx4: You are the reason I keep fighting every day. Nothing has given me more pleasure than being your mom and you are all amazing human beings. You are the best parts of both your father and me and I am extremely proud of each of you.

Amy: My BFF. Sorry your namesake was Fletcher's second choice. But you are my first choice always! You have known me forever and seen every part of me. The Good. The Bad. The Ugly. And everything in between—and you still continue to be friend anyway. I love you more than I can ever say.

Julie and Carrie: I am so glad we reconnected and were on team *doing stuff.* I have been fortunate to have met many amazing women during my life and I'm lucky I get to have both of you as friends.

Tania and Christy: Thank you both for continuing to drop whatever you are reading to pick up my unpolished work and diving in. I value your feedback and I'm so happy to have both of you in my life.

Anna: For the first time, I haven't written a book with a sister in it---but I still need to say how much I love having you as my sister.

Leddy: I can't believe this is book number nine for me. I'm not sure what I did to be blessed with such a talented writer as a friend. Thank you for holding my hand when I needed it and pushing me to spread my wings. I will always be grateful for your guidance and friendship.

To Robin at Wicked by Design Covers: Thank you for transforming my vision into a work of art and creating a perfect cover!

To Kerry at *writersresourceinc.com* thank you for being my editor extraordinaire. Your insights, corrections, comments, and feedback help make the words of my book so much better.

To my readers: Thank you for taking a chance on me. I am extremely grateful to each of you that decided to read Fletcher and Ivy's story! I hope you enjoyed it!

Also by Greenleigh Adams

CALLAHAN CLAN Series:

Love Burns (CALLAHAN CLAN #1)

Butterfly Girl (CALLAHAN CLAN #2)

Heart Pieces (CALLAHAN CLAN #3)

Empty Room (CALLAHAN CLAN #4)

Hard Nox Life (CALLAHAN CLAN #5)

Baywood Hospital Series:

The Distraction Project (Tobias and Paisley)

The Travel Assignment (Em and Finn)

The Destined Proposal (Boone and Melissa) releasing later in 2025

Standalone Novels:

To Start a Heart

The Only One for Me

Vine Around my Hart

About the Author

Greenleigh lives on the Eastern Shore of Maryland with her husband and four children. Being an ER nurse for two decades and married to a firefighter, she write stories about what she knows. Coffee and chocolate are everyday must haves in her life, but fishing and relaxing at the beach are her favorite pastimes.

After a pancreatic cancer diagnosis in 2019, Greenleigh began to check things off her bucket list—one of those things being "write a novel." Today she is healthy and continues to write whenever she can, so she can get the stories in her head down on paper. She is inspired by people that chase their dreams and is a firm believer in happily ever afters, so you will find her characters and their stories mirror these ideals.